THE FIRST WIDOWS

S.E. REED

Storm
PUBLISHING

Ebook ISBN: 978-1-83700-186-6
Paperback ISBN: 978-1-83700-188-0

Cover design: Lisa Horton
Cover images: Shutterstock

Published by Storm Publishing.
For further information, visit:
www.stormpublishing.co

ALSO BY S.E. REED

The First Wives

For my children—I would do anything for you...

PROLOGUE

Betrayal—it's a knife in the back. Or in this case, a heavy, pointy, glass "Doctor of the Year" award jammed in the neck...

"Just leave the girls out of this." My voice is hoarse from all the screaming. Hot, stinging tears streak down my cheeks as I scramble to my feet. There is a massive gash on the side of my head, where I've been hit with a chair leg. I drag the back of my forearm over my face, trying to clear the blood away. I search the room, looking for my assailant, or a way out of this mess.

The house is completely trashed. Broken glass, scattered papers, furniture turned over in every room. I had no idea she'd be so strong. Or violent.

Not that it would have stopped me from fighting to protect what's mine. The two little girls, hiding in the closet upstairs. If I don't protect them right now, when they need me the most, who will? Their dad? No, Mitch is dead. There's been so much death— am I next? I choke out a cry when I step on a piece of glass.

I limp from the dining room, calling her name, heading into the kitchen. I strain my ears, hoping to hear the sound of sirens racing through our neighborhood. The police should be here soon—I just have to keep her from going upstairs and finding the girls.

"SARAH! BAILEY!" she screams from the living room.

"Don't you fucking say their names," I growl and lunge forward with my arms out, slipping on some of the broken glass and falling to the floor. I'm so tired. I guess I should have taken those classes at the gym, but with managing the house, the girls, and everything else I've been dealing with the last six months—I just didn't have the time or energy.

She laughs at my crumpled body. "You're pathetic." She spits the words at me. Her eyes are blazing like she's possessed by the devil.

I grab her ankle before she can take a step up the stairs. "Please, I'll do anything. Leave them alone!" I cry. Then I muster enough upper body strength to pull her leg out from under her, but she doesn't lose her balance, instead she shakes the leg I have a hold of. But I'm not letting go. She'll have to beat me to death.

Which is exactly what she tries to do.

She bends down, pounding my head with her fists. "Let go of my leg."

"Fuck you." As long as she doesn't go upstairs, I'll take every beating she can dish out. That's when I hear something, between the punches, like a child whimpering in the hallway. I think I see Sarah holding my phone up, but I can't be sure. Between the fist hitting my head and the blood in my eyes, everything is a blur.

Police sirens wail down the block. Finally! The police are almost here.

She starts screaming at me, but I can't make out all the words. My head feels like I'm underwater or maybe my ears are just filled with blood.

"... ruining... plans... life..."

She's so full of herself. She thought she could show up tonight and—what? I'd just sit back and let her hurt my girls? I would rather die than let anything happen to them. Which might happen if she keeps hitting me in the head. At this point I'm not even sure if she's still using her fist. It feels more like a hammer.

Thankfully, even with my damaged ears, I can hear the sirens and see red-and-blue lights cascading through the windows. The police will arrive any second and save me and the girls. But she's a smooth talker—the smoothest I've ever seen. She already said her plan is to pin everything on me. Which means there won't be anyone to protect Sarah and Bailey.

So with the Herculean strength of a mother lifting a car that's rolled on top of her child, I shove her away from me and get on my feet, grabbing the first thing I see. Mitch's prized "Doctor of the Year" award.

She turns to run toward the police officers who are shouting in the foyer. But there's no way in hell I'm letting her reach them and spew more of her lies. So without any hesitation, I slam the award, point first, into the back of her neck.

She doesn't scream as the glass severs her spinal cord. Her body just tumbles face forward in a heap of flesh.

Then I collapse, succumbing to my own injuries. As I'm blacking out, I swear I can hear Sarah and Bailey talking to the police. Something about a video. But it's hard to tell—my head is killing me.

"Mommy and Fifi were fighting," Sarah sobs.

"Are they dead?" Bailey asks.

PART 1

ONE

REBECCA HENDRICKS

Six Months Earlier

"Well, don't you have a spring in your step this morning, Rebecca?" Justin, one of the medical assistants, says to me as I stroll by the nurses' station.

"Living my best life, Justin, that's all." I singsong the words and even do a pirouette before I grab a clipboard, and head toward the clinic rooms. I can hear the other nurses and medical assistants snickering. I try not to let it bother me. I mean, who the hell are they anyway? I don't care what any of them think about me.

They're just jealous that I can see my own patients and they can't.

"Mr. Torez, good morning," I say brightly to the elderly gentleman sitting on the exam table. "Now, why are you back so soon?" I close the door behind me and start my day.

I see patient after patient.

Doing my best to put on a performance of a lifetime for each and every one of them. And by that I mean being attentive, engaging, and compassionate. I might throw in a little singing and jazz hands for them now and again, especially for my favorite patients, the ones who clap and cheer for me. It's the least I can do, considering most are impoverished and battling chronic conditions. What a miserable life that would be.

I know I'm never going to realize my dreams of being on Broadway—so being the best damn advanced practice registered nurse at the free clinic in downtown New York City is what I've got. Even if my co-workers are less than cordial. *Turds*, as my eight-year-old daughter Sarah would say. It's not my fault the doctors here all kiss my ass because of who my husband is. Or that the patients prefer me over anyone else because I write prescriptions with the most refills.

"Last one." Justin hands me the final clipboard of the day. "Suture removal."

"Is it five already? The day just flies by when you love what you do."

Justin groans and rolls his eyes. I know he hates this place, along with everyone else. Which is why I get such satisfaction rubbing in how much I love it.

I quickly glance at the clipboard before strolling into the clinic room. Sophia Carter... That name sounds familiar. Once I see her face I'll remember. Oh, maybe it's that cat lady, the one with the blue hair.

"Good evening, Ms. Carter, now let's get those stitches out," I say as I open up the door and breeze in, expecting to see an elderly woman covered in fur. I gasp when I see who it really is. "Sophia!" I exclaim. It's the woman I met last month during our annual team-building activity at the art studio. One of those guided classes where we all painted the same ugly bowl of fruit. Apparently mine wasn't so ugly, as she wandered over from the gallery to strike up a conversation.

"Hello, Rebecca." She smiles. "You mentioned you worked here, and I, uh—" She holds her finger up.

"Need some stitches removed?" I laugh.

"Do you mind?"

"Do I mind? Of course not!" I hope she can't see the color in my cheeks. God, how embarrassing! Not only did she remember my name, but she remembered where I worked.

"My regular doctor is out until next week, and, well, these stitches are killing me. I need them out and it looks fine," Sophia explains as she takes off the bandage covering her left pointer finger.

I take her hand and inspect the finger. Whoever her doctor is did a horrific job stitching the wound. He didn't even use the right sutures. She's going to have a nasty scar.

"Now, see, I would have used a much thinner gauge suture or even just liquid wound adhesive with a cut like this." I put her hand down and putter around the room, setting up the tray of items I need to remove the stitches.

"Oh. I'll let my physician know his work was subpar," Sophia says in a low tone.

I cock my head slightly. I can't tell if she's joking or serious. But then I see the sides of her mouth turn up.

"Relax, I'm kidding," she assures me. "I know how doctors are. Their egos are so delicate."

"Right? Like, what's with that?" I ask and laugh. "Did I tell you my husband is a physician?"

"No, you didn't mention it. Does he work here, with you?" she asks, raising a brow.

I shake my head. "He's a pediatric heart surgeon. His home base is here in New York, but he spends most of his time working internationally." I hope that didn't come off like I'm bragging. Because I'm not. It's not the glamorous life you'd think. Mitch is never home and when he is, he's always distracted.

"Wow, that's incredible," she says.

I crack half a smile and nod, hoping to hide my disappointment. If I'm honest, it's annoying that everyone thinks Mitch is so amazing.

Then Sophia adds, "*If* you're into your husband working

unforgiving hours, traveling the world without you, and let me guess—having an ego the size of Texas?"

I set down the small scissors I just used to remove the stitches and look her in the eyes with renewed faith in this woman's potential to be—dare I say—a friend. "What state is bigger than Texas?" I ask.

"Alaska?"

"Yes. An ego the size of Alaska."

She snorts.

"Well, Sophia, everything looks fine. A little antibiotic ointment for a few days and no soaking your hands in water for about a week."

She examines her finger. "Brilliant." She smiles. Her gray steely eyes reflect the terrible halogen lighting, making them almost sparkle. "Rebecca, would you like to go have a drink with me? I mean, if you don't have to run home to wait hand and foot on *Alaska*."

Hmmm... A drink with a strange woman that I hardly know anything about... except that she was in awe of my painting at the event, walking from the gallery side to the studio side just to introduce herself to me. She's clearly wealthy—those are real Louboutins on her feet and a genuine Hermès purse sitting next to her on the exam table. I don't think someone like that would be "up to something."

"Yes, I'd love to have a drink." Why the hell not.

"Lovely." She stands up. "Shall I wait for you in the lobby?"

"Oh god, no, you saw it, disgusting. Just wait here. I'll go put my things away and grab my purse."

Sophia smiles as I slip out of the clinic room. The team is busy finishing up their notes and end-of-day tasks around the office. I drop my clipboard at the nurses' station, then pull out my cell phone to call my irritating housekeeper, Mrs. Melnyk.

"What?" she answers.

"Can you stay and feed the girls dinner and put them to bed? I have to work late."

I can tell by her husky deep breathing she's annoyed. But it's not like she has anything better to do. She's a single, fifty-year-old woman, who, as far as I can tell, has no family in the States.

"I charge double for late night."

"Fine." I hang up before she can hear me growling. It's really hard to find both a competent housekeeper and one with a good attitude for what I'm able to pay on my salary. If my husband would get off his high horse and help me with the expense, I could afford a live-in. Someone who would actually help me with the kids.

I walk back to get Sophia from the clinic room. Half expecting her to be gone when I open the door. Why would a glamorous, stunning, wealthy woman like Sophia want to hang out with me anyway? But when I open the door, she's still there waiting.

"There's a little coffee and wine bar down the street," she says.

"Perfect." I'm glad she knows where to go. I don't usually hang out in the city after work. It takes close to an hour to drive home to our secluded, wooded neighborhood on Long Island—so I'm always the first out of the building at night.

We use the employee entrance on the side of the building and walk toward the bustling street. My car is parked in the garage— hopefully the bar isn't too far... I glance at Sophia's feet as she leads the way. In those shoes, it must not be far.

"Right there, is that okay?" She points at a narrow building with a blue-green exterior designed to look like a European coffee shop. Neon lights in the window say "WINE"and "COFFEE". I don't know how I never noticed it before. We're less than a block from the free clinic. I guess I don't pay too much attention when I'm driving to and from work.

"This is nice. I, uh, don't have a very active social life—I can't remember the last time I went out for a drink with a friend," I tell her. Although I immediately regret the words. Now she's going to ask me about the last time I went out with friends.

"Oh, me neither, it's been ages. I'm always so busy. But I vowed if I met someone interesting, I'd make more of an effort," she says and winks at me. Then she opens up the door to the coffee shop for me.

As I walk past her, in my navy-blue scrubs, feeling grimy from a day of working—I smile and hold my head high. She just called *me* interesting.

TWO

I've opted for a decaf latte, while Sophia's having a glass of deep burgundy merlot. As much as I'd love to join her, I can't risk driving home in the dark with wine in my system. If I got pulled over, I'd lose my independent nursing license. And they aren't just giving those things away. It took years of extra classes from my alma mater, NYU, to earn my master's degree to qualify.

Which is what I'm currently telling Sophia.

"So is that what you always wanted? To be a nurse?" The wine has caused her cheeks to warm, which looks good on her. If we were actually friends, I'd take a picture and tell her to color match that shade of blush.

"Oh god, no! I came to New York to be on Broadway."

"Really? I adore Broadway. It's the only music I listen to," Sophia says. She takes another sip of her wine and leans back against the polished wood in the booth-style seat. Her face falls into a scowl, and for a split second I think she's going to tell me how pathetic I am for giving up my dreams to work in a free clinic. "God, these seats are terrible. You think a cute place like this would have cozy velvet couches."

I throw my head back and laugh. "This is New York. People piss everywhere, and you can't wipe down velvet."

"Ew, yuck, I never thought about that."

"I can tell from your accent you aren't from New York—but I can't place it."

Her shoulders relax against the unforgiving wood seat. "I grew up outside of London, but I consider myself a woman of the world. I've lived all over Europe, China, and the United States."

"Wow. That sounds exciting." But then I think about my husband, traveling the world, and a pang of jealousy erupts in my chest.

She studies my face before answering. "If you say so."

"Well, if you didn't find living all over the world exciting, why did you do it?"

"Work and family obligations," she answers quickly. "But now, it's just me. So, I thought I'd move somewhere I've always wanted to live. The city that never sleeps seemed fitting, because I rarely sleep these days."

"Insomnia? I can prescribe you something for that," I offer.

"No, no, thanks anyway. I'll sleep better once my flat is finished and I'm out of the hotel I'm stuck in. The contractors are taking a very long time. Something to do with the workers' unions. I don't really understand American laws."

"Ohh, that makes sense. I never get a good night's sleep in a hotel. That's part of why I don't travel with my husband. That, and our two daughters."

"Children are hard to travel with. How old are they?"

For the next hour, Sophia listens attentively as I talk about the girls, life with a famous surgeon husband, and my abandoned dreams of starring on Broadway. She doesn't share much more about herself, which, as I'm driving home, I realize might have been my fault. It just felt so good to have someone ask about me— and seem to genuinely enjoy listening. I don't even know what Sophia does for a living. Maybe old money? She was browsing the ridiculously priced art in the gallery attached to the paint-and-sip studio when we met. Hmmm. She mentioned being alone—that her previous world travels were tied to family... Maybe her parents died, leaving her an inheritance? Or a husband? Although, she doesn't strike me as a woman who would enjoy being married. The next time we speak, I'll have to spend less time talking about myself, and more time asking her questions.

Because I'd love to see her again. This time we exchanged phone numbers.

"I'm not doing this every night," Mrs. Melnyk says as soon as I walk in the door. "Hire live-in."

"I'm sorry. But, Mrs. Melnyk, how often do I ask you to stay late?"

"Too often." She crosses her arms.

I roll my eyes. That's a lie. This is only the second time in six months.

She's muttering under her breath in another language as she collects her purse and coat. I've got to defuse this, or she might not show up at all tomorrow. With Mitch out of town the rest of the week, I'm relying on Mrs. Melnyk to be here when the kids get off the school bus.

"I'll pay triple for the extra time tonight. Please don't be angry with me," I say as I follow Mrs. Melnyk to the door.

She turns around slowly. What I imagine passes for a smile in her mind, spreads over her face and she nods once. "See you tomorrow."

"Bitch," I grumble as soon as she leaves.

It's already nine thirty.

I should go to my room and get ready for bed, but instead I pour myself a glass of wine, collapse on the oversized living room chair, and turn on the television. I navigate to YouTube, then go to my saved pages. West Valley High in Akron, Ohio, mailed out a notice to former graduates that their technology class had uploaded all the old footage from football games, pep assemblies, school musicals—basically any old footage they could digitize was going online. I couldn't help myself. I had to log on.

Watching a young, starry-eyed Rebecca on stage singing her heart out, leaves me feeling both comforted and with an ache in my chest. Every hope and dream of stardom glimmering in her eyes. I sip my wine and sink deeper into the chair, flipping from the musical junior year to a pep assembly. There, in the front row of the cheer squad, that body was tight and perky in all the right places. It looks so easy—I'd be lucky now if I could kick my leg up waist high.

"Turn, pivot, hips, boom," I cheer for the girls onscreen.

Then young Rebecca puts her face in the camera and smiles before shouting, "Woooo! Go, Bobcats!" and flashes a peace sign, sticks out her tongue, and spins around before running and doing three cartwheels in a row, without skipping a beat.

I let out a long sigh...

What's the saying about the good old days? You don't know you were in them until they're gone. Something about that feels like a comfort and a curse. Maybe these days I'm living right now are my good old days. Or maybe they're long gone.

"Mommy?" Bailey calls to me as she wanders down the stairs, holding her blankie and rubbing her eyes.

"Back to bed." I hate when she gets up. If I give in, it becomes this vicious cycle all night. Water. Snack. Story. She gets more and more whiny, until it turns into crying and I get angry.

"Carry me," she begs with her arms open wide. She's so cute, but I can't give in to her.

"No. Bed. Now." I'm firm.

From the corner of my eyes, I see her head fall in defeat. She doesn't say anything else before turning around and walking back up the stairs. I wish Mitch was here to see how well it works. He always caves, then leaves, and it's on me every other time Bailey gets up. If he would just use my method, it would be so much easier. On all of us.

The happy teens bouncing on the screen only remind me of

shattered dreams, so I turn it off, set my wine glass by the sink, and trudge upstairs to my room.

"Mommy," Bailey calls out as I walk past her dark room.

Wait. Why is it dark? Why isn't her kitty lamp turned on next to her bed? I pause, debating if I should go in there to turn on the night-light, knowing it will probably lead to endless up-downs all night long.

I let out a sigh before going into her room. I turn the knob on the small lamp, and the shade with cut-outs of kitties illuminates the walls with shapes.

"Thank you, Mommy," she whispers and rolls over without any other requests.

Well, that was easier than expected. My shoulders relax as I leave her room and tiptoe past Sarah's open door. Once I reach my bedroom, I'm in the clear. I lock my door—strip off my scrubs and crawl naked into my bed. One of my guilty pleasures when Mitch is out of town. It's only as I'm about to drift off that I realize I forgot to wash my face. Not that it really matters—I stopped caring about my skincare routine a few years ago.

Flawless skin, brows, and makeup takes a lot of time and energy. With the girls and work and a husband who seems less and less interested, why bother? It's not like I'm going to auditions anymore. And my patients at the clinic still love me no matter what I look like.

That's when Sophia's beautiful face flashes in my mind. Perfection. I would have never guessed she suffers from insomnia. She looked refreshed, glowing, absolutely pristine. I suppose it wouldn't kill me to get up and go wash my face and moisturize. I'm sure all my old serums and creams are still under the sink.

I drag my tired, naked body from the bed and go to the bathroom.

When I flick on the light, the woman staring back at me is disgusting. She doesn't look anything like the girl on the YouTube videos. I'm ashamed, seeing the roundness of my belly and the dimples on my thighs. My hair is dull and my complexion is sallow.

Why on earth did someone like Sophia Carter strike up a conversation with flabby, hideous, me?

After washing my face and applying some clearly expired products, I slink back to bed, ready to roll over and cry myself to sleep. But my phone lights up with a text.

> Rebecca, thank you for a lovely evening. If you're free on Friday, I'd like to take you to dinner. You're the first nice person I've met in New York. I could use a friend.

My heart quickens. I do like Sophia, even if I don't know much about her. And she thinks I'm nice, which is something. Maybe spending more time with her would be good for me. Maybe it will motivate me to get my groove back.

> I would love to. I just have to make sure I can get a babysitter for the girls. I'll let you know tomorrow.

> Brilliant.

So instead of crying myself to sleep, I close my eyes and imagine what it would be like to be Sophia's New York friend. I'm sure she has glamorous friends all over the world in the places she's lived. One bosom buddy for every city she's traveled. I like the idea of her choosing me for New York. It feels like being chosen as the lead in a Broadway production... Sophia mentioned she loves Broadway. Maybe, if dinner goes well, we can go see a show together. Mitch hates going with me anymore, he says I'm moody and depressed afterwards. Which is not true. I just like to relive the show in my mind, thinking about the work that went into it: building the sets, the rehearsals, costume production. I've tried explaining it to Mitch, but he doesn't understand.

"Don't you imagine the surgeries before you perform them?" I asked once, trying to use a medical metaphor he might understand.

"Yes, but that's because I'm actually going to perform it. You're not going to be in the show."

Maybe I was depressed after hearing that.

But it was Mitch's fault. He said that on purpose to cut me. Sophia will be different—I can feel it in my bones. I bet she's even seen shows in London's famed West End, somewhere I've dreamed of going. And the same place sleep drags me into just moments later.

THREE

"No."

"But, Mrs. Melnyk, please, I'll pay triple," I beg my stone-faced housekeeper the next morning when she arrives.

"No. I have church."

"On a Friday night?" I scoff and fold my arms over my chest. I want to stamp my foot, like Sarah when she's annoyed with her little sister, but I refrain. I'm not sure a temper tantrum would be an effective method of bargaining with Mrs. Melnyk.

She ignores me and heads for our laundry room to start her work, washing, folding, and ironing. I can see this conversation is over. But I don't have anyone else I can ask. None of the staff at the clinic have teenage girls—and even if they did, I think I'm the only one who lives this far east of the city.

I follow Mrs. Melnyk to the laundry room.

"Could they go to church with you?" I'm desperate. I want to go out with Sophia so bad I can taste it.

She turns slowly from the big front-loading machine where she's shoving towels and narrows her gaze at me. "You don't believe in God."

"Yes, but isn't that one of your goals, to convert the non-believers?"

"You want me to convert your children?" She smirks.

"If it means you'll watch them Friday night, you can give it a go." I don't have time to keep arguing with Mrs. Melnyk. I've got to get the girls to school and on the road soon, or the traffic will be unbearable.

"I'll think about it."

That means yes. I can see it in her eyes. Triple pay and the chance of bringing faith to my "heathen children"—her words, not mine. Just as long as the girls don't tell Mitch they went to church with Mrs. Melnyk, it will be fine. And it gives me time to research and find an actual babysitter I can use in the future—if this dinner goes well with Sophia and she wants to do it again, I need to be prepared.

After dropping the girls off at school and barely making it to work on time, I've talked myself out of the girls going to church on Friday night with Mrs. Melnyk, even if she says yes. What was I thinking? I hardly know Sophia. Is it really worth sending my children to church for a chance at some adult company with an interesting woman who seems desperate to be my friend? But when I walk through the back door of the clinic, and the smell of Bengay and vomit hits my nostrils, I change my mind again.

Yes. I deserve to go out. I deserve to have some friends. Mitch never takes me anywhere. He hardly even talks to me these days. I've been lonely.

I quickly take out my phone and text Sophia.

> I have a sitter for Friday. Have you been to the restaurant Table 60?

I follow the cast of *Hamilton* on social and they were eating at Table 60 after one of their shows a few weeks ago. It's a very posh restaurant on the sixtieth floor of a Manhattan skyscraper, overlooking New York, and seems like a fitting place to dine with someone like Sophia. I've got my fingers crossed that she hasn't already eaten there. It would be fun to experience it for the first time together. Even if the meal will cost me a small fortune. I'll have to use "my money" because Mitch would throw a little hissy fit if he saw the charge pop up on his bank account.

> You must have read my mind. I've been dying to try it. I'll make reservations. Have a nice day at work.

No one has told me to have a nice day at work in, well, I can't remember the last time. I'm sure she's just being polite, but it still puts a smile on my face.

> Great.

Before I can say anything else, I'm being handed a clipboard and a quick brief on my first patient. I slip my phone in my pocket, check the name on the chart, and turn on the charm before I open the door.

"Good morning, Mr. Taylor. I'm sorry to hear you've been—" I look at the chart quickly. "Oh, um, rectal bleeding. Now, that's no fun for anyone. Let's get you into a gown and take a look."

My hunch was correct, thank god, and Mrs. Melnyk agreed to take the girls with her to her Orthodox church tonight. I was worried the girls would be upset with me and scared to go with our strict housekeeper. But whatever she's told them has them both excited on the way to school this morning.

It's going to be hard to hide the church thing from Mitch if the girls have fun. They are a couple of jabber-jaws.

Well, I'll just tell him it's his fault. Since he never takes me out, I don't have a babysitter I can trust. And would he rather I left them at home with a stranger from one of those online services or with a woman we've trusted to clean our house and cook our dinners for the last two years? I think the latter.

"Now remember, listen to Mrs. Melnyk. Don't whine or carry on—just do as she says and—" I glance in the rearview mirror to see if they are paying any attention to me. But they're already focused on unbuckling and getting out of the back seat.

"We're gonna have so much fun, Mom, don't worry," Sarah exclaims. "Come on, Bailey, let's go." They climb out, excited for another day in kindergarten and third grade. Sarah slams the door shut and I drive off, realizing I didn't say *Goodbye* or *I love you*—just gave them a warning about behavior.

I'm sure they know from my actions how I feel. I mean, my mom told me she loved me every day, but those were empty words. She was more concerned with appearances and keeping up with the Joneses to actually love me. All my lessons and the activities, those were so she could parade me around like her personal show pony to inflate her own ego. Which is why I haven't put the girls in any extracurriculars yet—I want them to be old enough to choose their own passions.

Plus, I don't want them turning out like me.

I left home truly believing I could be a star, because of how often my mom told me it was my destiny. And I'm not an idiot. I could tell how disappointed she was every time we spoke and I hadn't made it to the top. She was actually angry when I said I was going to stop auditioning and go to nursing school.

I'm *never* going to do that to my daughters.

They can grow up and live their own lives, and I won't interfere.

I look over my shoulder to change lanes, still lost in thought about my style of parenting versus my mom's, when a car speeds up behind me and cuts me off. Missing me by mere inches.

"Fuck you!" I honk the horn and flip them off. Blood rushes to my head from the surge of adrenaline. "Aaaannnd now my day has really started. Thank you, New York drivers."

I've got the first honk out of the way—so I turn on some music and spend the rest of the drive singing at the top of my lungs and pumping myself up for a day at the clinic followed by my night out with Sophia.

"You got a hot date or something?" Justin asks when I exit the employee bathroom.

"Jesus, you scared me," I gasp, dropping my shoes. I thought everyone had already left for the night—the clinic isn't open at the weekend, and no one lingers on a Friday. "What are you still doing here?" I've spent the last thirty minutes fixing my hair and makeup and changing in the bathroom.

"Luis is running late and I didn't want to wait in the back alley... You were putting on quite the show in there," he says.

Oh yeah, I guess I was belting the songs out. I can't help it. I'm nervous and excited to see Sophia again. It's obviously not a date, but I have butterflies in my stomach. "I have a thing tonight."

"Becky, Becks, Beck-a-roo," Justin says, followed by a smirk. Then he shakes his head from side to side, showing off his perfectly chiseled jawline. He's the only one who calls me something other than Rebecca around here. "Tsk, tsk. Are you sneaking off to an audition? I thought you'd given up on all that." Then he narrows his gaze, giving me a once-over. "Hair, makeup, something mildly fashionable. I'm impressed."

I roll my eyes and bend down to pick up my sneakers. "No. Not an audition. I'm done with all that. I'm actually meeting a friend for dinner. She's new to town and I thought it would be nice to show her the city." Even if it was Sophia who asked me out to dinner, not the other way around. Justin doesn't have to know that.

His phone buzzes and he looks at the screen. "Luis is here. Gotta run." Then he looks back at me. "Becks—"

"Yeah?"

"You're kinda a bitch and all, but you do have the singing chops. You shouldn't give up on auditioning." Then he shoves open the back door and leaves me alone in the dark clinic.

He's stupid. I haven't auditioned for a part in years. I'm sure as hell not about to start doing it again. The toll it took on me was tragic.

Sigh... I look around the dingy clinic. Actually, that's how I ended up here. After the last time I went to an audition. It was when Sarah was a baby—I was feeling overwhelmed and fat and like I needed something just for me. Mitch was surprisingly supportive, watching baby Sarah so I could go to the open call.

He told me I looked beautiful.

When I returned home, I told him I made it to the final round before being cut.

Which was a lie.

I didn't even make it on stage for the first round. I had a meltdown in the lobby while I watched all those perfect, skinny, pretentious Juilliard grads rehearsing together. I ran to the bathroom to hyperventilate and saw baby vomit down my shirt and bags under my eyes. My husband was a liar. Beautiful? Hardly. I was a fool.

I ran from the theater in a panic and down the street. I walked around the city for an hour, a dazed, delusional mess of a woman until I stumbled upon the free clinic. I walked in with every intention to check in as a patient. I needed to talk to someone, anyone, about the racing thoughts in my head. I was scared and I wanted to hurt myself. I mean, I was seriously contemplating jumping in front of a taxicab.

But the receptionist looked at me and asked, "Are you here for the RN interview?"

I smoothed back my hair, stood up tall and proud and said, "Yes, actually, I am here for the RN interview. I was referred by my husband, Dr. Mitch Hendricks, the pediatric surgeon." Then I tugged my jacket over the vomit and smiled brightly—I've always been able to turn on the acting when I've needed to.

Of course the impromptu interview went amazingly. As soon as they knew who my husband was, I landed the job. I could have had a second head growing from my shoulder and they still would have given it to me. But I was determined to prove that I deserved the job, regardless of who I was married to.

When I got home that night, Mitch was so proud of me for having a positive attitude, even though I didn't get the part in the Broadway show. I could see the relief in his eyes, and it made my blood boil. He never really wanted me to get the part. I waited a week before I told him about the job at the free clinic—which was another fight entirely.

Buzz.

Sophia. Oh, thank god. I have to get out of my head.

"Hello?" I answer.

"I know our reservation isn't until eight, but I'm bored. The problem with being a widow, too much free time. Let's get a drink before we go to dinner."

Oh my god, she's a widow? I swallow hard. "I'm just finishing up at the clinic. But yes, I'd love to have a drink first, and I'm sorry to hear about your—"

"I was hoping you'd say yes." She cuts me off. "I'm at the wine and coffee bar down the block. I'll order you a drink. What would you like?"

"Surprise me," I say and hang up.

FOUR

SOPHIA CARTER

I order Rebecca a glass of champagne, because I know she deeply desires to be celebrated. Which is exactly what I'm going to do tonight when she arrives—give a toast to her, my recently acquired *bestie*, as the American girls love to say. A title I'm very certain she is going to accept. We've only been talking for a week, but I've been watching and studying her for a month, and I know she needs me just as much as I need her.

I knew she was perfect when I laid eyes on her at that shitty "art studio" I'd been lured to. The owner, a crass woman I met at a bar, had made promises of her niece's raw talent that just had to be seen—*She's the next Picasso, I'm telling you, just come by and take a look.* I knew I'd have better luck selling something I pulled from the trash bin as soon as I saw it. But I pretended, for the sake of decorum, and the hunt.

Ever since I arrived in New York six months ago, I'd been hunting.

Not for the next Picasso, but for someone. With my husband, Blake, finally out of the picture and Hannah and the twins living their best lives in Iowa, I was feeling—oh, I don't know... alone? No, that's not right. I don't mind being *alone*. I was living on my own in Beijing for years before I moved to Florida. But I always had Blake to talk to and Hannah to watch online. And when I finally met Hannah in person, she'd been everything I imagined, and more. She really was the best friend a girl could have.

Oh, and the twins!

God, I miss them.

Rowen's funny little sense of humor. Ruby's confidence.

Sigh... I wasn't upset about being alone. What I was feeling was loneliness.

That's why Rebecca caught my eye. She too was lonely, I could practically smell it wafting off her plump frame. She wasn't binge drinking and gossiping with the other people in her group. She stood near the back, focused on her painting—which wasn't all that bad.

"I'll have to get back to you about your niece," I said to the owner of the wannabe gallery and do-it-yourself art studio, placing my hand on her arm, making her feel like there might be hope.

"Fabulous, I'll tell my niece you think she has potential." Her eyes lit up. It took all the strength I had not to vomit. *Potential* was the last word I would use to describe her talentless hack of a niece.

I made my way from the gallery to the art studio, where Rebecca was painting, and introduced myself. Our conversation was easy. She glowed from even the tiniest compliment. I could see the beautiful and bright woman she was hiding under the extra fifteen pounds of fast food and self-loathing.

Now, you wanna talk about potential.

Rebecca Hendricks has potential. At least, that's what I saw.

So for a month, I've tracked her. Driven past her house on Long Island. Followed her to work in the city. Learned her routine. All from a distance and without Rebecca or her husband, Dr. Mitch, mister self-absorbed *Doctor of the Year*, noticing.

I might not have done so much in-person watching if she had a larger presence on social media. But unlike Hannah, Rebecca has very few followers, doesn't post very much, and—from what I can tell—only set up social media a few years ago when her daughters started school. Based on the date of her master's degree program and when she received her APRN designation from the state, she was probably too busy with babies and school to have much of a social life. Which is great for me. Fewer real-life friends to contend with.

Still, I have to make sure she is the one.

And so far, so good. She seems to be the perfect candidate. Here we are on a Friday night, getting ready to have a real girls' night out, with drinks and dinner at a Michelin-star restaurant.

"Sophia!" Rebecca exclaims when she sees me.

I stand slowly. Is it too soon to open my arms for a hug and a kiss on the cheek, I wonder? Her shoulder blades hitch up in preparation for a hug. So I quickly open my arms. "Rebecca!" I exclaim. "You look fabulous. New dress?" What a stupid question. How would I know if it's new or not? Until she invites me into her home and I can snoop in her closet.

She wraps her arms around me, tighter than I expect, but I don't let on.

I give her a kiss on both cheeks, and she giggles, then I motion for her to sit.

"I ordered you a glass of champagne." I look at the glass. Then I grab mine and hold it up. "A toast. To you…" I stare deep into her eyes, pausing long enough for her to know I really mean it. "And our blossoming friendship."

She clinks her glass with mine. "To our friendship, may it be, uh—" She blushes. "Better than all the rest." She takes a sip of her drink and shakes her head. "Sorry, that was tragic. I've always been terrible at those sorts of things." A nervous laugh escapes her lips.

I lean forward. "Well then, we'll have to work on it—a woman like *you* should know how to give a killer toast." I wink. Was that too much?

She makes a sour face but tries to hide it with a glance over her shoulder.

Yes, too much. I need to backpedal. "Doesn't your husband drag you to hospital fundraisers and other events all the time?" I already know Dr. Mitch loves that part of his job—I spotted him in nearly every photograph on the hospital's philanthropy page. But I didn't spy Rebecca in a single one.

Her face relaxes and she takes another sip—no, a large swallow—of her drink. "Ohh, yes, well—yes, there are so many events, but I rarely go these days. What with the girls and all, plus, I'm not on any of the boards. So there's really no reason I'd give a toast. But I see what you mean."

I smile and nod. Phew. That was awkward.

"It's really like putting on a performance. And you said that was your dream, to be on Broadway. Here, let's have a do-over." I hold my glass up again. "To our blossoming friendship."

She smiles and clinks my glass for a second time. "May it be filled with long walks on the beach, starry nights, and, uh..." Her eyes dart around.

"Rebecca, is this a toast or an advert for a dating website?" I tease, laughing.

For a split second I think she's going to get embarrassed or angry—or worse, she'll stand up and walk out. But instead, she starts to laugh. Not just a polite chuckle, but a full belly laugh. It tickles me to see her laugh this much, because I know it's probably rare for her... She's alluded to the fact that she doesn't have many friends and her husband is a dud.

"Oh, Sophia, I've never met anyone like you before," she says and wipes the tears from the sides of her eyes. "It feels good to laugh. It feels like it's been a long time."

"I know what you mean." And I really do. It's been ages since I've laughed with a friend. Is it weird that it feels like I'm cheating on Hannah? Maybe I should call her and tell her I'm seeing other people? No, I doubt she wants to hear from me.

Now it's Rebecca who's leaning forward. "Tell me, Sophia, I want to know about the last time you really laughed." Her eyes focus on me.

I purse my lips. Hmmm... I wondered if she'd turn the tables and start asking about my life tonight. That's what friends do, right? Share stories. Have a healthy back-and-forth. But what if I don't want Rebecca to know the real me? What if I just want to be her rock? The person she can count on, so that she always wants and needs me in her life. Like a sister. Like family. All I want from Rebecca is a home—somewhere that I can go for Christmas. Somewhere I can retreat to when I need to recharge my batteries. A real home.

I put my finger to my mouth, pretending to think.

I know the last time I really, truly laughed. It was with Hannah and the twins. We had a dance party that ended with a doggy pile and tickles on the floor. "I honestly can't remember the last time I had a good laugh. I guess I met you just in time."

"Would you believe me if I said the same thing? I seriously feel like I met you just in time. God, I've really been in a slump lately," Rebecca says.

"You know what's good for getting out of a slump?" I ask.

The corners of her mouth turn up.

"A melt-in-your-mouth dinner with a view... I'm famished." I stand up and reach a hand to Rebecca. She clasps my fingers. Her skin is rough—probably from all the antiseptic soap she uses at that disgusting free clinic. I swear I was going to catch hepatitis just walking through the front door. I really can't understand why she works there... but I'm going to find out. It's high on my list of things about Rebecca I need to unravel to make sure she's the one.

FIVE

I told Rebecca I'd never been here before, to the restaurant Table 60, but that was a lie. I've dined here several times. They say it's the best in the city, but in my opinion, it's trying too hard. But I'll pretend, for Rebecca's sake.

And for the next three hours we wine and dine.

By the end of the evening, I'd say our first will-we won't-we-become-best-friends dinner date was a success. Not only did I learn *why* Rebecca works at the clinic, I also learned another helpful tidbit about the dynamics in her home. Helpful, since it's a place I'm hoping to frequent in the near future.

First, the job at the clinic.

It's not because she loves caring for the less fortunate. No. Working at the free clinic is a lesson in spite. Her husband, Dr. Mitch, loathes the free clinic.

He finds it *a disgusting place and an utter waste of her time—* his words, according to Rebecca. I don't disagree with his assessment of the clinic, however he's an asshole for saying it to her face.

Why can't Mitch see that Rebecca is the kind of woman who needs purpose outside of the home? I spotted that within five minutes of meeting her. Mitch might be an internationally known pediatric heart surgeon, but he's clearly an idiot. If he had any brains at all, he'd realize that if he stopped bad mouthing the clinic and constantly telling Rebecca she should stay home with the kids, she'd most likely quit on her own and find some other activity he finds worthy of her time.

It's a classic power struggle dynamic.

One I can use to my advantage in the future, if it ever comes to that.

The other thing I learned about Rebecca tonight over dinner: she has zero maternal instinct. Which is probably part of the reason she seems to have no desire to be a stay-at-home mom. All of her stories about her two girls reminded me of my mother and not at all of Hannah. The two women I can safely use to compare maternal instincts.

It's midnight, and we are standing near her car after catching a cab from the restaurant. "Will you call me when you get home? Or text me?" I put my hand on Rebecca's shoulder.

"Of course." She looks around the dark lot where her car is parked. "Are you sure I can't drive you back to your hotel?"

"No, I'll take a cab. It's in the opposite direction," I remind her.

We stand together for a quiet moment before Rebecca throws her arms around me. "Thank you for a wonderful night." She squeezes me.

I wasn't expecting a bear hug goodbye, but I don't flinch. Instead I squeeze her back. It feels nice to have someone hold me this tightly.

She laughs a little, before releasing me and crawling into her car. I wave, then make my way to the street to hail a cab. I give them the address to my flat. Sure, I told Rebecca I was living in a hotel, but that might have been a white lie. I *was* living in a hotel for about two weeks when I arrived in the city and my flat was being painted. But six months? I would never.

The somber night bellman lets me in the building and calls the elevator for me.

As soon as I get up to my floor, I slide off my uncomfortable Manolo Blahniks and stretch my feet. Then I take off my dress and slip into a silk robe. I'm not tired—I never am. So I pour a glass of wine and walk over to look out the big windows overlooking the city. My flat has an amazing view of the city that never sleeps—the lights, the movement, the hustle. You'd think that living in such a vibrant city with a killer art scene, I'd feel more at ease.

But something about this place, it just doesn't feel like home.

It makes me anxious—which I find to be the most irritating emotion.

It's why I need this thing with Rebecca to work out.

I linger a little while longer by the window, visualizing the next few months of my life, watching them play out in my head. Then I roll my head and stretch my neck. I'm a little stiff, so I head for my room to sprawl out and lounge on my bed with a book, waiting for Rebecca to call or text me that she arrived home safely to the suburbs.

But I can't focus on the words.

I start replaying our dinner over in my head.

Rebecca's disdain for her husband is completely valid. The man in all of her stories is selfish and arrogant. I'm not sure how she ever fell in love with him in the first place. She was a little evasive when I asked how they met and how long they've been together. A decade or so, she said. I think in the hospital where she was working as a nurse. I suspect there's more to the story—maybe they were secretly dating to start. Oooh, maybe her doctor husband was already married?

"Rebecca, you little slut, did you start off as the other woman?" The idea is titillating, but also gives me cause for concern. Rebecca's home should be a stable environment... I don't need her out prowling around for married men.

I sip my wine.

Then I chuckle. "What am I worried about?" I shake my head. Whatever she was like in the past, the Rebecca I know doesn't have it in her to hook up with a married man. No, if anyone was cheating, it was her arrogant husband—that must be why she couldn't say how long they'd been together. He told her he was single, but was technically still married. He's probably scared if that information got out it would ruin his reputation with his colleagues.

I swear to god every man in New York is a pig.

That's why the first thing you have to do is look at their ring finger. Do they have a tan line? Or is it a little narrower around that finger, where they've been wearing a ring for twenty years?

Hmmm... I bet that's part of the reason Rebecca doesn't have any friends. They all disapproved of her dating a married man. Well, it will be easy enough to find out if he was married before. I reach for a pencil on my nightstand and scribble on my notepad where I keep a list of things I'm working on.

Currently it says:

- *Get to know Rebecca*
- *Was Mitch previously married?*

Not a huge list.

My only real fantasy with Rebecca involves a loving home. A warm and welcoming place that I can go for holidays. Which makes me a little worried about the underlying contempt she seems to have for her young school-aged daughters, Sarah and Bailey. That could cause a problem for me down the road... like if Rebecca invites me for Christmas, and when I arrive, she's fighting with the girls and declares, *Santa is dead.* Go figure, it would be like Christmas in my home growing up, one of the very few I spent at my parents' estate, instead of my boarding school.

If *my* mother had just had a sister, or an aunt, or a fun friend—someone to give her a stiff drink and make her laugh, that might have changed the trajectory of my childhood. I decide that it's my responsibility to be that woman for Rebecca, in order to save her children.

"Don't worry, I will fix you, Rebecca. I promise," I announce. I glance at my phone. She should be home soon. My stomach rumbles—the dinner portions were microscopic and my sugar buzz from the cheesecake is waning. What I need is a bowl of potato chips and more wine.

I keep the chips hidden in the back of my pantry, just like Hannah used to. Which is silly, since there's only three other things in my pantry—a jar of chutney, a tin of biscuits, and a package of sesame crackers—and they aren't hidden. And there's no one living here to hide them from, like a judgmental mother or asshole husband.

Armed with my salty snack and a fresh glass of wine, I crawl back on my bed and check my phone.

> I made it home. Thank you again for a wonderful dinner.

> Wonderful, but not that filling. Current mood...

Then I snap a picture of my hand reaching into the bowl for a chip and text it to her.

> Gasp! You mean that 1oz meal didn't fill you up?

> Not even close. Next time, we should go family style, with heaping plates of Italian. Chicken parm, linguini with clams, you know, the works. We could even bring your kids.

I know. It's a stretch. And after five minutes with no reply, I think I spooked her. But I need her to know that this friendship—if it's going to progress—involves her family. I want her to start imagining me at their dinner table for Sunday meals. And when she pictures the holidays, she makes concessions for me—like which guest room I'll sleep in, and where my stocking will go on the mantel. It's the only way I'm going to get what I want out of this.

> Sorry... crying five-year-old...

> No problem, it's late. Sleep well.

Damn. I did spook her. She's not ready to think about me as

someone she could bring around her children or include in a family meal. That's okay—I knew it was a stretch. I need to solidify our friendship first. Maybe I can invite her to yoga or to get our nails done or shopping. Then, to my surprise, she texts me back after a few minutes.

> I know a great Italian place, but it's on Long Island. Not sure you want to leave the city.

> Are you inviting me to your house? You said you make the best spaghetti in all the land.

> LOL! Actually, I am.

> I'd love to.

Well, well, well, so I didn't come on too strong. She does see me sitting at her table having Sunday dinner with her family. Brilliant.

I let out a yawn. Interesting. I'm suddenly overwhelmed with the desire to sleep—which I haven't felt in a long time. I'm like the children from the poem, "'Twas the Night Before Christmas," but instead of sugar plums dancing in my head, I have visions of a big family dinner at Rebecca's house.

SIX

True to her word, a few weeks later, Rebecca calls and invites me to dinner at her place with Mitch and the girls. I'm looking forward to it, because we haven't seen each other much this week. Her husband has been home, which has meant no after-work drinks or dinners. Of course we've been texting. And I stopped by the clinic once, mid-week, to drop off a honey latte and a little gift for her, something I knew she'd go crazy over. A pair of Kristin Chenoweth's stage-worn earrings from the set of *Wicked*. The real deal, not some knock-off.

I know because I bought them from Kristin.

A fact I'm not going to tell Rebecca, because her ego is too fragile right now. If I tell her I know a real Broadway star, she'll never believe that I want to be friends with her. I meet all kinds of people through the art world, but I always keep my clients' identities confidential. After my husband, Blake, took advantage of my connections, I'll never make that mistake again.

I have my driver stop at one of those great big suburban grocery stores on Long Island, close to where Rebecca lives. As I wander the aisles in search of something sweet for her children, and flowers and wine for her, I wonder if this is the same store she shops at. And if it is, how can she stand it? American grocery stores scare me. They are so big and bright and overwhelming. I much prefer small markets and individual shops that specialize in something, so you know the items are higher quality. I do love that part about New York. There's a bakery a few blocks from my flat —close to a cheese shop and produce stand. That's really all I need.

Not all this.

Endless cans of beans and corn, aisles of soda, shelves as tall as the ceiling with things I've never heard of. My heart starts to palpitate. Maybe this is a bad idea, going to Rebecca's house. What if she's arguing with Mitch the entire night? What if her children are little monsters who start crying and claim I've pinched their arms? What if Rebecca turns into a different woman in front of them?

It would all be rather disappointing. I've built this up in my head. I need Rebecca to be the missing link, the person to fill me up, so I'm not lonely all the time.

After quickly paying for my items and running outside for fresh air, my phone rings.

"Hello?" I answer without looking.

"Hey, just making sure you aren't having any trouble finding the place. The girls are exhausting me with their 'When will Sophia get here' chatter." Rebecca sounds like herself.

My shoulders relax.

"I'm just down the road, had to grab something at the store."

"Oh, I hope you didn't think you needed to bring anything on our account," she says, as I slide back into the car.

"Not at all. See you soon," I say cheerfully and hang up.

The driver resumes his route and I look out the window at a familiar view. This isn't the first time I've been here. I've come at least three times, to scope out the neighborhood. It's idyllic, with the tree-lined streets and sprawling driveways leading up to big homes. It's nothing like where I used to live in Florida, with its bright flowers, palm trees, and steel and glass houses overlooking the ocean.

This feels older, settled, more like being on the outskirts of a village in England than in a suburb of New York City. I think I could grow to love it here.

"Sophia!" Rebecca exclaims when she opens up the front door. "Oh my gosh, flowers? Wine? I told you not to worry about bringing anything. Mitch"—she looks over her shoulder and bellows into the house—"Sophia brought me flowers and wine. Isn't she amazing?"

I don't hear Mitch respond. He's probably hiding in his office, pretending not to listen. But I do spy two small heads peeking from around the edge of the hallway beyond the front entry.

"And, if you don't mind terribly, I brought some treats for the little darlings." I hold up two Cadbury Crunchie bars, with their inviting yellow-and-purple wrappers. I was surprised to find the UK candy on a shelf, but that grocery store was enormous, chock-full of all kinds of unimaginable items. The girls dart back behind the wall, and I feel like the witch from Hansel and Gretel, caught red-handed trying to lure them into a cage where I can fatten them up before throwing them into my boiling pot.

"I don't mind that you brought candy, but they'll have to wait until *after* dinner." Rebecca's tone shifts, ever so slightly, and if I didn't know better, I'd say she was jealous that I brought her children candy. I quickly stuff the bars into my purse, and follow Rebecca into the belly of her home. It's clear she did not have a decorator. Her style is a menagerie of bargain finds from discount chains like Home Goods and Wayfair.

Even so, it's cozy, lived-in, dare I say loved?

I suck in a deep breath. "It smells absolutely delicious." I compliment Rebecca's cooking. And it does. There's no denying the mouthwatering smells coming from the kitchen.

"Well, after our micro-meal at Table 60, I wanted to make sure you left stuffed. So I made stuffed shells with homemade marinara and beef short ribs." Then she leans in and whispers, "Mitch hates my homemade sauce, so I always make it for company."

A chuckle escapes my lips. "I assume he compliments it in front of guests?"

"He puts on quite the show. He's the king of backhanded compliments." She heads to the cupboard and grabs two stemless wine glasses.

"Well, then we should play a little game tonight," I suggest and take the wine when she hands it to me.

"Ooooh, what sort of game?" Her eyes light up.

"Like the Tony Awards. But we can make our own categories... You know, like most obvious lie, most forced smile, that sort of thing."

"Aren't you funny, I love it." Then she grabs me by the hand and pulls me out of the kitchen. "Time for the tour."

As we wander around Rebecca's home, she spouts off facts and anecdotes about various items and pictures.

"We got that in Austin, Texas... I ordered that from a store in Seattle... Mitch brought that home from Australia..."

Their home is much larger than it appears from the outside. Complete with a fully finished attic, filled like a shrine to Rebecca's glory days in high school. She has costumes from school plays on mannequins, a cheer outfit is framed and hanging on the wall, there's an entire wall covered in medals and trophies. I know she's proud, but also ashamed that she didn't become more.

We don't linger for long in the attic.

But it's definitely a place I want to go snooping around in again. I spot several boxes sealed up in the corner that look interesting. I wonder if Rebecca is hiding anything else up there, besides the shame of not becoming a superstar on Broadway.

"What's behind that door?" I ask when we get back to the main level. It's the one room we haven't entered, besides Mitch's office. She knocked, but he said he was on a call and we walked away.

"Oh, nothing. Just the basement where the girls play and my housekeeper does the laundry—I'm sure it's trashed. You know how kids are, never putting anything away. We don't have to go down there," she says.

"Your housekeeper doesn't clean up after the girls?" I ask. Something about it seems strange.

She laughs. "Mrs. Melnyk? God no. She's basically worthless. She cleans the kitchen and bathrooms and does the laundry. Then she sits around and watches TV until the girls come home and she feeds them a snack." She shrugs. "If Mitch would help me with the cost, I could afford a proper live-in."

This is a sore subject, I can tell, because it's the second time she's brought up wanting a live-in housekeeper. Surprising, because the house isn't all that messy. I could tell the kitchen was sparkling clean, same for the bathrooms. So Mrs. Melnyk is doing her job, even if it's not as thorough as Rebecca would like. What Rebecca wants is someone to actually take care of her children full-time. A nanny, not a housekeeper.

"Is there anything I can help you with to get dinner ready?" I ask.

"No, you're my guest. Just sit and visit with me. Here, let me top you off." She adds more wine to my glass, then starts to sing as she putters around the kitchen. I take a seat at the island, watching and listening.

I'm not saying anything, because I don't want to interrupt her song—she really does have a beautiful voice. But after a few minutes, she stops and looks at me.

"You're bored, aren't you? You were expecting something more." She knits her brows.

"Not at all! I was very much enjoying your song," I praise. She cocks her head and narrows her gaze as if she doesn't believe me. A darkness spreads over her face. Something I've not seen in her before. The hair on the back of my neck raises and I'm not entirely sure what's happening, when the timer dings on the oven and Rebecca claps her hands. Her face brightens again.

"Perfect timing. Dinner is ready," she exclaims. "Would you mind going upstairs to get the girls? You remember where their rooms are?"

I nod. "Yes, of course." I slide off the stool and make my way up the stairs. I glance back over my shoulder, but Rebecca has exited the kitchen, heading in the other direction, presumably to get

Mitch from his office. I'm feeling a little uneasy as I climb the stairs, and I'm not sure why.

What just happened with Rebecca?

That was very strange.

And now she's sending me up to see her children on my own, like some kind of test. Which is fine. It's not like I don't know how to be around children. When Hannah was sick and I spent two weeks at her house, I had so much fun with Ruby and Rowen.

There's no reason I can't have fun with Sarah and Bailey.

I reach Sarah's door first. It's partially ajar, so I push it the rest of the way open and peer around. Empty.

I continue down the hall toward Bailey's room.

When I walk into the room, I can hear soft whispers from the two little girls, but I don't see them anywhere. "Time for dinner," I announce.

No response.

But then I hear, "Shhhhh..." I pinpoint the sound to the closet, but when I open the door, it's empty. Well, not empty, it's filled with small dresses and sweaters and coats and smells like clean laundry—everything is neatly organized. So Mrs. Melnyk isn't just cleaning the house and doing the laundry, she is organizing the closets. No easy task. I know firsthand from my time with Hannah's kids, it takes a lot of work to iron and hang small clothes.

"I'm hungry," a little voice says.

"Shhhhh, Bailey, she'll hear you."

There. Coming from behind the winter boots. But, how?

"I promise I won't tell anyone about your secret hideout. It's time for dinner and your mummy won't let you have the treats I brought you if you don't come eat first."

That's when a panel slides open in the back of the closet, and Sarah and Bailey crawl out. Sarah quickly replaces the wood panel and Bailey makes sure the clothes are neat and the shoes in order. How on earth did a five- and eight-year-old find a hidden crawl space in there? I'm impressed. Especially with the way they keep it tidy and organized in front of the panel so you'd never know they'd been there.

They have big eyes, like Rebecca, and dark hair—which must come from Mitch.

"You're pretty," Sarah says. Bailey is standing next to her, holding her hand and nods.

"Well, so are you... Sarah. And this must be Bailey." I squat down and reach my hand out to give her a little tickle. She giggles and then lets go of her sister's hand and runs out of the closet.

"We better get down there or Bailey might eat it all," I tease and turn around to leave. "You coming?"

"You promise? You won't tell Mommy about our hiding spot?" she asks.

"Cross my heart." I drag my finger in a cross symbol over my heart.

"I like how you talk," she says as we exit the closet. "It's like Mummy Pig from *Peppa*." Then she runs as fast as she can out of the room, her ponytail swinging side to side. I don't know many children's shows, but that's one reference I do understand.

When I touch down off the stairs and turn the corner back into the dining room, Rebecca is crying while she's putting a napkin on Bailey's lap.

"Rebecca, what's wrong?" I rush to her side. "Are you injured? Is Bailey hurt?" I'm searching for blood or something to make sense of the crying.

"Mitch left," she whispers.

"What?" I don't understand.

"A heart donor... emergency surgery..." Her words trail off. She's hovering over Bailey, who looks nervously from her mum to me and then puts her hands over her face, as if she wants to hide.

"Mommy, please don't cry," Sarah says.

"I'll cry if I want to," Rebecca snaps at her daughter.

Sarah inhales sharply and puts her head down. My heart hitches in my chest. I'm pretty sure I know why Rebecca is angry: because Mitch refused to meet me when he had the chance. But that's no reason for Rebecca to shut down and yell at Sarah. I walk around to Rebecca, put my hands on her shoulders and guide her to a seat. She slumps down and puts her face in the palm of her hands.

I decide to dish up everyone's plates. Food typically makes people feel better.

"Mommy, are you okay?" Sarah asks.

But Rebecca doesn't respond. I shouldn't get involved, but if this is going to be my home away from home, I need it to be happy, healthy, and welcoming. So I decide to take a stab at smoothing over this situation to salvage our night. "Sarah, sweetheart, I think your mommy is sad because a little girl like you died. Your daddy had to go to the hospital tonight to do a heart transplant. Which is super special because that means a different little girl gets to live... But it's still sad."

Rebecca scoffs. She clearly doesn't agree or approve of my attempt to smooth over the situation for her daughter. Well, what would she rather I say? Probably nothing. I should have said nothing. The silence is awkward and I'm second-guessing being here.

Then Sarah slides off her chair, walks around the table to Rebecca, and places a small hand on her shoulder. "Don't be sad, Mommy, the first girl still gets to live, her heart will go on."

Rebecca straightens up and wipes her eyes.

"Yes, you're right. Her heart will go on. You know, there's a song about that very thing," Rebecca says.

"Will you sing it for us, Mommy?" Bailey asks.

Rebecca nods, then opens up her mouth and belts out Celine Dion's famous song, "My Heart Will Go On" from the movie *Titanic*. When she finishes, Sarah, Bailey and I all clap furiously. It really was a hell of a performance. No wonder Rebecca had aspirations to be on Broadway.

"Bravo!" I shout.

"Bravo, Mommy!" Sarah and Bailey chant.

"Thank you, thank you." Rebecca smiles and clutches her hands to her chest. "Well, what are we waiting for? The food is getting cold." She picks up her fork and takes a bite of the stuffed shells. "Mmmm." She closes her eyes, enjoying the fruits of her labor.

I'm so excited to try Rebecca's food. It looks amazing. It really is too bad Mitch isn't here so we could play our little game with him. The stuffed shells are tender and I load up my fork before putting it in my mouth. I realize all eyes are on me as I'm chewing.

I pray my new friend and her daughters can't see the horror in my eyes...

It takes all of my strength to feign a smile while I swallow. Then, in my best fake voice, I say, "Rebecca, you dear, this is absolutely delicious."

But Mitch was right.

Her sauce is repulsive.

SEVEN

Thankfully, I'm quite the actress. I had years of practice—around my parents and sister, Lauren, at boarding school, with Blake, and finally with Hannah. Although, I was most like myself around Hannah. Which is what I was hoping I could be around Rebecca. *Myself.* But damn this is hard.

The sauce is a test.

What other explanation is there?

It smells incredible, but it tastes like rotted meat, sour and putrid. Does Rebecca really make this every time they have guests? I wonder how often that is. I suspect the answer is rarely. Did Mitch fake a heart transplant just to get out of eating this dinner? Is that why Rebecca was crying? Does she know how disgusting it is?

"Don't run off just yet, I'll be right back," Rebecca says and excuses herself to use the restroom when we finish eating. I glance over at Sarah's and Bailey's plates. They've finished everything I dished up for them without complaint. They must be used to their mother's foul cooking.

I get up and retrieve the two candy bars from my purse, giving one to each child before their mother can return and change her mind. She did say they could eat candy after dinner. And I'm sure they'll be grateful after what we've all just eaten.

"Thank you." Sarah grins. "Come on, Bay, before she comes back." She grabs her little sister's hand and they dart up the stairs, presumably to hide in the closet and eat their treat. I check the time. It's getting late, I hope Rebecca doesn't blow a gasket when she realizes they are eating sugar before bed.

She's gone for five minutes, then ten, then fifteen. I'm starting to think maybe she lay down and fell asleep somewhere. So I wander around the house, not really snooping, just looking for Rebecca. As I walk, I imagine what it might look like decorated for the holidays, with twinkle lights and garlands, a big tree in the living room. I pause when I reach the guest room, picturing myself with a suitcase full of gifts I've collected on my travels. Come to stay and recharge my batteries and spoil the family who's adopted me as one of their own.

"You can spend the night if you'd like."

I jump.

"Jesus, Rebecca, you scared me." I spin around and look at her. She's changed out of her clothes and put on pajamas. Her face is red and bloated—she was either vomiting or sobbing. Or both.

"Sorry," she shrugs.

If I was just some random woman she'd met and invited to dinner, this would be the point I'd run out of here, block her number, and nervously laugh about the psychotic nurse I thought I could be friends with all the way back to the city.

But I'm not a random woman and I don't scare easily.

"Yes, I'd love to sleep over."

The pajamas Rebecca has provided me are incredibly soft and smell like lavender. Mrs. Melnyk really knows her way around that washer and dryer. I know Rebecca is disdainful of the woman, but after tonight, I'm a fan.

"Sorry again about earlier, I was just so mad at Mitch. He knew I was excited about you coming over, and he could have easily come out of his office to meet you. Or said hello before he left," Rebecca says when she sits down on the couch next to me. She hands me a bowl of popcorn then pulls a blanket off the back of the couch and puts it over her legs. "Wanna share?"

Yes. This is exactly what I wanted.

Snuggling up on a couch with my new best friend, snacking, gossiping, about to watch a movie. I pull the blanket over my legs and set the popcorn bowl in the middle so we both can reach.

"Don't worry about Mitch. Honestly, I don't really care if I get to know him or not." I reach my hand in the bowl. She popped it homemade with real butter and salt. Not the kind from the microwave that tastes like cardboard. She might make a horrendous red sauce, but her popcorn skills are perfect.

"Really?" She raises an eyebrow. Her face has resumed its normal shape and color. As soon as I accepted her offer to spend the night, she brightened quickly.

"Yes, really... I've never had any desire to visit *Alaska*," I tease.

She smiles and laughs for what feels like the first time all night. Our little inside joke about her husband has done the trick.

"Mommy, can we have some popcorn, please?"

I turn my head and see Sarah and Bailey standing at the bottom of the stairs. I smile and wave at them, but they are both hyperfocused, staring at their mother. When I look back at Rebecca, she's stiffened. The smile gone from her face.

She lets out a long sigh... "No."

"Please?" Bailey whispers.

"Oh, Rebecca, it's fine, we've got plenty. I'll go grab them a bowl." I crawl out from under the blanket and walk to the kitchen and open the cupboards until I find a small plastic bowl. When I return, the girls are hugging Rebecca. I'm not sure why, but it surprises me.

"Aw, cutest thing ever," I say.

I scoop out some popcorn into the bowl and give it to Sarah.

"Thank you," she says, before she and Bailey run back up the stairs.

"Your children are lovely, very well-mannered," I compliment

Rebecca. She smiles, but this time it's strained. I'm sure she loves them, but she clearly doesn't enjoy motherhood. Maybe I should give her something to feel superior to me in this moment. "I can't have children."

"Oh my god, Sophia!" she gasps. "I'm so sorry."

I don't tell her it's because I had a hysterectomy to guarantee I'd never have any. Because I didn't trust that my husband, Blake, wouldn't kill them if we did. "It's alright, I've accepted it," I say instead. Letting her believe whatever she wants about why I can't have children, or how it makes me feel.

"Sometimes I forget how lucky I am," she says softly. We sit silently for a minute, which turns into two, and I realize if I don't say something quick, Rebecca might spiral.

"Do you know what's fabulous with salty, buttery goodness? A glass of rosé. I think I spotted a bottle on your shelf, do you mind if I—" I pause to gauge her reaction.

"Please do, rosé all the way," she cheers and jumps up from the couch to get us each a glass of wine.

Thankfully, the rest of the night is exactly as I imagine a sleepover with Rebecca to be. We watch a silly, over-the-top rom-com movie where the guy gets the girl even though he's a big goofball, and giggle like teenagers. We eat every last crumb of popcorn, drink the entire bottle of rosé, and tell stories from our childhoods. We bond over the fact that we both have less-than-stellar mothers. Although her mother is still alive—but they went no contact before the girls were born. I can tell she harbors some guilt for not speaking to her. As opposed to me, whose mother is dead, which is a relief.

It's well after midnight and Rebecca yawns a few times.

"Well, should we call it a night?" I suggest.

"Yes, bed." Rebecca drags her body off the couch. She throws her arms around me as we walk down the hall.

"Thank you for staying, what a fun night," she says and gives me a hug.

"The best. I hope we have many, many more." I squeeze her back.

She stands in the doorway and watches me go into the guest room and lie on the bed. For a moment I think she might walk over and crawl into the bed with me. I wouldn't tell her no—she clearly needs human contact. But I would flag it as questionable on her part. I'm open to having a female sexual partner, but I'm not attracted to Rebecca in that way.

"Good night," she says and shuts off the light and closes the door.

Okay, so she's not going to try and sleep with me. My body relaxes and I snuggle into the bed, reveling in the fresh smell of the sheets and bedding. I haven't had a good night's sleep in a long time—and I'm not sure a new bed is the place it's going to start, but within minutes, my lids close and I'm drifting...

EIGHT

REBECCA

Something about Sophia staying over did me good. I slept like a rock. And the next morning, she said the same thing. We laughed and hugged, as if we'd cracked some secret code. That was six weeks ago. And since then, we've spent as much time together as we can. She comes by the clinic every day to bring me coffee or lunch and we whisper like schoolgirls in the breakroom. She's spent two more nights at the house with me, since Mitch left for another work conference abroad.

I don't know what it is about her, but I truly feel so much better when she's around. Which scares me. Because I know it's all going to end... Everything good in my life always comes to an end. That's why I have such a hard time being a—

Snap!

Sophia snaps her fingers in front of my face. "Earth to Rebecca." She waves her hand. "Do I need to call Mitch? Rebecca, are you okay?" she asks in a panic.

We're at the park—the girls are playing on the equipment and we are sitting on a bench drinking coffee. I blink a few times. "What? No. I'm sorry, I'm fine."

"Are you sure? That was scary, you just left," she says. "I

thought you were going to have a seizure." She looks like she's seen a ghost.

"No, it's okay, I promise. Um, my migraine medicine, the dose was adjusted yesterday. I'll let my doctor know, it must be too strong. I'm sorry." I shake my head. "What were you saying?"

She knits her brows and stares at me. I'm not entirely sure she believed my quick-thinking excuse. Or if she knows it was a lie.

"Well, if you're sure you're okay... I was just asking if you'd like to take the girls to the aquarium this afternoon—but I think if your medicine is off, we shouldn't worry about it, we can visit the aquarium another day. I think we should get you home to rest. Why don't I call my driver?" She stands up.

No. I don't want to go home and rest. Or go to the aquarium. I mean, yes I do. But I know it's foolish because I need to stop all of this. I just have to work up the strength to tell her that we should end our friendship before it goes any further. It's really better for both of us if it ends now. I shake my head—I'm afraid if I open my mouth my voice will crack. Thinking about it makes my chin quiver and tears well up in my eyes, threatening to bubble over.

"What's wrong?" she asks. "Is it Mitch? Did something happen?"

"No," I manage to squeak out. "It's you."

"Me?" she asks. Her face scrunches as she tries to make sense of what I'm saying.

I take a deep breath to regain my composure. I have to get this out. "Please, sit down," I ask, reaching my hands out to her. She takes them and sits back on the bench with me. I turn and face her, then I open my mouth and just let the words pour out. "Sophia, you're too good to be true. I've needed a friend like you for a very long time... I'm scared you're going to get bored being my friend, because I'm just some basic woman. And then all of this will be over."

Sophia's eyes soften.

I know I'm holding my breath, but she hasn't gotten up to run away. That's a good sign. Right? Then she says to me gently,

"Rebecca, you lovely woman. Thank you for being brave enough to tell me how you feel. If we're going to be best friends, we have to be able to share our feelings. And I want you to know, I'm not going anywhere."

The air hisses from my lungs when I exhale and my shoulders slump forward. I didn't realize just how tense I'd been. "Brave? Hardly. But I'm glad I've told you how I feel."

"Actually, Rebecca, darling, I have something I want to discuss with you as well." She smiles, then looks over at the girls. They are waving and shouting.

"Sophia, look at this!"

"Watch! Sophia!"

I want to yell, *Shut up and stop trying to hog Sophia's attention!* But instead I force myself to clap and cheer as they race down the slide.

She smiles watching them, then turns her head slowly back to me, the breeze blowing her dark hair. "My contractor sent me a message this morning that they got the final permits in place and—"

Oh great. This is the part where she says she isn't going to have time to keep hanging out and that it's been nice being friends and all, but she's moving on. I knew it! I fucking knew it. So why did she have to lie and blow smoke up my ass about being brave? My stomach twists and turns and I think I might get sick.

"He said it would be about four months to finish the job. But I can't bear to live in the hotel a second longer. So I was wondering if you could speak with Mitch—and maybe I could stay with you for a while? I'll pay rent and for all the groceries and—"

"Oh my god, yes!" I shout. Startling her.

"Uh, wait, shouldn't you speak with Mitch first?" She narrows her gaze.

"No. Why should he have a say? He's getting ready to go to Berlin for a month anyway—teaching at some surgical program. He won't care," I assure her. I want to add, *And when you're around, I feel better, like I matter*, but I don't because she might find that too needy. She's asking for a room to rent, not to become my emotional security blanket.

"Lovely. As long as you don't think Mitch will mind. I don't want to be a bother to you or your family." She stands up and walks towards the girls, who see her coming and quickly scramble to get on the swings.

"Push me!" they shout in unison.

Sophia turns to look at me and waves her arm.

I want to warn her, if you push them once, we'll be standing here for thirty minutes while they beg and plead for more and more. But right now I don't even care. I'll stand here forever, next to my stylish, wealthy, kind, and completely unexpected best friend. A best friend who wants to live with me. My day seriously just got so much brighter.

"You really don't mind?" I waited until Mitch was already in Berlin to ask him about Sophia moving in. She's arriving later today with her suitcases, regardless of his answer.

"I said it's fine. You've been moaning for a live-in for years." Mitch is breathing heavily. He's walking from his hotel to catch the U-Bahn underground railway to the university where he's teaching. I can hear the bustling sounds of the foreign city in the background and a pang of jealousy settles in my gut.

"Sophia isn't going to be our live-in," I scoff. "She's a wealthy art dealer. She's going to be my guest for a few months while her apartment is being finished."

He chuckles. "Sure, Rebecca... Regardless, the girls seem very fond of her, and maybe with Sophia around, you'll find more joy in our home."

"What the hell is that supposed to mean?"

"You know what it means. Anyway, I've got to go, my train is here." He hangs up without so much as an *I love you* or an *I'll call you later*.

"Prick," I say to my screen. Does he really think that with

Sophia here I'm suddenly going to want to quit my job and be a stay-at-home mom? We've gone over it so many times. He knows I can't just sit around all day while the girls are at school. I'd go crazy.

As long as I've known my husband, he's known I have an inner drive. I mean, sure, when we met he found me crying in a closet at the hospital, but I'd just had the most disappointing audition of my life.

I remember it like it was yesterday. My skin still crawls from the embarrassment. I was in the final round. It was just me and two other girls. One of us was going to get the lead and one would get the understudy. Or maybe even two understudies! This was a huge production, after all. There was no way I wasn't getting my first role. I was smiling from ear-to-ear—it was my time! I could feel it with every fiber of my being.

"Not that one, she's too happy." The director walked into the casting call, as if he was God, and pointed right at me.

"But, sir, she's actually our number one—just listen to her and watch—" the head of casting protested.

"I SAID GET HER OUT OF HERE!" the director shouted like a deranged psychopath. His face turned red and he stomped his foot, then threw his coffee at me.

When I got to the hospital, where I worked back then, I was in a daze. What had I done that was so wrong? What did that even mean? *Too happy?* I wasn't happy. I was the least happy person in New York. I'd been auditioning for eight years without any luck. I'd changed my style so many times to fit what each casting call was looking for, I didn't even recognize myself. I was so unhappy I'd rather be dead. So I hid in the closet, with a bottle of pills I'd stolen from the med cupboard, prepared to end it all...

And that's when I met Mitch.

He fancied himself my knight in a white lab coat when he opened that closet and found me. I should have known better. That a man like Mitch has one purpose in life—*to save.* Which is what he spent the first few years of our marriage doing. Saving me from myself. Now he just seems bored and distant. He doesn't even care that I'm moving Sophia into our home—a woman he's only met once.

I quickly dial Sophia. "Are you almost here?"

"Look out your window."

I rush to the dining room window and watch a long, black limo pull into my driveway. I laugh. Of course she hired a limo. She probably has twelve suitcases. No wonder she's anxious to get out of the hotel. Renting a suite in downtown New York City for months on end must have been so uncomfortable for someone like her. Not to mention, it probably cost her a small fortune.

The driver gets out to open the door for her. I expect her to get out, like a movie star, in stilettos, a pencil skirt, silk top and dripping in jewels or a wearing a big hat. Like Audrey Hepburn in *Breakfast at Tiffany's*. But Sophia surprises me. She's wearing yoga pants, a tank top, and—I squint—are those flip-flops? No way.

"You look so—" I pause when I open the door for her to come inside.

"I found my Florida flip-flops in the back of the closet." She laughs. "I was thinking they might come in handy if we go to the beach."

"Only if you want to see a beached whale," I tease. But she doesn't laugh, she cocks her head a little to the side. I realize she doesn't understand. "Because I'm fat, you know, like a whale?" I clarify.

"Rebecca, you are not fat."

The driver puts two large suitcases on the porch and Sophia thanks him.

"Is that all you have? I expected more." I raise an eyebrow.

"Oh god, no. This is just what I'll need while I'm here. I have a storage unit in the city for the rest of my things." She winks. "Thank you again for letting me stay in your home. I was going crazy at that hotel."

"You don't have to keep thanking me. With Mitch gone for the next month, it'll be nice to have an adult to talk to," I say as I help her bring the suitcases to the guest bedroom.

It feels smaller than it did this morning when I was making sure Mrs. Melnyk changed the sheets like I asked. My heart quickens and I have a moment of panic. There's no way Sophia's going to want to stay in this tiny spare bedroom for months until her apartment is finished.

Why didn't I consider turning the extra room above the garage into a guest house? Instead it's just Mitch's medical book graveyard. I swear that man has enough books to fill a small library.

There's a noise coming from the basement.

The girls.

Oh god—once Sophia realizes how needy the girls can be and how little Mitch does to pitch in... she really is going to want to run away, back to a hotel in the city. Ughhhh... Why did I agree to this? It's going to ruin our friendship. This sinking feeling growing in my gut is making my knees weak. A bead of sweat runs down my back.

Sophia looks around and smiles, before she flops down on the bed. "Home sweet home, I love it here," she says and lets out a long, satisfied sigh. "Thank you again."

The sweat evaporates.

Okay, maybe I'm just being paranoid.

She loves it.

NINE

Sophia said she loved it here the first day she arrived. So why do I keep having this sick, gnawing feeling that she's lying to me?

For the last two weeks, on the surface, everything has been perfect. Sunshine and roses. But I swear to god, every smile on Sophia's face is fake and forced. And I think I know why. She's spending too much time with the girls—just like I feared—and she's not cut out for motherhood. It's all too much for her. *I can just tell.* Yet, she insists on helping. I think she believes she has to earn her keep. But she already gave me a ten-thousand-dollar check the day she arrived. More than enough for renting a room for a few months and covering the very small amount of food she eats.

Every day she's up before dawn, getting Sarah and Bailey ready. Then she drives them to school in Mitch's car. Sure, it's made my mornings a lot less stressful, but at what expense? Her happiness? No way, this has to stop.

"Sophia, can we chat?" I drop my keys and purse on the kitchen counter after work. I spent all day preparing my speech.

She's sitting on a bar stool, looking at her laptop, drinking a glass of wine. "Of course. How was work?" She looks up from the screen.

"Work was fine."

"Do you want to change first?" she asks. "You have a little something on the front of your scrubs..." She looks at my chest.

I look down and see dried vomit on my scrubs from my last patient, a toddler with an impressive projectile ability. "Oh, yuck. Umm... yes, let me go shower first." My shoulders slump. I really need to get this off my chest—not the vomit, but what I want to say to her. That she's supposed to be my guest, not my live-in nanny.

"Oh, I got you a surprise today while I was out doing some shopping. I left it in your bedroom for you," she says before I leave to go upstairs.

"Aw, you didn't have to do that." I scan her face for signs of resentment.

"I know, but I was walking along Main Street, for a little local inspiration. And you know those shops you think are snobby, well, you're right—they are super snobby. But there was one that had the most delicious bath oils and lotions, imported from the UK. I don't know, it reminded me of my sister." She feigns a smile.

Her sister.

She hardly speaks of her. All I know is she died. I'm not sure if I should be flattered or offended she wants me to smell like her dead sister.

"I got some for myself as well. I hope you enjoy."

Okay, so maybe she was just feeling nostalgic. I get that. It's why I make those thick-frosted sugar cookies every Easter. They remind me of baking with my grandmother. I soften... Maybe tonight is not the night to talk to Sophia about my fears that she's spending too much time with the girls and I'm scared she's going to grow to hate living here and this is going to ruin our friendship.

"You're so thoughtful," I say as I leave the room and head up to shower.

Sitting on my bed is a basket. Inside I find the bath oil and lotion, along with a beautifully bound leather notebook, a candle, and some dark chocolates. I wonder if it came like this or if she put it together herself. Those women in the shops on Main Street are vultures, convincing the tourists to buy all their crap.

I turn the notebook over in my hands. Jesus. Did she really spend sixty-five dollars on it? What the hell am I supposed to do with it anyway? I haven't written in a journal since, well, since Mitch and I were first married and I was here in this big house—where I had no one and was feeling very alone. It helped to put my emotions on paper—like once I wrote them, I could forget about them entirely.

Maybe I should do that again... No, that's stupid.

"Or is it?" I say. I have been feeling very emotional lately. So I set the notebook on my nightstand. Tonight before I go to sleep, I'll try.

After I shower and get cleaned up, I head back downstairs to find the girls and Sophia at the table. "Perfect timing. Dinner is served," she says cheerfully.

I really don't know why she goes to so much effort to cook. With Mitch gone, it's usually frozen pizzas. Not savory roast chicken and vegetables.

"Mmmm... smells good enough to eat." I sit down and Sophia dishes up the plates, one by one, passing them around. She always takes such a small portion for herself.

"So, what was it that you wanted to discuss?" she asks, just as I've put the first bite in my mouth. She catches me off guard. Making the explosion of flavor turn to ash on my tongue. "Oh, sorry," she chuckles. "That was rude of me, finish your bite before you answer."

I half smile and nod. Chewing fast and swallowing it down like a lump.

"No, it was nothing. I, uh, just wanted to let you know if you need to use Mitch's car to go into the city and check on your apartment, you can." I quickly make up a lie.

"That's generous of you, but I can take the train or call a driver.

I really don't like to drive in the city," she says. Then she turns to the girls and asks questions about their day at school, even though I'm sure she already grilled them when she picked them up today. This is all a show—for my benefit. She doesn't really care about what they did at school. She just wants to prove something to me—but I'm not buying it.

"Rebecca," Sophia says and touches my arm.

"What?" I blink a few times and look at her.

"Sarah just said her music class is performing scenes from the musical *Annie* and asked if you'd help her practice," she says, then leans in and whispers, "Are you alright?"

"Yes, yes, I'm fine. I, um, yes, *Annie*. I performed that in middle school. You know, I'm not very hungry." I set my fork down and get up and walk out of the dining room. My head is swimming. I think I need to lie down.

"Rebecca, wait..." Sophia chases after me and grabs my arm. "What's the matter? I thought you'd be so pleased and want to help Sarah."

"I need to lie down, I don't feel well. I'm sure you can manage." I have to get out of here. I jerk my arm from Sophia and march up the stairs, slamming my bedroom door, much harder than I mean to. What the hell was that? Why is Sarah's elementary school performing a musical anyway? I don't want my daughter getting involved in musical theater. It will only set her up for heartbreak. The same heartbreak I've had to bear for my entire adult life.

I sit on my bed, ready to close my eyes, when I remember the notebook on the nightstand. Maybe I'll just jot down a few things, to get them off my chest...

TEN

SOPHIA

My plan worked. I'm staring at Rebecca's confidently inked private thoughts. Feeling a bit shocked at her very accusatory first entry.

She used the beautifully handcrafted leather notebook to purge her feelings last night after her bizarre escape from the dinner table. I got the idea of giving Rebecca a notebook she could journal in when I remembered the attic and that strange shrine to her high school days. I'd spotted a box in the corner marked "Year-books, Journals & MISC".

Of course, I haven't gone back to open the box, but I can imagine it's filled with swirly bubble letters, heartfelt diary entries, and notes a young Rebecca passed in class with her peers. I'm sure they are all about her dream of becoming a Broadway star. As opposed to the entry last night. In which she sounds like a jealous kook.

I'm not even sure where to start! Sophia moving in was supposed to be different. She's all style and grace and practically movie-star material, but since the moment she arrived she's been cosplaying motherhood. Why is she cooking? Women like her don't cook. Why is she helping out with the girls? Women like her aren't supposed to like children. What is her game? And why the hell would she encourage my annoying lackluster daughter to audition for a part in the school musical? Doesn't she know it'll only end in heartbreak? JUST LOOK AT ME!!!!

"This is worse than I thought," I say and put the notebook back exactly how I found it. I knew things had gone sideways with Rebecca since I'd moved in. I'd thought she was going to be the perfect best friend and that we'd wear matching pajamas, watch *Love Is Blind*, play with the girls, take trips to the beach, and create incredible memories together. Then I'd move home to my flat in the city, having solidified a family-like bond with Rebecca. A bond that I could tap into anytime I want.

Because I've got job requests from all over the world—to track down art and curate exclusive pieces for the mega-rich. But I'd hate to travel right now, without a home base. A tether. I don't know why, but I need to have someone, somewhere, that cares about me. A person I can wake up and text.

And Rebecca is supposed to be that person.

But she's clearly not ready. She's too much in her own head. Paranoid about my motives. She wants me to make her feel more like a star, while I want her to be my family. I see that we are in a sort of paradox. Each one wanting and needing the other one to be something else. But I'm the only one who knows what is going on.

Not to mention, now that I'm here, I realize how much Sarah and Bailey need me. I knew Rebecca wasn't very maternal. I'd spotted that right away. But it's much worse than that. I think she loathes her daughters. Probably because she loathes herself.

I walk out of Rebecca and Mitch's bedroom, not wanting to be caught by Mrs. Melnyk, who moves around the house like a laundry ninja—stealthily carrying a basket from room to room. Not that she'd care if she found me in Rebecca's room. I'm sure she's done a full snoop of every room, cupboard, and drawer. I mean, that's what I would do if I worked for a family like this. Even if she finds me, I know she'd never tell Rebecca, because she despises her. And it would give her something to lord over me.

"Has she always been this way?" I say casually to Mrs. Melnyk when I get back to the main floor and sit down in the kitchen.

She's in the middle of making lunch—leftover roast chicken on toast with brown gravy. She sets down the knife, narrows her gaze, and crosses her arms. "Why you care?" She raises an eyebrow.

I appreciate her no-nonsense and that I don't have to explain myself. She knows I'm asking about Rebecca. "I just wondered if it's something that can be fixed, or if it's who Rebecca is."

"She always this way. Angry. Sad. Depressed. Happy. Loud. Crying. She up today, down tomorrow." Mrs. Melnyk grabs a second plate from the cupboard, dishes another helping, and slides the plate to me.

I nod with thanks. Still wondering, while I'm eating, what's really gotten into Rebecca. The way Mrs. Melnyk is describing it, it sounds like Rebecca has bipolar disorder. But I haven't found any antipsychotic meds in her cupboard. And with being an APRN, wouldn't she have noticed? Or Mitch. Rebecca's husband is a doctor, for Christ's sake, you'd think if it was true—if she has bipolar disorder—he'd at least have prescribed something for her. She is the mother of his children, after all.

You'd think he'd want her stable.

"Hmmm... I don't think her mood swings can all be about never making it on Broadway. There's definitely more to it. What do you think?" I prod Mrs. Melnyk. She's got to know more, she's been in this house five days a week for the last two years.

"Yah, I know."

I set down my fork and bat my lashes at her... waiting.

She lets out a sigh. "The doctor, he cheats. I think she knows."

"Well, that definitely explains some of it." So Mitch is a cheater. This throws a wrench in my plans... Because if I want

Rebeca to be my tether, I have to get her to a happy place. Where she feels good about herself, her children, her marriage, all of it. I am going to make it my goal to fix Rebecca's life. *If* she was happy, then maybe Mitch wouldn't feel the need to cheat on her. I think back to my marriage with Blake. It was always so much easier to be around him when he was happy. Being with unhappy Blake was like being slowly tortured to death. And even if Mitch doesn't stop cheating entirely, if Rebecca can get to a happy place, then maybe she'd be strong enough to divorce him and start over. Not ideal, but she'd probably get to keep the house.

"I'm going to help her fix things," I announce to Mrs. Melnyk.

Mrs. Melnyk lets out a loud, singular laugh. "Right. You fix her. That's rich." She rolls her eyes.

"Well, do you have a better idea? I know you love Sarah and Bailey. Do you really want them growing up with this version of Rebecca as their mother?"

She looks at me and scowls. "No. But what you do to fix her? Broken people not so easy to fix like broken vase."

"Maybe so... but I'm going to try." I set down my fork and stand up. "Can you pick up the girls from school? I need to run into the city and pay a visit to a potential client. I'll be home before Rebecca."

Mrs. Melnyk nods.

Walking back into my flat after spending two weeks at Rebecca's house feels—strange. It's mine, but it's too quiet, clean, empty. It doesn't look lived-in and there's nothing that makes it warm or cozy. Not like Rebecca's home, with its mishmash of styles, over-sized furniture, and little signs of the girls dotted throughout. In my apartment, there are no family photos on the walls or smells coming from the kitchen or the humming sound of household appliances.

I've only stopped here so I can change into something a little more appropriate for the meeting I scheduled while riding the train into the city.

I glance at my reflection in the mirror—very *dramatic*. Perfect.

I'm wearing a red dress with black trim, a pair of glossy black Jimmy Choos, and of course as many diamonds as I can. I've covered up with a long fur-trimmed coat and a pair of wide sunglasses and thrown on some red lipstick to complete the look.

Now, all I have to do is convince the director of the new Broadway musical *Happily Never After* to hire Rebecca for the lead. I'm sure the very large check I'm going to write will do the trick. But I need more than that. I need to convince the director to make Rebecca believe she's earned the role fair and square on her talent alone. I need him to waste his precious time holding auditions and put Rebecca through the same exercises as the other women. That's the only way she's ever going to have the confidence boost she needs to pull herself out of this depression.

At least, that's what I'm hoping will happen...

"No." Grant F. Baker III (the third, no less) leans back in his chair and sets his hands on his balding head.

I'm sitting across from him, dripping in diamonds, showing as much leg as I can, not that it matters—I'm quite sure Grant is gay. I lean forward. "I respect that you are a businessman. Just tell me how much it will cost, and I'll write a check to the production company right now. Rebecca is a star. You'll see."

"The part is not for sale," he says a little too loudly, stands up, looks around, then closes his office door and lights up a cigarette. I pull a cigarette out of my bag. They are for social environments only now, as I've tried to cut back since I'm living with children.

I take a long drag, so I have time to think. Hmmm... okay, so maybe Grant has professional morals. But everything is for sale, for the right amount. And typically that amount is much less than one might think. I've already offered to put money into the show, which I thought he'd go for, since I read online he's helping to finance the production. But he must be more savvy than I gave him credit for. That's probably not his money, he's probably raised capital through friends and family. I do understand his concern. As far as he knows, Rebecca might be terrible, and cause the whole show to flop. What would sway him then, enough to risk the production on some unknown actress?

I narrow my gaze.

"I'll cut you a *personal check* for one million dollars."

ELEVEN

He's already deposited the check by the time I get on the train heading back to Rebecca's house and texted me with the date, time, and location for the first round of fake auditions. They are taking place in two weeks. "I like your style, Grant, no messing around," I snicker to myself. Now I really am glad I decided to wear my expensive clothes home to Rebecca's house, instead of changing at my flat. If Rebecca wants me to be movie star adjacent, well, that can be arranged. I don't have a lot of time to waste, I need to get her on board with this audition tonight. Two weeks to get her Broadway ready is gonna take a miracle.

It's dark when I arrive and the front door is locked. I search my purse, but I realize I've forgotten my key. The lights are still on inside, it's only eight, so Rebecca should be awake. I ring the doorbell and wait. I'm about to walk around to the back of the house to peer in the windows when the door opens.

"Sophia. You're so fancy," Sarah exclaims and runs out to hug me.

"Where's your mother? Should you be answering the door by yourself?" I remember how paranoid Hannah was of the twins answering the door—and we lived in a gated neighborhood for the filthy rich. This neighborhood isn't even gated.

"She doesn't feel good. She's in her room." Sarah hangs her head and lets out a sigh.

I lift her chin with my finger. "Well, next time, sweets, do me a favor. Don't answer the door. Safety first." I boop her on the nose. "I'll go check on her. Do you have any homework?"

She shakes her head.

"Well, why don't you help Bailey put on her pajamas and I'll come tuck you both in after I check on your mother." I make sure to lock the door after Sarah scurries up the stairs.

·

Knock, knock.

I gently rap my knuckles on Rebecca's door.

No answer.

"Hey, can I come in?" I crack open the door and whisper.

"Oh, so you decided to come back?" Rebecca snarls.

I'll take that as an invitation to enter. The lights are dimmed and I spot Rebecca curled up in a chair in the corner of the room. She's still wearing her scrubs. She must have had a rough day at the clinic.

"I have the most delicious news, Rebecca." I turn on the charm. "Do you mind?" I walk over and flick on the lamp next to her bed to brighten the room up and to emphasize my glamorous look. "You'll never guess where I was today."

She looks at me—like, really looks at me. Her eyes start at my head and work to my toes and back up again. Her hunched shoulders straighten, and she sits up, as if maybe she's interested.

"Where?" she says. Her voice is flat, but I know I've got her attention.

"Well, I was in the city with a new client—a very famous actor. Of course he made me sign an NDA, so I can't tell you who he is, I'll just say he tried to task me with an *impossible mission* with the piece of art he wants."

Her eyes grow wide.

"Anyway, he had to step outside to take a call and I was chatting with his personal assistant and we started talking about the shows coming to Broadway this season. Have you heard of a production called *Happily Never After?*" I don't wait for her to answer. "Well, apparently they're holding auditions in a few weeks. The assistant's cousin, or roommate, or some such person is trying out. I happened to mention how talented you are and they gave me the information."

"What information?"

"For the auditions, of course. So you can try out—you know, to be in the show."

"Why would I do a thing like that?" She knits her brows.

"Well, because you're so talented. And this has been your dream for forever, Rebecca. I know you're destined to be a star, I can see it in you. I mean, I have been around the ultra-famous and the mega-rich—royalty, even. I know what I'm talking about."

She blinks her eyes a few times, as if she's coming out of a trance. A smile spreads across her face and the light I'd seen in her when we first met seems to be floating back to the surface.

"Sophia, I... uh... really? You think I compare to those kinds of people?"

"Why would I lie? I want you to be successful." I knew it wouldn't take much to pull Rebecca out of her funk. And Mrs. Melnyk thought it would be hard. What does she know? "I'm dying to get out of this dress. Do you mind unzipping me? These designer zippers are more fashion than function."

I want her to see the tag in my dress.

I want her to look it up online and see it cost ten thousand dollars. She'll be able to feel by that damned zipper, it's legitimate couture. I'm not sure I can turn on my own personal star vibes much more than this. I'm just hoping it's enough for her to want to do the audition. I'll trick her into going if I have to. Because she's not missing it. Not for the price I paid for her to get the part.

She unzips me and I can tell she's checking out the label.

"Thank you, for telling me about the audition and believing in me. I'll give it some real thought."

"Brilliant." I smile as I exit her room to go down and change. That's when I remember I said I'd tuck the girls in for the night. I quickly run downstairs, fling my stupid dress on the bed, ditch my jewels and heels and throw on a pair of comfy pajamas. Not the kind a glamorous, wealthy art broker would wear, according to Rebecca. But I don't care. I want to lean over and give Sarah and Bailey each a great big good night hug. The kind Rebecca no longer gives her daughters, since she practically has no contact at bedtime anymore.

I slip into Sarah's room first and sit on the edge of her bed.

"I think I gave your mother some news to make her feel better. She should be more like herself now." I smooth Sarah's hair from her face, tuck the blankets around her, then lean in to kiss her on the forehead.

"Promise you won't leave."

"Why would I leave?"

"When she doesn't feel better again, promise you won't leave. Daddy used to try and make her feel better. But then he just started leaving."

"Oh, sweets." I lean down and give her that big hug. "I'll stay as long as you and Bailey need me."

She seems satisfied with my answer. I flick on the little nightlight by the door before I go. Then I tiptoe into Bailey's room. She's already asleep, curled up with a stuffed animal.

"I promise, I'll never leave you." I make a vow not to leave the girls, as long as they need me, because what Sarah and Bailey don't know is I need them as much as they need me.

TWELVE

REBECCA

Mitch is coming home tonight and I'm dreading it. The first few weeks with Sophia here were an adjustment period, but we overcame it, and now I feel stronger than I have in years with her by my side... She really is the best friend a woman could have. She dotes on me and the girls. She really seems to enjoy this entire domesticated housewife thing. At first, I thought she was pretending, but now—I think it's more like she's trying to have what she never did in her life up to this point. And I'm glad I can give it to her. Because of what she can give me.

My dreams.

There are so many wonderful things about Sophia, but if I'm being truthful, the most wonderful thing is that she has access to the right connections. Something that always eluded me before now.

I know it was fate that she was in the right place, at the right time, to find out about the audition tomorrow for *Happily Never After*. And I know I'm just going to be a face in the crowd when I go, but there's something that feels special, different. Almost like I was personally invited to audition, through Sophia's connections.

And I'm not going to take that for granted. If it ever got back to Mr. Movie Star's assistant that the hot tip he gave Sophia ended up with me embarrassing myself, I'd never live it down. That's why I've been working my ass off—researching the show and learning the songs. I even decided to dip into my sick time at work, so that I could spend the last five days really pushing myself. Just like I used to, when I was auditioning full-time when I first arrived in New York. One thing I'll never forget is that singing and performing day in, day out can put a serious strain on your vocal cords. So by putting in the work now, if I get a call back, I won't have vocal fatigue. Call backs are usually even more intense than the first day of auditions.

"Rebecca, love, would you like some tea?" Sophia pops her head into the formal living room turned dance studio. I haven't just been rehearsing my vocals. I've been dancing again too. I have no idea the direction the director will go with the auditions—could be vocal heavy, dance heavy, or both.

"Sure, that sounds good. Thanks." I grab my towel and wipe the sweat from my brow. I'm not at all in the shape I once was, but dancing is kind of like riding a bike. Once Sophia helped me move the furniture and Persian rugs out of this room, it became the perfect space for dancing. And after a few hours, most of my old moves came back to me.

"Meet me in the kitchen whenever you're ready," she says and smiles.

I take a few deep breaths to slow my heart rate. After the last three hours of freestyling, I should be exhausted. But I'm not. Maybe it's all this nervous energy about Mitch coming home. I really wish he was staying in Germany permanently. Or at least until my audition is over.

"Are you going to tell Mitch about the audition tomorrow?" Sophia asks when I walk into the kitchen.

"I don't know. What do you think?" I pick up the tea she's poured for me.

"What I think doesn't really matter, he's your Alaska." She winks before closing her eyes and tilting back her mug, savoring the sip, as if it's the best thing she's ever had. I have to admit, her tea is pretty incredible.

I laugh. "God, you're right. He's going to be so jealous. Even if I don't get the part, just knowing I'm strong enough to audition again, it's going to drive him insane!"

Sophia cocks her head. "He's a fool for ever thinking you weren't strong," she says.

I set down my mug and reach out my hands. She sets down her mug and clasps my fingers, squeezing.

"What would I do without you?" I ask. As I'm about to pull her into an embrace, the door to the basement opens and Mrs. Melnyk walks through with a basket of laundry.

"I interrupt big moment?" she snorts.

God, she's such a bitch.

"Ekaterina, here, let me help you with that." Sophia rushes to Mrs. Melnyk's side. I really don't know why Sophia insists on using her first name. And look at Mrs. Melnyk, just forking over the basket, like I'm not even paying her. She turns around and goes back down the stairs to the basement.

"You don't have to help her. I pay her," I remind Sophia.

"I don't mind. You should go back to rehearsing anyway, we'll have to put all the furniture back in a little bit, before Mitch comes home." She starts walking away with the laundry and I'm disgusted. It's beneath her. Laundry. Then she spins back around. "But once you get the part, we are moving all the furniture again, and Mitch can just deal with it. You'll want a place to rehearse on the weekends."

She does a perfect twirl on her toes, while holding the laundry, before waltzing out of the room. Jesus. She can dance too?

I smack the side of my head with my open palm three or four times. "Stop it. Stop it." I try to quiet the intrusive thoughts in my head. Who cares if Sophia wants to help with the laundry? Who cares if she can dance? None of this is about her. This is about me —and I need to go back to rehearsing.

Mrs. Melnyk re-emerges from the basement with another

basket of laundry. She gives me a funny look. Did she just see me pounding my head? It wouldn't be the first time. It's a little trick I learned after Mitch found me in the hospital with a bottle of pills. Something about it resets my thoughts and then I can keep going.

As soon as Mitch gets home, I know something has changed. He's happy. He looks healthy. As if being away from me and the girls for a month has given him a new lease on life. And I'm fucking pissed. Why should he get even more joy out of his life? He already has everything he ever wanted.

We are all sitting around the table having dinner. Even Sophia. She didn't want to, she said we should have a nice family dinner without her there to alter the dynamic. But I insisted. Because I knew if I decided to tell Mitch about my audition, I'd need her here to remind me I'm strong. I deserve this. I've been working hard and I'm not going to come home and pout if I don't get the part; I'll come home and keep working hard.

"You seem different," Mitch says to me as he takes a bite of his salmon. "Mmm... this is nice. When did you learn to cook fish?"

"Sophia prepared it... She's been so helpful, since I've been rehearsing." I take a sip of my wine. I wasn't sure I was going to tell him. But if he thinks I'm different, then maybe something I've been doing the last two weeks is working.

"Rehearsing for what?" He sets down his fork.

"I'm trying out tomorrow for a part on Broadway."

"Mommy's been practicing every day, Daddy," Sarah says. Mitch ignores me and smiles at Sarah.

"Well, that's exciting for Mommy." His voice is jovial and the girls look at him like he's some kind of hero. He glances over at me and says, "Good for you, Rebecca. Glad to see you're getting out there and doing something you're passionate about." Then he takes another bite of the fish and goes back to chatting with Sarah and Bailey.

He doesn't look at me again, or ask me anything about the

production I'm auditioning for. He doesn't tell me it's stupid to try, like he used to, he doesn't seem to care whatsoever. About me or the audition. I don't understand what's happening. My husband has never been so nonchalant about me or the things I want to do.

This is extremely strange behavior.

I feel like I'm on the outside, watching my family have dinner. Mitch is talking to the girls and Sophia. The girls are laughing and eating. Sophia smiles and nods. And all I can do is stare at all of them. A growing knot forms in my stomach, twisting and writhing. They keep talking, and all I can do is watch as this feeling inside of me grows and extends like some kind of alien creature—through my veins and blood vessels, expanding into my muscles, taking hold over me and gripping my flesh. Every fiber of my body clenches and I reach up to clutch my throat because I can't breathe. *I can't breathe, someone help me!* I scream, but they can't hear me.

You're having a panic attack, Rebecca. Dr. Nakamura's voice echoes in my head.

But I don't have panic attacks anymore, do I? I look around. I'm not sitting at the dinner table any longer. I'm in Dr. Nakamura's office, the one in the city, that overlooks Central Park. It looks exactly the same as the last time I saw it, ten years ago. I'm lying on the couch, and from here I can see out the windows. *How did I get here?* I ask.

I told you to come see me whenever you have a panic attack.

But I mean, how did I get here, to your office right now this very moment? I was in the middle of having dinner with my family, I explain.

You're still having dinner with them—look, right there, see— your family is all laughing and doting on your cheating, piece of shit husband. Dr. Nakamura points at his coffee table, where there's a miniature version of my dining room all laid out perfectly. And miniature versions of Mitch and Sophia and the girls, and then me. My tiny figure is clutching at her throat. *He just told them he's going to Europe again, and leaving you with the children. Those fucking brats he insisted you have, even though you never wanted to have kids.*

"Wait, wait, what are you talking about?" I shake my head and blink a few times, freeing myself from the impromptu panic attack visit to Dr. Nakamura's office.

"I was just telling Sophia that it's perfect timing you're auditioning again, because I've accepted another month-long teaching position. I'll leave in a few weeks. This time it's in Amsterdam. I'm the only pediatric surgeon in the world who's used the Velature system for neonatal cardiac malfunction repairs."

"Oh, I see." So he's leaving again. That's why he doesn't care if I'm auditioning.

"Yes, and these European hospitals are willing to pay me quite a pretty penny to come and teach their teams. Anyway, I'm sure you'll get the part, Rebecca. Sophia says you've been putting in a substantial amount of effort." He sounds surprised. As if he didn't know I had it in me.

"Yes," I reply and fold my hands in my lap. "I have."

"Sophia thinks you could land the lead—and when I look at you now, I really see it. You do have a star quality about you."

"Oh," I whisper. That's the nicest thing my husband has said to me in as long as I can remember. There's no way in the world he would ever speak to me like that—unless he wants something from me. Something big. Not just going back to Europe for a month, but even bigger. I run through what it could be in my head. A vacation? No, he knows I don't like to travel with the children. New car? No, he'd do that without even asking me. A new house? Yes, maybe, but he always says this is the best neighborhood in New York.

That's when it hits me. He does want a new house. Just not here. He wants to move us to Europe. I'd bet my firstborn on it. But if that's the case, why hasn't he suggested me bringing the children over to visit while he's teaching? Sure, I don't like to travel with them, but this would be different.

Okay, so maybe it isn't moving to Europe with him. Maybe he wants a divorce so he can move there on his own?

As long as I get a part when I audition, I really don't care, whatever it is. If Mitch wants a divorce, fine. If he wants to move us to Europe, fine, he can go and take the girls. I'll stay here until the show is over. Okay, that's not so bad... A few years ago, the thought of a divorce would have debilitated me, leaving me bedridden for weeks. But the longer I'm with Mitch, the less charming I find him and his ego. I swallow hard. I can deal with whatever my husband is up to and hold my head up high.

"I'm going to go up and shower and rehearse a few more times before bed. If you don't mind doing the dishes and putting the girls to bed," I say to Mitch as I stand up, but he's smiling at something on his phone. He's entirely forgotten about me.

Sophia looks at him, then me, then the girls.

"I'll take care of it. You go get in the zone. This time tomorrow, I intend on popping a large bottle of champagne to celebrate your success."

THIRTEEN

It's been so long since I've gone to an audition. I'm not sure I'll know what to do. Sophia desperately wanted to come with me, but I knew that would just throw me off my game, having to keep an eye on her. I mean, I'm not her babysitter or tour guide. Sure, she might have told me about this audition, but I'm the one who has to get up on stage and perform. And I don't need Sophia holding me back.

"Rebecca Hendricks. You're up," someone calls my name. The young girls in their twenties, the professionals, snicker next to me. I don't know if they are snickering at me or about me, but it fuels me to get out there and show them what I've got.

"I'm here," I yell and march out on stage.

The director is balding, sweating to the point of pitting out his jean shirt, and is he smoking? Do they even still allow smoking in buildings in New York?

"Rebecca?" He says my name again, looking at his papers. "Start at the bridge during the act two solo," he barks. The pianist shoots him a strange look, but I don't have time to decipher their interaction, I barely have time to flip the papers I was given and find the spot to start singing. The music starts quickly, there's no time to have any nerves, there's only me singing—at the top of my lungs, and walking out on stage.

The director seems interested, using his hands to encourage me. "Yes, give me more." He stands up and swooshes his arms. "More, more!" He can't contain himself. "Arms out, can you move?" he asks. "Like this." He demos the move he envisions the lead performing during this part of the show. It's a shuffle ball change step with some kind of mambo hips.

I follow his stage direction as best I can, while looking at the music, trying to sing, following the tempo, keeping a smile on my face, and trying to remember everything I'm supposed to do while performing.

"STOP!" he screams. "Go—over there." He points to the other side of the stage. I nod once and move to a small group of performers stretching and lingering, trying their best not to look smug because they know they made the first round of cuts.

Holy shit.

I've *never* made it to this side of the stage during auditions.

In all the years I tried, I was never part of this group. Sure, I earned a few call backs, but never did I get the first-day bump to the "safe group."

I really don't want to get my hopes up. The director is clearly erratic and very artsy, so who knows what he's thinking. But I'm also not going to sabotage myself. I've earned this spot. I've been working my entire life for this.

"You lot, tomorrow, ten a.m." The director waves his hand at our group after the auditions are over. "All day, bring gear and food."

I keep my face as straight as I can. I watch the others as they fist pump and nod to one another. They know this is the next step to landing the role. I wonder how many times they've been invited back to this stage? How many productions have they all been in? I'd ask, but I'm scared if I open my mouth, I'm going to jinx all of this. So I grab up my stuff and head for the door.

"See you tomorrow, Rebecca," someone says to me. I glance

over my shoulder and smile before rushing out of the theater. I race around the side alley and throw up on the street. My entire body is shaking. I made it to the second round. Not just a call back. But an actual day of auditions—the director said bring gear and lunch. That means I'll be here all day, that means he's seriously considering me for a role in the show.

Me.

I pull out my phone and call the only person in the world I want to share my joy with. Sophia.

"Hello? How'd it go?" Sophia asks as soon as she answers.

My breathing is labored, and my saliva is still tangy from stomach acid. "They want me to come back tomorrow. Not like a call back, but like placement auditions. I think maybe I'm getting a part."

Sophia coos on the other end. "I told you. You're amazing. Now, get home so we can celebrate your success."

"Oh no, no celebrating. Not until I'm one hundred percent that I have the part. I'm going to come home and meditate. Do you mind feeding the girls and doing their homework with them and putting them to bed? I can't deal with kids right now."

"Of course, not a problem," she says.

"Is Mitch home?"

"I haven't seen him."

"Good. Maybe he'll stay in the city at the hospital all night. I don't want to see him until I know for sure if I have a part. He'll only say something to piss me off." Like last night. What was that? Since when is he supportive of me auditioning? It felt very performative, his behavior, like he was trying to impress Sophia, not me. He's never once before said I was a star. I don't know why he'd suddenly start thinking I am one now.

He's spent the last ten years treating me like something that might break.

Not like someone strong enough to perform.

FOURTEEN

"Mitch is having an affair." I say the words out loud as I weave in and out of traffic. My hands shake and I grip the wheel to keep them steady. Then, with a different intonation, I say it another way. "Mitch is fucking another woman!" I shout. No, that's too in-your-face. My heart rattles against my ribs. "My husband is sleeping with—"

HONK!

"Fuck you!" I blare the horn at the woman who just cut me off.

She flips me the bird in New York fashion, which makes me laugh, then scream at the top of my lungs. Once I get that off my chest, I take a deep breath of recycled car air, push my hair back, and relax my shoulders.

"Now, where was I? Oh yes... My husband is sleeping with... I don't know—some random fucking bitch." I know my Mitch revelation will catch Sophia off guard. Especially because she thinks I'm coming home to tell her whether or not I've landed the lead role in my very first Broadway production.

But my marriage is falling apart.

It should be addressed. I can see it now— Sophia will gasp, then throw her hands up in the air, and rush to my side, offering a hug. She'll hold me to her chest and comfort me. Of course, then she'll ask, *How did you find out?*

I'm not sure I want to tell her how I know, *but I know*. After that episode at dinner the other night, I got scared that I might have a breakdown during an audition—so I decided to see if I could refill some old prescriptions for the antipsychotic stuff I used to be on. If the state wasn't so strict, I'd just write myself a new, valid prescription, but oh no, that would be unethical.

Anyway, that's how I found out about Mitch's cheating.

I was at that little pharmacy by the hospital this morning, standing near the front window examining an old paper script and trying to decide if I could turn 2015 into 2025 without it looking suspicious, when I saw my husband walk by on the street. So I abandoned my attempt, ducked out of the pharmacy, and followed Mitch for a while. He didn't see me, because he was on the phone talking to someone.

He laughed and tossed his head back, running his hands through his receding hair. "Ohhh, you darling girl," I heard him say and laugh again. "Really? You'd do that for little ol' me? You're so naughty." He was smiling and happy.

Darling? Little ol' me? So naughty? My claws extended and I almost reached right out to slash him across the jugular.

What had I done that was so fucking wrong that he stopped calling to talk to me like that? Or laughing and smiling when I said something cute? I know I'd convinced myself that if he wanted a divorce, I wouldn't care, as long as I got a part on Broadway. But there's a twinge of something in my chest—sadness? No. Bitterness? Yes, maybe. Anger? One hundred percent.

Twenty minutes later I pull into the driveway. I'm mentally and physically exhausted. I've talked myself out of telling Sophia about Mitch's affair in any kind of dramatic fashion. Instead, I walk in, hoping to just sneak upstairs to my room without even seeing anyone.

"Rebecca, is that you?" Sophia calls out from the kitchen the moment I walk through the front door. Damn. So much for sneaking upstairs without a big fuss. "I want to hear everything." She walks out with a smile on her face. For some reason, that smile gets under my skin... Why should she be so happy when I'm feeling this way?

"My husband is having an affair." I blurt out the words.

She frowns and cocks her head. "Well—yes, I think he is... but can we talk about that later? What about the audition?" Sophia puts her hands on her hips. "Can we celebrate yet? Four days seems excessive. Did you get the part or not?"

I laugh uncomfortably. I just told her that I think my husband is having an affair, and instead of reacting, she just agrees and moves on and wants to know if I got the part in the show. "Yes, I actually got the lead." This was not at all how I expected to tell her. And where's my fucking hug? I thought she'd be holding me right now, not whatever it is she's doing.

Sophia squeals and does a little dance.

Although, I suppose it's sweet she's so happy for me. I soften and decide I should be happy. I mean, I did just get the lead in a Broadway show.

"The director, Baker, said he knew the moment I stepped on stage and started singing the part was for me, but he's been trying to place the rest of the cast around me. That's what the delay has been for." Truthfully, I could tell by Baker's demeanor by the end of the second day that I had the part, but I wasn't ready to say anything to Sophia. Because I wanted to know how my husband was going to react if I kept coming home with news that I was moving on to the next round of auditions. He continued to maintain this newfound supportive behavior Which is another clue about his affair. There's only one reason he's being so nice... Because he's in love—it just isn't with me.

"Brilliant." Sophia claps her hands. "Baker wanted to build a cast around you. What a testament to your talent, Rebecca. Now, you can't tell me no.... I've been itching to pop this bottle of champagne all week." She unwinds the metal around the champagne and throws a towel over the top, then pops the cork, like she's done it a thousand times.

Which she probably has.

I look at her. She's more glammed up than she has been all week.

"Are you going somewhere?" I ask. I realize there's no smell of dinner. The house is rather quiet for a Friday night. My brows knit.

She sets a champagne flute in front of me and pours.

"I thought I'd take you out to dinner. Mitch is working late and Mrs. Melnyk took the girls to church with her. So it's just you and me and this champagne."

"Really? You planned to take me out?" I ask. "What if I hadn't gotten the part?"

"I was prepared for a girls' night in. I have a bottle of American whiskey, matching pajamas, and the pizza delivery on speed dial."

"Oh, that's sad. I'd much rather go out. I need to shower quickly and change." I toss back the glass of champagne, then run upstairs. I don't have anything near as glamorous as the royal blue satin slip dress Sophia is wearing, but I do have a black dress I wore to a funeral. It's nice enough for a dinner in town. Maybe it will fit a little better since I've actually lost a few pounds from all the rehearsing.

Knock. Knock.

"Can I lounge on your bed while you get ready?" Sophia peeks into my bedroom and asks. I'm wrapped in a towel, about to step into the shower.

"Sure thing." I push the bathroom door shut enough so she doesn't have to see my naked ass. But she can still hear me.

"I'm so proud of you, I knew you'd get the part," she yells.

I quickly lather up with soap and water, making sure not to get my hair wet. I really appreciate how proud Sophia is, but there's something that doesn't feel genuine about it. Like she's trying way too hard. I mean, what's in it for her? Why does she care if I got the part or not? She doesn't go around bragging about her famous connections. So I don't think she wants to use my leading role in a Broadway production to her advantage. Or maybe she does. I've never seen her out with other people. Maybe she brags all the time. Just not to me.

Maybe you should just ask her point blank while you're at dinner, Dr. Nakamura says.

I shake my head and take a deep steamy breath from the shower. Now is not the time to have a panic attack. *I'm back on the meds, Doc. I don't need to come see you every time I'm struggling with the thoughts in my head.*

Are you sure, Rebecca? Because you remember what happened last time you didn't come to see me? You ended up in that closet. And—

Shut the fuck up! I hiss at Dr. Nakamura. I turn off the water and open the door to my shower, releasing the steam and helping set me back into reality.

Don't be mad at me, just because you don't have the nerve to ask Sophia what's in this for her, Dr. Nakamura yells from a distant place, but the words dissipate with the steam as I wave my hand around. I reach over and flick the fan on, clearing the rest of it out of the bathroom. Then I use my hand and swirl a spot on the mirror for me to see my reflection. Sometimes I don't even recognize myself. I see someone else—one of Mitch's exes or this new woman. Or the woman I used to be... before kids and life got me down.

I let my hair out from its clip, shaking and fluffing it with some dry shampoo spray, then I spritz some eau de parfum on my naked body, and slide into a clean dress. When I look back into the mirror, it's me this time—staring back at myself.

"You look lovely," Sophia says when I step out of the bathroom. "A car is waiting. I thought we could go to that little seafood place down on the water."

But suddenly, I don't want to go out to eat.

Even in a little black dress, I'm nothing compared to Sophia.

She looks amazing—and I'm overwhelmed in her presence. "You know what, I don't want to go out. But don't let me stop you. You look incredible. I'm sure you can strike up a conversation with anyone at the bar. There's always men around looking to pick up a date. That's probably where Mitch goes before he comes home."

Sophia puts her hands on her hips. "Nope. I'm not letting you self-destruct right now. I know it's been stressful the last four days and now you're having some imposter syndrome. But I won't let that get the better of us tonight. Come on, put on your heels. Let's go, Becks."

Ugh. I don't want to. And since when does Sophia call me Becks? Has she been talking to Justin at the clinic? "Really, you're going to force me to go to dinner with you?"

"Yes, I am. I know you're hungry. And I'm famished, so come on, let's go." She grabs my hands and pulls me. I let out a long sigh, then I follow her out of my room and down the stairs. Oh fine, I guess she went to the trouble of getting Mrs. Melnyk to babysit and she ordered a car for us and she's so excited for me. Maybe I need to relax. Maybe I should celebrate—it is a pretty big deal that I got the lead in a Broadway production.

I smile. "Sorry, I don't know what came over me. Of course I want to go celebrate with you. You're the best, Sophia. Thank you."

But even though I told myself I could do this, go out and enjoy an evening with Sophia, our dinner is off to a really weird start. I feel like I'm moving in slow motion. Or everyone else is moving around me really fast. Maybe I shouldn't have taken those pills—turns out I can in fact turn 2015 into 2025.

"Order whatever you want tonight, my treat," Sophia says, loud enough for the entire restaurant to hear. "I'll have a glass of Chablis Grand Cru Raveneau and a plate of oysters for the table. Becks, what would you like?"

I'm still trying to make sense of my menu, and turn it upside down and backwards, because the words are spinning on the page. "I'm not sure," I whisper.

Sophia gives me a look, and I want to smack it off of her face. Tears well up in my eyes and I open my mouth to tell her that she's really being unfair, bringing me out to this nice restaurant when I can't read the fucking menu. But she starts talking first, and asks about today's special and whether the fish is locally sourced and about the heirloom vegetables. Our waiter is fawning over her and eating it up, but I'm annoyed because I don't even know what I want to drink. The waiter finally leaves to get her drink and she looks at me.

"Is everything okay?" she asks.

"Dandy... Now, why don't you be a dear and go tell the waiter I'll have a glass of red?" I say and point to the bar.

She looks puzzled and doesn't get up.

"You're being strange," I accuse her.

"Me? Jesus, Rebecca, if I didn't know any better, I'd think you're on drugs. Landing a leading role on Broadway is something you've wanted for a really long time. Why aren't you acting more excited?"

I shrug.

"Is this about Mitch? I'm sorry, I know what you said when you came home tonight, about him having an affair. But I didn't want that to spoil your night." The waiter returns with her drink and the oysters. She thanks him and orders a drink for me, several other starters and salads for both of us.

Maybe that's it.

Maybe that's why I'm feeling this way. She didn't act surprised or like she even cared that I said my husband is having an affair. I guess it made me feel like she doesn't really care about me.

"Yeah, I guess I'm feeling bad about Mitch, and that's really overpowering my ability to enjoy getting the lead." But that's a lie. The more that I think about it, the more I actually don't feel bad that Mitch is having an affair. I'm relieved. I'm done dealing with his overinflated ego and bending over backwards to please him, when he's never really given me very much in return. I want him to leave. I want him to go away and never come back.

Sophia frowns. "I'm sorry, Rebecca, I should have been more sympathetic and not rushed you out of the house for dinner. Of course you're out of sorts. What woman wouldn't be? This is my fault. Can you ever forgive me?"

For the first time all night, Sophia seems genuine. "Of course I can forgive you," I say. "And you're right, I was a bit distracted. Now, tell me what it was you ordered for starters, they sound delicious. And look at these oysters." I think my second pill must have kicked in.

"They do look fabulous," she says and smiles as she picks up one of the little half shells. "I know, let's toast." She holds out the shell to me.

I laugh—what a silly idea. Toasting with shellfish. But she doesn't look like she's joking at all. So I pick up the oyster and hold it out. "Should I make the toast?" I wink. When I did that the first night we went out for dinner, boy, what a disaster.

"Oh my gosh, yes please," she says.

"Here's to a fabulous dinner between two fabulous people." Then we clink the edges of the shells together. I put the shell up to my lips and suck down the salty, briny oyster—chewing slightly to release the flavor. It's perfect. Just like the rest of our meal.

The food is delicious.

Sophia's company is wonderful.

I've completely relaxed and forgotten all about Mitch and Dr. Nakamura and having the blues. Before the meal is over, I get a text from the director—Baker—setting up a group chat for me and the other lead actors in the show. My heart swells. This is everything I've ever wanted. But there's this nagging feeling that just won't go away. Something is missing. I just can't put my finger on it.

FIFTEEN

SOPHIA

I wasn't sure if Rebecca had the temperament to pull off being a lead actress on Broadway. Not after her meltdown the night she came home and announced she'd gotten the lead. She was absolutely unhinged and I was certain she was high on something.

But it's been a little over a week and so far she seems to be holding her own with the cast and crew. At least, I assume so, because the director hasn't called me to say the million dollars isn't enough for putting up with Rebecca. And she hasn't come home crying and sobbing about the working conditions or any strange Broadway hazing incidents.

She actually seems to be flourishing. She holds her head up higher. She has purpose in her steps. Which is great, it's what I wanted. To pull her out of her spiraling depression. So that she could be the wife, mum, and best friend that I wanted her to be.

But I'm thinking I might have pushed her too far, with the whole getting-the-lead-in-the-production. I should have thought it through. But at the time, I just wanted Rebecca to be happy and I thought the fastest way to do that was to get her a leading role.

What I didn't know was just how much she would change...

First, she quit her job at the clinic. Fine. That was to be

expected. She can't very well be at rehearsals and work at the same time.

Second, Rebecca has become super distant with me and with the girls. She comes and goes, sometimes not even acknowledging any of us are in the room. She breezes in, does whatever she's doing and leaves, not even having made eye contact or started a conversation. It's unnerving, especially for Sarah and Bailey. I've told them she's probably running lines and songs in her head and that's why she doesn't say anything to them... But I'm not sure they believe me.

If I wasn't here to help out, I can only imagine how lonely and even scary it might be for Sarah and Bailey. So I've made taking care of them my new mission.

Which means I need to buy a car. Owning a car is completely impractical for living in the city. That's why I don't currently own one. But being out here in the suburbs of Long Island, well, what the hell.

I have the money.

And having my own car will give me a lot more freedom to take the girls places. When I move back to my flat in the city, I can sell it, or gift it to Ekaterina.

"Why you buy mommy car?" she asks when I return to the house the next day with a Range Rover.

"Why do you think, Ekaterina? So I can drive the girls to school and pick them up."

"Ah, so you want to play mommy."

I roll my eyes. "Oh please. I know you feel sorry for those little girls. I just thought while Rebecca is rehearsing, it would be nice if I stepped up to spend more time with Sarah and Bailey."

"What happen when Dr. Mitch divorce her and they sell this house and everyone move away? What you do then?" she asks. She's whisking up another batch of her almond meringue cookies.

They melt in your mouth and I could eat a thousand of them. They are also Sarah's and Bailey's favorites.

"If I have anything to do with it, that's not going to happen."

"Oh, what, you control rain too?" She puts the baking sheet in the oven.

"If that's what it takes to keep Rebecca and Mitch together, then yes, I'll learn to control the rain. And in the meantime, I'm happy to do what I can to make the girls feel wanted in their own home." I spin on my heels and walk away. Mrs. Melnyk just likes to argue. It's in her nature. But if she knew how persuasive I can be and the lengths to which I would go to get what I want, then she wouldn't argue with me about it.

I know I can keep Rebecca contented and in this home.

All I need to do is figure out how serious Mitch's affair is. If he divorces Rebecca, this entire thing will have been for naught. The Hendrickses' won't be my home away from home. Rebecca won't be my tether. There won't be any family Christmases to come home to, because there won't be a home. I've played it down to Rebecca, but it does have me worried.

I've snooped and read Rebecca's journal, but I've not gone and poked around in Mitch's office. I doubt he'd keep anything about his affair in his office, anyway. No, I'm going to have to be sneakier to find out who he's banging. Another good reason to have my own car. I can follow Dr. Mitch. Which is what I plan on doing the next few days until he leaves for Amsterdam. I'm also going to call an old friend of mine, someone that used to help out Blake when he wanted to dig up dirt on his associates.

"I'm going to run some errands before I pick up the girls from school, do you need anything?" I ask Mrs. Melnyk before I leave.

She shakes her head no as she carries a basket of laundry up the stairs.

"I'm bringing home dinner," I call after her. Since she spent the morning baking cookies, maybe she'll appreciate not having to cook. "I thought I'd pick up a couple of pizzas. I doubt Rebecca or Mitch will be around, if you'd like to stay and eat with me and the girls."

She throws a glance over her shoulder.

I don't really care if she stays to eat. I've spent the last five years eating dinner on my own for the most part. And with Sarah and Bailey, I'm never really alone, they always have so much to say. But I know that forging an alliance with Ekaterina is important. I don't know when or how, but I feel like she's going to be useful to me.

"I might. I might not," she says, then continues her march up the stairs with the laundry.

I smile and shake my head. As soon as I step outside, I make a phone call, then I climb into my new car.

"Hello, Barry Whitemore, what can I do for you?" he answers.

"Mr. Whitemore, hello, my name is Sophia Carter. You did some work for my late husband. I was wondering if you're still working as a private investigator?" I ask.

"Oh, well, not much these days. On account of my bad knees— real hard for me to get around. But what kinda work you need, Mrs. Carter?"

"Just a background check, for a friend of mine. Her husband is having an affair. We just want to know how serious it is. Her name, whereabouts, you know—that sort of thing." Okay, so it's more than a background check. It's some deep dive kind of stuff. But that's what Barry does. Or at least, that's what he used to do.

"Hmmm... Well, let me think... Hmmm..." he says. I imagine he's stroking his chin, trying to decide how much work it would be to uncover the affair. Would he have to do much walking? He must remember my husband, who would have paid him a small fortune to investigate potential wife and mother candidates. I bet he's wondering how much I'll pay for this job.

"Mr. Whitemore, it's a simple yes or no." I'm getting impatient.

"Well, yes, of course. I'll text you my fee and the items I need to begin." Then he hangs up. I'm still driving, but my new car reads the text messages out loud and lets me respond using voice commands.

Five thousand. Send picture of birth certificate, social, current address, and employer. Results can take up to 30 days, depending on how sneaky this guy is.

Provide me payment instructions. I'll send you the information you need tonight. I'd like the results as soon as possible. I'll double your fee for expedited results.

Done. PayPal link to follow.

Okay, so that was easy enough. Hopefully Barry can figure out who the hell Mitch is sleeping with ASAP, because Mitch is leaving on Saturday for his month-long teaching post in Amsterdam, and I'd like to know what I'm up against before he goes. Is it some nurse at the hospital here? That'd be easy enough for me to get rid of her while Mitch is gone. But if it's some woman in Europe, that's going to be harder for me to combat.

I'll figure it out though, no matter who it is.

It's worth it to keep Mitch and Rebecca together in their marriage. If not for my own selfish desire to have a home away from home, but for Sarah and Bailey to have their mommy and daddy stay married. If Mitch was to divorce Rebecca, I really think she might actually lose her marbles.

I'll need to snoop around to find the things Barry needs. I'll have to do it tonight, after I feed the girls, before Rebecca or Mitch come home. I'm sure Mitch has got his birth certificate and Social Security card locked up somewhere in his office.

"I've got you, Dr. Mitch. Time to put an end to your little extramarital affair," I say as I zoom down the road toward town. I want to pick up more of that lotion from the little shop. Then I have to stop at the grocery store. Jesus, I'm really becoming a suburban-housewife type.

. . .

"Becks, I'm surprised to see you home so early," I say when Rebecca walks in while the kids and I are eating pizza later that evening.

"The crew was going out for drinks again, but I was tired. That pizza smells great, I'm going to go shower fast. Oh, Mitch pulled in the driveway right behind me," Rebecca says and runs up the stairs, just as Mitch comes waltzing in the door behind her.

"Mmmm, what smells so good?" Mitch says when he enters the dining room. "Oh, Sophia, you picked up pizza from Massimo's, my favorite." He takes off his glasses and rubs the bridge of his nose.

"Daddy, sit by me," Sarah exclaims.

"No, me," Bailey begs.

Mitch chuckles, grabs a plate, loads up some pizza, then ruffles Sarah's hair. "Sorry, ladies, I have some work to do in my office. I've got to finish up my curriculum before my trip." Then he wanders off toward his office, carrying his pizza.

Shit.

I guess I'll have to stay up late and break into his office after everyone goes to bed tonight. I need to get those things for Barry if I want to know who Mitch is sleeping with before he goes to Amsterdam. Because I can't stop his affair, if I don't know who it's with. You'd think Rebecca would be more interested in figuring it out. But she hasn't even brought it up again since she landed the leading role in the show and we had our celebratory dinner.

She doesn't end up coming back down to get pizza.

I don't really blame her. How can she sit at the table with him and the girls and not just feel like total shit? Well, don't you worry about it, Becks. I'm going to get to the bottom of this and fix your marriage for you. So you can be the mum you're supposed to be and the best friend I need you to be.

SIXTEEN

He doesn't lock his office. Or his desk drawers. This is so easy—
why did I never look in here earlier? It's two a.m. and I can safely
assume Rebecca, Mitch, and the girls are all upstairs sleeping
soundly. I haven't heard any footsteps or coughing or toilets
flushing in hours. I guess it's a good thing my bedroom is on the
main floor, along with Mitch's office.

I'm sitting at his desk. The leather chair is extremely comfortable. No wonder he likes to sit in here so much. Seriously, I should
look at the brand. I rub my hands on the armrests, deciding where
to begin. His computer is tempting, but I have no idea what he
might use as a password, and the things I need for Barry are probably going to be filed as hard copies.

I use the flashlight on my phone to assist my eyes so I can flip
between the folders in his desk drawer. "Bingo," I whisper when I
come across a folder called "CREDENTIALING PAPERWORK", which
I bet has copies of everything I need. Thumbing through, it's
exactly what I need. It's got a copy of his birth certificate, driver's
license, Social Security card, as well as all of his medical credentials and paperwork for foreign travel.

I take pictures of each item and text them to Barry, before

putting them back in the folder. When I slide the drawer shut, it sticks and doesn't close all the way.

"Oh, don't be a little bitch," I say as I open and close the drawer over and over. Each time it feels like it's sticking more. I put my hand in and feel around, seeing if it's catching on a rogue folder. I try to close it several more times, once I think I have everything lined up. But I still can't get it to close. I'm about to leave and say fuck it, when I stick my hand in one more time, this time to the back of the drawer, in case a pencil or something fell in the back and that's what's causing the hold up. My fingers clasp around the edge of something. I tug and maneuver it out of the back of the drawer. Then I slide the drawer closed and it fits like a glove.

Phew. That was annoying. I quickly glance at the culprit. An unmarked folder. The only thing inside of it is a sealed manila envelope with the word "PRIVATE" written on the front. Well, this seems like it could be something interesting.

Clatter.

Scrape.

I look up at the ceiling. Someone is awake upstairs and moving around. Shit. I can't stay in here. I look at the envelope. I mean, I could, but I risk someone walking downstairs and finding me. I'll just take it to my room, lock the door, and open it up there. I turn off my flashlight, grab the folder, and tiptoe back to my room. I glance down the hallway to make sure it's not Sarah or Bailey wandering around in the dark. But I don't see anyone, so I duck into my room and lock the door. My heart is beating loudly in my chest, which is silly. I'm sure there's nothing in this file that's of any importance. Just like Mitch has his file of credentialing papers, this is probably the mirror file for Rebecca, and when I was opening and closing the drawer so many times, it slid off the row and got itself wedged in the back.

There's only one way to find out.

Open the manila envelope.

In the drawer of the nightstand next to my bed, I have a small pair of scissors for trimming loose threads or hairs from my clothing. They are very small and sharp, and the edge of one of the blades works well to slide under the tongue of the manila envelope. I should be able to glue it back together later so I can put everything back like I found it.

Once I unseal it, lift the flap, and turn it over, the contents slide out and land on the bed. I've convinced myself it's going to be school records for Sarah and Bailey or a copy of Rebecca's nursing license or maybe Mitch's college entrance letter. So when I see what looks like a hospital discharge sheet on top of the papers, it takes my mind a second to understand what I'm looking at. I read through it quickly, trying to remain calm.

Admission Date: 02/10/2015
Release Date: 04/01/2015

Patient was admitted via court order after being found by police with the body of a dead infant. Provided antipsychotic medications, antibiotics for UTI, and IV fluids. After two months of observations, the clinical team determined that with home care and medication management for MDD, the patient can resume normal activities. Including work. Due to the court order, these records will be sealed.
Patient to follow-up with primary healthcare physician for monthly medication management and evaluation.

"Holy shit," I whisper. What the fuck am I looking at? The police found Rebecca with a dead baby?

Now my heart really does have a reason to rattle loudly in my chest. I want to know more, so I look at the next few sheets in the packet—it's a redacted police report, judge's statement, and court order for mental health treatments. Black spots scatter the papers, covering up the names of the victim, the police, attorneys, and even the judge involved.

Even with all the names removed, my mind paints the picture of what happened... Rebecca came home from the store, unloaded the groceries, and accidentally left her newborn baby in the car seat in the garage. Then she lay down and fell asleep on the couch, and when she woke up hours later, and realized the baby wasn't inside the house with her, it was too late. The baby was dead, frozen to death, because it was the middle of winter and the garage was too cold. Rebecca wasn't charged with killing the baby. She was admitted to the hospital. And everything was ruled an accident.

Based on the dates, that was just a couple of years before Sarah was born.

I can't imagine losing a child, being forced to stay in a hospital for two months, being put on antipsychotic meds, and then getting pregnant again so soon after. I'd need a decade to recover if something like that happened to me. Or more!

This explains so much about Rebecca. God, I feel terrible for her.

I imagine a postpartum Rebecca, her belly still partially swollen. Clasping on to her dead baby, screaming, crying, begging God to forgive her. Tears well up in my eyes. And the more I think about Rebecca's pain and agony, the more it reminds me of the day the Italian Polizia showed up at my villa to tell me about Lauren's accident. It was before Blake paid everyone off and constructed his own narrative of the deaths of her and their twins.

The pain and agony I felt that day, I can still feel it, like a terminal disease—eating at my insides. It's my fault they're dead. I didn't mean for it to happen, just like Rebecca didn't mean to fall asleep and for her baby to freeze to death in the car. But it was still my fault—for sleeping with my sister's husband. Just like it was Rebecca's fault—for sleeping and not getting the baby out of the car.

I'm about to put all the papers back in the envelope, because this is all really disturbing and I need some time to process how I'm going to bring it up with Rebecca. Or maybe I should just hide the fact that I know she had a baby that died, and that she was in the hospital for two months, recovering from a mental breakdown. Yes. I'm never going to say a word to her about it, and some day maybe she'll open up to me and tell me on her own. Until then, it will be my secret.

I'll just take a quick flip through the rest of the papers.

To make sure there's no other big family secrets.

That's when I find a stapled packet, that looks to be the pediatric medical records for a child named Annie Hendricks, date of birth, February 14, 2013. Which would make her too old to be the baby that died in the car.

"No, no, no." I shake my head and my heart palpitates. "Is this about to be what I think it is?" I close the folder.

I cannot read about another dead baby.

But I'll never be able to sleep if I don't just finish looking. Maybe it's not that at all. Maybe I'm overreacting. I quickly scan the documents—well-baby visits, vaccine records, just the basic things you'd expect in an infant medical record. According to the notes Annie was growing normally. That's when I reach the last page.

The printed note from an on-call hospital physician, dated March 28, 2013.

Patient DOA. Patient found in asystole. Code protocol initiated on arrival. No return of spontaneous circulation. Time of death pronounced: 8:15 a.m. by Arnold Lewis-Riggs, MD.
Appears to be a 6-week infant, well-developed, nourished, cool to the touch, no sign of struggle. Evidence of postmortem lividity. Initial determination, SIDS.

Sudden Infant Death Syndrome. My sister, Lauren, was horribly afraid of SIDS with her children, refusing to let them sleep in the bed with her. "What the fuck, Becks, did you really have two babies that died?" I ask the papers, as if I'm talking to Rebecca herself. Oh my god. If I still had a uterus, it would be clenching right now.

I just can't believe it.

I mean, I completely understand why Rebecca never told me

about any of this, the heartbreak she must have experienced. First, she loses a baby to SIDS and then two years later she has another baby and accidentally leaves it in the car and it freezes to death.

I can only imagine the intense and painful feelings of guilt she must have. Especially because her husband is a pediatric surgeon—and his entire job is rescuing and saving babies and children from life-threatening illness and injury. But the two things that killed their children are things her husband couldn't fix, no matter how talented he is.

This explains so much about the kind of person and parent Rebecca is. It's not an excuse for her lack of maternal skills, but it does explain a lot of her behavior. Why she has a hard time connecting with her daughters. I bet when they were little, she always thought the other shoe was going to drop. After losing two children, it's a wonder she even had Sarah and Bailey at all.

I wonder if Mitch worries that Rebecca will eventually break. Maybe that's why he was always harping on her to be a stay-at-home mum. He is worried that if she does too much, she might be forgetful again, or do something she'd regret. Not just threatening his career as a doctor, but her career as a nurse. I doubt many medical clinics want to hire someone on antipsychotic drugs with two dead babies as part of their personal history. Doesn't really lend to the credibility or effectiveness of being a healthcare professional.

I'm not entirely sure what to do with all of this new information, but perhaps I'll be grateful for it depending on what Barry finds out. Maybe I can use some of it as leverage to threaten Mitch. He's obviously gone to some lengths to hide this information. Otherwise, I would have come across it when I googled Rebecca when we first met. Nothing about this comes up in any basic internet searches. Hmmm... I wonder if I asked Barry Whitemore to do a background check on Rebecca what he might find? Is this her biggest secret, or is this just the tip of the iceberg?

"You know what, it's none of my business." I put all the papers back in the folder. Knowing this information about Rebecca doesn't change anything. It doesn't change the fact that she's become my best friend, she's been letting me live at her home, she's going to be my tether so I can start traveling the world again for work.

Even if she's had a few off days lately. It's not her fault she's out of sorts because her husband is cheating on her. It doesn't change who she is now.

I look around. I don't have anything in my room I can use to seal up the envelope. But I know the girls have a glue stick in their basket of art supplies in the bottom cupboard in the dining room. Tomorrow I'll seal it up and put it back. Until then, I need to put it somewhere safe. So I put the envelope back in its folder, lift the edge of the mattress, and stuff it under.

No one will find it there.

SEVENTEEN

"Where is it?" I panic. The folder containing the manila envelope with Rebecca's medical records and the information on her two dead babies is gone. I know I shoved it under the mattress for safe-keeping until I could put it back in Mitch's office. There's no way anyone saw me, unless there's a camera in my room watching my every move.

I look around at the mirrors and artwork.

Could there be a camera behind one of them?

As much as I want this friendship to work with Rebecca, I'd have to seriously reconsider things if I find a hidden camera. That would be a big red flag. I won't tolerate her spying on me. I peek behind the mirror. Nothing.

"Oh, this is stupid," I say to myself as I check behind the lamp. Rebecca isn't smart enough to install secret cameras. She can barely use even the most basic features on her phone. She is not tech savvy.

I stick my hand under the mattress one more time, shoving it as far back as I can. My fingertips brush the edge of something. It's the folder. My heart rate settles down to a normal rhythm. Okay, phew, I just didn't stick my arm back far enough the first time. Jesus, I must have been very paranoid when I stuck it in there in the middle of the night to have pushed it so far under the mattress.

Now, time to return it to its place in Mitch's office. Everyone is gone, except for Ekaterina. But she's upstairs cleaning Rebecca's bathroom. I can hear her in the tub with that steam-cleaning device she's obsessed with. Not that I blame her, I've watched her use it, and it is a cleaning miracle.

Gross, I really have turned domestic.

I need to get things under control here fast and schedule a business trip to somewhere like Tokyo or St. Petersburg, before I completely forget how to behave around my regular clientele: billionaires and royalty.

I set the file down on the bed, open up the little purple glue stick I borrowed from Bailey's backpack this morning, and I'm about to seal the manila envelope shut when I realize it might be to my advantage to have copies of everything in this folder. *Just in case.*

So I dump the contents out again and quickly take a picture of each page, then return them to the envelope and glue it shut. It almost feels like I'm a mixed media artist, with all the various papers, folders, envelope and glue. Mixed media isn't usually my forte, but maybe I'll have to start paying more attention to it. Then I rush to Mitch's office and shove the file in the back of the drawer like I found it, but without it wedged against the mechanism, so that the drawer will still shut.

"What you doing in there?" Ekaterina asks as she walks by.

"Trying to find out who Mitch is having an affair with." I decide it's better to be mostly honest.

She snorts. "Obviously woman in Europe. Why else he go back again so soon?"

"That's what I thought too. I just wondered if I could find her name, maybe I could look her up online and see how serious it is. I don't want it to break Rebecca—she's doing so much better now that she's landed a role in a show."

Ekaterina rolls her eyes.

"What? You don't think she's doing better?" I ask and follow her down the hallway.

"You don't want to know what I think," she says.

"Yes I do, or I wouldn't have asked." I take a seat on a stool at the kitchen island while Ekaterina puts her steam cleaner away in the cupboard. She turns around and narrows her gaze.

"She doing better for her. But not for anyone else. Not better for girls. Not better for husband. Or you or me or this house. She a selfish, godless woman. You see. She stab you in the back to get ahead," Ekaterina says and wipes her hands with a dish towel. That's the most she's said on the subject of Rebecca since I've been here. And rather bold, considering I'm supposed to be Rebecca's best friend. She doesn't seem worried that I'm going to run and tell Rebecca, though.

"Do you think I'm friends with Rebecca?" I ask.

"No. You using her." She sets down the towel and goes to the fridge. She narrows her gaze at me before she opens up the door. "I can't figure out why, because woman like you don't need woman like Rebecca." She starts pulling out ingredients and plunks a stick of butter down in front of me, followed by a paring knife and cutting board. "Cube that for crust."

I oblige and start cubing the cold butter.

"You're wrong, Ekaterina. I do need Rebecca. I need someone here in New York, like a home base, to care about me when I travel for work. I need someone I can call and they'll ask me how I'm doing and they'll remind me to get enough sleep and take my vitamins and come home for the holidays," I explain as I finish cutting the butter for what I've determined must be an apple pie, based on the ingredients sitting on the counter.

Ekaterina dumps a scoop of flour into a bowl. She pauses, looks at me and shakes her head. "You an idiot if you think Rebecca that person. She selfish woman. Only care about herself. Never care about anyone else. Not husband. Not children. And definitely not you."

I hand the cutting board with all the cubed butter back to

Ekaterina and watch as she puts it in the flour and begins to cut it in with a pair of forks to form it into a crust. Maybe she's onto something… Maybe Rebecca is never going to be the person I can count on when I'm traveling the world.

Especially now that she's starring in a Broadway show.

It will be months, six months at least, before the show is over and Rebecca resumes her normal life. But she might never be satisfied as a nurse again. And she might audition for another show on Broadway—and depending on how well she performs in *Happily Never After*, she could conceivably get another starring role on her own, without me paying off the director.

Which means…

Yes, Ekaterina isn't just onto something. She's one hundred percent right.

"Well, fuck. Now what? I have to start over? Find a new best friend?" I moan. Ekaterina hands me the bowl of apples.

"Start slicing. Nice and thin."

"Maybe you can be my person?" I raise an eyebrow.

The housekeeper throws her head back and laughs. A great big belly laugh. "Oh please. I don't give a shit if you take your vitamins or come home for Christmas." She laughs so much tears come out of her eyes and run down her cheeks. She uses her arm to wipe them away, still laughing.

I scowl at her. "Oh, shut the fuck up."

"Don't be mad… Look, I make you deal. I care about you, *if* you promise to take little girls." She side-eyes me. "Protect them."

Hmmm…. That is a strange thing for her to say. Why would I take Rebecca's children? Take them where? With me when I travel the world for work? Can you even imagine? Dragging two little girls with me to view priceless art. And what am I protecting them from? I mean, I know Rebecca and Mitch are both pretty self-centered, they don't seem to care much for the girls. But that's a far cry from children needing protection from their parents. And the thing with the two dead babies, I know Ekaterina doesn't know about that. How could she? Even if she did, those were accidents. Rebecca didn't cause their deaths.

The house phone rings and Ekaterina sets down the ball of dough she just finished forming to answer it. Leaving me to keep pondering what the hell she meant. Her English isn't the best. I must have misunderstood. I'll have to ask her to repeat it, because whatever she's trying to say, isn't coming across as she intends.

"You go to school. Bailey is hurt, or something, needs pickup," she says in a hurry when she comes back into the kitchen.

I don't have to be told twice. I grab my keys and rush out of the house. While I'm driving I call Rebecca. It goes directly to voicemail.

"I'm on my way to the school to get Bailey. Call me when you get this."

Next, I try Mitch. Same thing. Directly to voicemail. I decide not to leave him a message. He can call his wife.

I reach the school in under ten minutes and fly into the parking lot, parking in a spot reserved for "Teacher of the Month."

"I'm here for Bailey Hendricks. We received a call that she was hurt," I say to the woman at the front desk. It's the first time I've been inside the school. I drop off and pick up the girls every day, but I've yet to have had a reason to come inside the building.

"Are you the housekeeper, Mrs. Melnyk?" the woman asks.

"No, I'm Sophia Carter." I'm not sure what title to give myself, so I don't bother with any. "Rebecca sent me," I lie.

"Ahhh, okay. Bailey's been asking for you. Follow me," she says and gets up, leading me down a narrow hallway covered in children's artwork. At the end is an office marked "NURSE". She opens the door. "You can go in to get Bailey. Just check out with me at the front desk before you leave."

Inside the nurse's office, Bailey is curled up on a small exam table. She looks like she's asleep, her eyes are closed. I look around for an adult or someone to tell me what's going on, but there's no nurse or anyone else in the room.

"Bailey, sweets, are you okay?" I walk over and check her forehead for a temperature. But she feels fine. "Is something broken? What happened?" I don't understand.

She opens her eyes, sees it's me, and shouts, "FIFI!" then scrambles to sit up and throws her arms around me and starts crying. I sniff the air—there is a strong whiff of urine in the room.

"I wanna go home," she cries.

"Of course, are you alright? Are you hurt? Did you throw up?" I ask the basic questions I assume you should ask a child in this situation.

"No, I wanna go home."

"Okay, you don't have to tell me what happened. Let's go home." I try to pick her up to put her on the ground, but she pulls away from me and gets off the table herself.

"What's wrong?"

"I'm wet," she whispers.

I look and see a wet patch on the paper on the small exam table. Then I look at Bailey's pants and realize they are damp in the middle and down one leg. So that's the urine smell. She's had an accident, but no one here has cleaned her up or given her extra clothes.

"Oh honey, I'm very sorry no one helped you change. Here..." I take my cardigan off and tie it around her waist to cover up the evidence that she's had an accident. Then I grab her backpack, sling it over my shoulder, take her by the hand, and march out of the nurse's office. We go right up to the secretary who led me to the unmanned nurse's office, and I look at her, narrow my eyes, and say, "You're a fucking bitch."

She gasps.

Another teacher in the office gasps.

Bailey giggles.

"I, well, um, I don't understand—" The woman's face blooms red. She's instantly flustered, picking up papers and setting them down.

"Really?" I lean in and hiss, "You left a child in soiled clothing alone in a back room. What sort of facility is this?"

"Um, well, it was her parents. They never sent extra clothing. Which is on the kindergarten list, because *accidents do happen*. And when I called Mrs. Hendricks to tell her what happened, she said she did not give permission for me to change her into the extra clothes we have around here in the lost and found."

"I don't believe you. Why would Rebecca say that?" I shake my head.

"I'm sorry." The woman hangs her head. "I wasn't sure what to do. That's why I called the housekeeper to come pick her up."

"What happened today is child abuse. You'll be hearing from my lawyer. I want Sarah Hendricks brought to the office right now. She will be going home for the day with me and Bailey." I turn around, so I don't have to look at the secretary or listen to her continuing to fumble around.

Thankfully, Sarah arrives at the office within minutes. She looks confused, until she sees me and Bailey. "Sophia." She runs and throws her arms around me.

"Come on, we're leaving." I take the girls and march out of the school.

I can't wait to tell Rebecca what lies this terrible school was spreading about her. She's going to lose her shit. Maybe she'll even take the morning off from her rehearsals to go down and scream at the principal and threaten a lawsuit. How could they say that she wouldn't give permission to change Bailey into extra clothes they had?

But there's a gnawing feeling in my gut.

One that I can't seem to make go away. One that says the woman at the front desk of the school was not lying. Maybe Rebecca did say that after all.

EIGHTEEN
REBECCA

Oh my god, I don't know why Sophia was so fucking upset over the incident at the school today with Bailey. I didn't mean to tell them they couldn't change her dirty clothes. They called and I was right in the middle of a big scene on stage. But the thing is, they didn't call my cell phone, they called the main office at the theater, which is the number I gave them for emergencies only. Meaning, broken bones or bomb threats. Not pissy pants.

That snarky, fat-assed woman Zena, who answers the phones in the theater's main office, came running out screaming, "Rebecca, your daughter peed her pants at school! What do you want me to do?"

And everyone laughed.

My castmates.

The choreographer.

But worst of all, Baker. The show's producer and director. We aren't supposed to call him Mister Baker or Director Baker. Or any other variation of his name. He just goes by Baker. And Baker is a theatrical genius. So to hear him laughing at me... Well, I guess I snapped.

"Jesus Christ. Go hang up. I told them to only call me if it was an emergency. She'll be fine!" I shouted, hoping to stop the laughing. I wasn't even sure which daughter. I assumed Bailey, because she's the youngest. Not that it mattered which it was. What exactly did the school expect me to do anyway? Drop everything and race there to clean her up? Isn't that why I sent a change of clothes for her at the beginning of the year?

That's when I remembered that I didn't send Bailey a change of clothes.

I'd meant to. I picked some out and set them on the table. But I'd been distracted by Mitch and something he said about leaving on a trip or some other such nonsense and I don't remember ever putting the clothes in her backpack.

Well—if that's the case, it's Mrs. Melnyk's fault. Because she would have seen the clothes and picked them up and put them back in Bailey's bedroom. Another reason not to trust that Eastern European bitch.

As soon as I'm earning the big bucks from my show, I am firing Mrs. Melnyk and hiring a more competent housekeeper and nanny.

"Sophia, I don't know why you're so upset. I appreciate that you went to pick up the girls, but I'm not changing their school. And I'm not going to march into the main office to, what did you call it? *Cause a fucking scene.*"

Sophia is pacing in the living room. "But, Becks, you don't understand, they left her in the back room, all alone, in cold, wet pants."

I let out a long sigh. I'm not sure she's going to let this go. "And then what? So I go there and cause a scene, scream, and yell. Give that front office idiot a real show, something she secretly films and posts on social media. That's not the kind of press I need going viral. I can see it now. *Broadway Star Goes Crazy.* If something like that happened, Baker would fire me." I want her to understand the repercussions if I get involved. I'm not letting a pair of peed-in pants derail my new career.

Sophia stops dead in her tracks and looks at me.

"You're right. I'm sorry, it was foolish of me to get so worked up." Her shoulders relax, and she walks over to the wet bar and pours herself a drink. She stands there for a while. I watch her as she picks up one of Mitch's awards and looks at it, then sets it back on the shelf. "If you win a Tony Award, you should display it on the mantel. Don't put it here next to these."

"Oh, I won't. I think having awards on the shelf of the wet bar is so tacky. But Mitch loves to stand there and stare at them when he mixes himself a drink," I snicker, then get off the chair, where I'd been relaxing after dinner, watching playbacks from today's rehearsals—until Sophia wanted to talk about the incident today.

I approach my friend and gently touch her arm. "I'm sorry. I know you have a life and you were probably busy today, and that's why you're annoyed. You had to go to the school and deal with my kids. And I know you don't want to be a mom."

Sophia inhales sharply.

Yes. I've hit the nail on the head.

That's why she wants me to yell at the school, because she's angry and I'm the mother.

She purses her lips, then takes a long sip of her drink. "Well, I'll let you handle it then. Good night, Rebecca." She takes a few steps away from me, then turns around. "Oh, I'm going on a trip and leaving tomorrow. I have to view several paintings in San Francisco. I'll be back on Sunday."

I'm supposed to go out with the crew for dinner and drinks this weekend. I wasn't exactly going to tell her that, I was going to lie and say we're having our costume fittings over the weekend—and there's no way she'd say no to babysitting the girls if it was for my show. She's been so encouraging about me getting the part.

"Ohhhh..." I let my bottom lip quiver.

"Is something wrong?"

"It's just, well, we're supposed to have costume fittings this weekend. I was hoping you could watch the girls."

"Really? On a weekend?" she asks and raises a brow. "Strange.

Don't you think it's strange they want to do costumes on the weekend?"

Shit. She's on to me. "Well, I don't know! I mean, this is my first show. How am I supposed to know what's normal or not? Never mind. It was silly—I'll just ask Mrs. Melnyk if she can watch the girls. Have a safe trip." Well, shit, I guess I will have to see if Mrs. Melnyk can watch them, if I want to go out with my new friends. Which I definitely do.

Sophia walks down the hall toward her room, and I go back to the chair to curl up and finish watching the playback.

As soon as I turn the video back on, a warm, fuzzy feeling envelops me—as if I'd chugged down a glass tumbler full of whiskey. But it's not a boozy warmth. Just seeing myself on stage washes away the stress of today, the stress of dealing with children, and their school, and Sophia and her demands, and it's all just gone. Watching screen-me sing and dance and perform with my castmates Chase, Violet, and Indra is a dopamine hit unlike anything else. It's better than sex, well, anything is better than sex —with Mitch. He couldn't give me an orgasm if his life depended on it.

I think about everything, and quickly realize, no... There's nothing better than this in my life. The only thing that came close recently was meeting Sophia, the rush I felt to have a woman like her want to be my friend, and the power I felt when I offered her a home while her apartment was being finished. I rewind the playback and watch it again from the beginning. This time there won't be any interruptions—the girls are in bed. Sophia has gone to her room. Mitch is gone. It's just me, watching myself.

A smile spreads over my face.

God, I'm so good. Look at me—dancing, singing, owning that stage. I'm nailing every beat. I'm so into it. I'm clearly the best actor in the show. I mean, Chase, Violet and Indra are amazing supporting actors. But it's all about me...

Have you been practicing those exercises like we discussed? Dr. Nakamura asks, interrupting me watching the playback.

What exercises? I ask and look around. I'm lying on the couch in Dr. Nakamura's office. I'm not sure why I'm here again. I've been taking my medicine and feeling fine. *Doctor, I'm not having a panic attack. I was actually having a really great time, watching myself perform in a playback video.*

The breathing exercises to ground yourself. Are you and your new castmates having too much of a good time together? he asks.

No, no, I promise, it's not like that. I'm not about to have a manic episode.

Dr. Nakamura raises an eyebrow at me. *We'll see, won't we... You know what happens when you have a manic episode.*

Suddenly, I jolt awake, and look around. It's dark and quiet. "Crap," I grumble. I've fallen asleep in the living room chair while watching TV. My neck is throbbing and I rub it with my hand while I get up and head to the kitchen to take some ibuprofen. Otherwise I'll be sore all day while I'm at rehearsal.

But before I can take the anti-inflammatory, I spy something on the kitchen counter. A piece of paper folded over and standing up like a little tent. My name is written on the front in Sophia's beautiful cursive writing.

> 12:30 a.m.
>
> Becks,
>
> My client called around midnight. He needs me for a morning meeting, so he hired a private jet to fly me there. Thank god, because I was not looking forward to flying domestic! You're asleep on the chair, and I didn't want you to worry when you woke up to see me and my vehicle gone.
>
> See you Sunday.
>
> Sophia

Hmm... It seems a little out of character for Sophia to just sneak off in the middle of the night—even for a client. I mean, I've only seen her working a few times since she's lived here and she seems to do it on her time, not her clients'. But I guess she does turn on the charm and dress up to play some sort of part for them. They're all ultra rich, and those kind of people get what they want, when they want it, regardless of how it impacts other people's lives. So if some mega-rich man from San Francisco wanted Sophia in the middle of the night, I guess he gets her.

A pang of something bubbles in my chest.

Jealousy?

Yes, I think so. But not because I'm jealous of Sophia getting to fly to San Francisco on a private jet. But because she has the freedom to go somewhere in the middle of the night for a job she loves. While I'm trapped in this house, making sure my children are fed and go to school and get to bed on time, when maybe I'd rather be living in the city in a high-rise over Broadway.

And like Sophia, my husband, Mitch, is also free to come and go as he pleases.

Why is that?

Like, where is my husband right now? Did he come home from the hospital last night and see me asleep on the chair and choose not to wake me up? He didn't even care that I might get a kink in my neck. He just walked up the stairs and crawled into bed, where he could sleep all alone, spreading his body out on the mattress, without me next to him.

Or is our bed empty?

Is he still at work? Or is he sleeping in some other woman's bed, in the city, a nurse or the mom of one of his patients? Someone he's met and finds more attractive than me? Someone who doesn't fall asleep in the living room. Someone who—

"Mommy." Bailey says my name and wanders into the kitchen. "I had a bad dream."

"Bed." I point.

"But, M-m-mommy." Her voice trembles as she stutters. I know I should feel something, but I'm tired and annoyed.

I snatch her by the arm and squeeze. She whimpers and I loosen my grip, tugging her along and up the stairs. She sniffles and cries. I'm sure she'd like me to pick her up and carry her to bed. But she's far too big for me to keep babying her. We reach her bedroom and I release my hand from around her arm. She runs to her bed, jumps in, and pulls the covers over her head.

I should go over and give her a hug and kiss good night, but she's probably already asleep again, and I'd just wake her up. There's no light coming from under my bedroom door, which means Mitch didn't come home.

He sleeps with the TV on and the volume going. A constant flickering glow. He says he needs the light and sound—he's used to it from his time in residency. I hate it. I prefer the dark and quiet to sleep, so my brain can disconnect. Mitch has never really cared about me.

NINETEEN

MITCH

As a pediatric surgeon, I've seen plenty of pregnant women. But until it happened to my wife, I really didn't understand the way having a child was going to affect me. She was in great shape, always lifting weights, and doing Pilates. One of her big things was not wanting to gain a lot of weight during the pregnancy.

Which meant a lot of extra pregnancy-safe workouts, all of which she wanted me to attend with her. Don't get me wrong, I enjoy a good workout. But usually I do them at the hospital gym, running on the treadmill while listening to my notes. I always record my surgical consultations, so I can go back before surgery to listen to them. But god, she's wanted me to do yoga, meditation, swimming, and about ten other trendy classes with her.

Besides working out, she's really trying to eat well and drink plenty of water. And again, that's great too. But she's not the best cook to start with, so you throw in her healthy twist, and suddenly her bland food is even more flavorless. Which means I've been hitting the drive-thru about three times a week and I still feel like I'm starving to death.

At least I can eat for free in the hospital cafeteria.

And the rep for this new surgical laser, well, she's all over me to try out their machine—so she's always offering to take me to dinner. I'm going to go out with her again tomorrow night. These surgical-device companies have so much fucking money, they don't care what I order. I can practically taste the steak and lobster with a side of garlic mashed potatoes. All that rich, delicious flavor.

The other thing I've been struggling with is the emotional side of my wife's pregnancy. I swear to god she is always crying and talking about how growing a new human being inside of her is affecting her mental health. I keep telling her she's doing a great job and how much I love her, but I don't think it's helping. She doesn't light up the same way she used to when I say, *I love you*. And she doesn't tell me she loves me anymore.

And maybe the worst part of it, she doesn't want to have sex. My dick has been limp for six months. Between the flavorless food, the crying, her obsession with working out, there's just nothing really sexy around here.

But that surgical rep, what's her name again? Something bubbly—she was probably a high school cheerleader too. Dani! That's it. Now, Dani, there's a sexy woman, and I bet at our next dinner, she'll order a rare steak to impress me, and she'll let the juice dribble a little down her chin. I'll try not to dominate the conversation. And if I wanted to fuck her in the bathroom of the restaurant halfway through our meal, I bet she'd let me. Her commission for selling my hospital her surgical device is at least six figures.

I take a deep breath to calm my libido.

I glance over at my very pregnant wife, sitting next to me on the couch, and remind myself I can't go around fucking the device rep just because it's been six months since I've felt the inside of a woman. No matter how badly I want that warmth wrapped around me, and a woman's arms holding me to her chest, reminding me that I'm loved and needed.

I decide to test out the waters. "Do you think you'll be ready to have sex again after the baby comes?"

"Mitch!" She slaps my shoulder. "The baby can hear you!"

Everything is about the baby. Nothing feels the same as it did before she was pregnant. It used to feel like she would do anything for me. That I was the sun and she orbited around me. Now it feels more like she would do anything for this unborn child.

"That doesn't really answer my question," I say it as playfully as I can, then lean in and give her a kiss, nuzzling my face in the crook of her neck. She smells heavenly, like that perfume she used to wear when we first met. I wonder if she's feeling nostalgic for what things used to be like before the pregnancy. It makes me hard.

I grab her hand and tug it gently down, and surprisingly, she doesn't stop me—she keeps going, reaching until she finds me, hard as a rock. "Please, I need you," I whisper and lean over to grind against her. If she'd just lean back and let me fuck her, it would be over quickly. Two or three pumps is all it would take.

"Mitch, honey, honestly—not right now, I think I'm getting a UTI and the baby is due in a few weeks. How can you think of sex right now?" She pulls her hand back and tucks her legs under herself, pulling her body away from me.

I let out a long, angry sigh, then I stand up. "You know, I'm meeting with that surgical-device company again. They are really serious about getting a pediatric surgeon to be the face of their brand. It probably means a lot of travel for work." I don't know why I'm even telling her, it's not like it matters. I could say I'd been nominated as president of the United States and she wouldn't care.

"As long as it's after the baby comes," she says and gets up and walks into the kitchen. "You want salad for dinner? I made a fat free, lo-cal alternative ranch dressing."

"No. I think I'm going to head back into the city to round on my surgical case from this morning. I don't trust the residents. I'll probably grab something to eat at the cafeteria."

"Okay, drive safe, call me if you're gonna be late," she says.

But in my mind it sounds more like, *Fuck you, Mitch, I don't love you.*

. . .

I don't really drive all the way into the city. Just thirty minutes away to Burger Shack and order a double with cheese, fries, and a chocolate shake.

"Oh, hey, Dr. Hendricks. Your wife still not feeding you?" Brittney, the high school blonde at the window, asks when she hands me my food.

A combination of the smell of hot, salty, greasy food and the shape of Brittney's breasts under her tight, white Burger Shack T-shirt, makes me hard again.

I grab the bag of food and grunt out a thank-you and speed out of the drive-thru. I drive down the block and around the corner into an alley behind an abandoned building. I lay my seat back, shove my hand down my scrub pants, close my eyes, and think about that bubbly, high school cheerleader Brittney who just handed me my food. Then I think about the even sexier, more eager device rep Dani. I picture her in a cheerleader outfit.

I know I have a type. My wife's shrine to herself in the attic would probably creep most guys out, but all those awards, they actually turn me on.

I'm done jerking off almost as soon as I start.

Six fucking months! I have *got* to get laid.

I wipe my hands on the extra napkins Brittney put in the bag—she knows my order too well, since I've been coming here three times a week for months now. I quickly scarf down my food, then I drive to a gas station and throw away the food evidence and use their bathroom to wash my hands and clean up a bit. I stare at myself in the mirror after splashing water on my face.

"What the fuck is wrong with you?" I ask my reflection.

The same thing I've been asking myself for years...

I thought I was over this sick cycle of self-loathing; eating fast food, masturbating in my car—it's how I got through the stress of medical school. Until I met my wife. She really understood me. She knew at my core, I'm a simple man. I just need to feel loved and wanted. And lately, I don't feel loved or wanted.

Things better change after this baby gets here.

. . .

"I told you not to let the baby sleep in the bed with you! Are you fucking stupid?" I yell at her. I'm shaking. I'm so goddamn mad. "Answer me!" I scream even louder.

She slumps on the couch and curls up in a ball and puts her hands over her ears. "Stop shouting."

But I keep screaming about how irresponsible she is and what a terrible mother she is. And how this is all her fault. Even though I know that it's my fault. If I'd been here tonight in my own bed, instead of fucking a blonde in the hallway of the unfinished new surgical wing in the hospital, maybe the baby would still be alive. I'm still screaming when I hear a heavy pounding on the door. I stop yelling long enough to go see who it is.

"Thank you for coming so quickly," I say. But it doesn't feel like it was quick at all. It feels like it's been days. The officer and EMT ask me some questions, but I'm in a daze. "Sorry, I'm just a little in shock here. Oh, yes, um, my wife is in the living room. The baby is upstairs. I performed CPR as soon as I got home and found them—but I'd say the baby was postmortem for at least two hours."

The baby.

I can't even say her name.

I look over at my wife. She's got her face buried in the palms of her hands. Is she going to make any attempt at helping? Or going upstairs with us to tell the police what happened?

When we enter the bedroom, we find the unmade bed.

There, in the middle of it, is my dead daughter, Annie Hendricks. I wasn't sure what kind of dad I'd be before she was born. I was battling with a lot of self-doubt issues. But the moment she arrived—when I saw her tiny, adorable face—I knew in my heart of hearts that everything was going to be okay. I was going to be a good dad—no, a great one. And my precious little girl, well, I had no doubt she was destined for greatness.

The police officer and EMT ask me additional questions. I do my best to answer. I tell them I was at the hospital all night, which is true. But I don't tell them I'm having an affair—what does that matter to them anyway? Why I was still at the hospital, even though I'd finished surgery hours before, well, that's none of their business.

"I'm going to head down to the ambulance and call the coroner. They might have us take your baby to the county hospital—or he might want to come out himself to get her. Give me ten minutes, okay?" the EMT says and pats my shoulder before he walks out of the room.

"Yes, sure, of course," I reply and follow him out of my bedroom. The police officer is behind us.

"I'll need to get your wife's statement now, Dr. Hendricks, if you don't mind getting her situated—maybe at the kitchen table if she can. I know this is horrible," he says. "I got a baby myself, ten months old, I couldn't imagine my wife if something ever—"

But the officer can't finish his statement, because as we all exit the stairs and walk into the living room to where my wife is lying on the couch, each of us notices her body looks unnaturally limp and is half hanging off the couch. A pill bottle is on the floor and pills have spilled out all over the carpet.

Everything happens so fast.

The EMT and police officer shove me aside and go into rescue mode. The officer radios for his partner, who was standing outside. He comes barging in, along with two more EMTs that were also apparently outside in my driveway. They are all shouting orders at one another, and I don't know exactly what I'm supposed to do right now. I'm sure I'd be no help. They've got her turned on her side, the EMT is putting a stomach flushing kit together, but based on the way she looks—I'd say my wife is dead.

TWENTY

REBECCA

2017

I've been extremely sexual during this pregnancy. Dr. Nakamura said it's from going off my meds. He said that my body is making new hormones and some of those are sex hormones. But my annoying husband, Mitch, refuses to have sex and I'm going insane. I really don't understand what his fucking problem is.

"I don't want the baby to see my dick," he started arguing when I was about five months along and really starting to show.

"Are you serious? You're a doctor, you know that's not how it works," I replied. But it was no use trying to convince him.

So now, I read spicy romance novels and dry hump my pillow when Mitch falls asleep until I give myself an orgasm. Sometimes I do it two or three times a night. I swear, if Mitch doesn't start fucking me again after this baby comes, I'm going to divorce him for cheating. Because if he's not screwing me, he's screwing someone else. I know my husband. And even if I have had some pretty rapid weight gain the last couple of months, he should still want to be inside of me. He's vain and egotistical, but I don't think his dick cares.

Plus, my doctor said it's just water weight.

It will go away quickly after the baby is born.

Which is great because I really want to get back out and start trying to audition again. There are some new directors on Broadway this season. That means they will want to find new, fresh talent.

"I think I'm going to take my paternity leave tomorrow," Mitch says to me.

I look at him and make a face. I can't help it. "What? Why? I'm fine. I'm not due until April tenth... That's like a month away."

"I know you're feeling fine. You say that every day. But that's what scares me... There's still work to do on the nursery, and if I don't take a few days off now, I know you'll try and finish the work on your own. I don't want you to hurt yourself, Rebecca," Mitch says. I can hear the genuine concern in his voice. But I don't know if he's worried that I'll hurt myself or I'll hurt the baby.

"Babe, I won't do anything stupid. I'm a registered nurse. I know what I can and can't do, and I promise, I'm not trying to do anything crazy. Anyway, I'd rather you wait and take your time off when the baby gets here, don't waste your days now."

"But the nursery room, you don't mind if it's not finished?"

"Why? The baby is going to use the bassinet in our room, it's not going to need its own room for months. There's plenty of time," I remind him as I glance at the big tan bassinet with its gender-neutral yellow bedding. I've positioned it a few feet from the bed. I wanted to leave it in the box until the baby arrived. But Mitch insisted we set it up months ago, complete with the bedding and a mobile that plays "Baby Mine." He said it was so we could get used to having it in our room. He made me swear that I'd never, ever let the baby sleep in the bed with me.

It's a little creepy in my opinion.

I'm not an idiot, I know the risk of SIDS as well as he does.

"I guess you're right. I don't need to take leave now. But I don't have any surgical cases, since I thought I'd be off work..." Mitch lets out a long, loud sigh.

I don't respond.

After a few minutes he says, "I guess I can go in tomorrow morning and check with Ross and Yaniff in the Emergency Department. See if they have any trauma cases that need a surgeon."

I roll my eyes. My husband is such a whiner. Seriously, what a baby. If he stays here until the actual baby arrives, he's going to be bored after a few hours, and anxious to get back to work. Leaving me alone with a newborn a few weeks after it's born—because he only has so much time off. I want his help with the actual human baby as long as I can. Not with decorating the nursery.

"Good idea, go see Ross," I echo his last statement. Now if he would just flip over to his stomach and go to sleep, so I can read my book and hump my pillow in peace, that would be amazing.

"Babe, can you turn off your side lamp? You know it's hard for me to go to sleep with that light on." Mitch sounds incredibly needy.

"Says the man who has to have the TV on all night... I'm going to read a few chapters, then I'll turn it off."

Mitch growls but doesn't say anything else—and before long he's breathing heavily with a light snore. The baby, on the other hand, is wide awake and doing flips in my stomach, making it look like I've got an alien in there. I rest my hand on it and whisper, "Go to bed."

Right then I vow: I'm not going to let this baby, or any other that might come later, dictate the kind of woman I'm going to be. Maybe I'll be good. Maybe I'll be bad. But I'll stay true to me. Unlike my husband over there, who's acting so strange I hardly know him.

TWENTY-ONE

SOPHIA

Present Day

Leaving Rebecca's house and navigating Long Island in the middle of the night was not on my to-do list when I woke up this morning. But neither was picking up Bailey at school with pissy pants and then listening to Rebecca justify her neglect with some excuse about the theater-office woman not passing on the message properly.

God, she's really making me sick.

I'm not sure how much more of it I can handle.

If this was about her ignoring me, that would be one thing, I could forgive that—because I don't need constant attention. But it isn't about her ignoring me. This is about her girls. She seems to have completely given up on her relationship with Sarah and Bailey. I just don't understand. Why doesn't she seem to care more about them? Especially considering her first two children died in infancy. You'd think she'd cherish every moment she has with Bailey and Sarah and do her best to make their lives picture perfect...

My eyes well up with those annoying tears, the kind you get

when watching something sad on the television. I'm not ignorant, I know Rebecca's never going to be Supermom like my former best friend Hannah. But bloody hell. A little fucking effort would go a long way to showing that Becks has a heart and she's not a monster.

I reach a hand up and dab at the corner of my eyes.

The more that I think about it, the more I realize I shouldn't be surprised. I pegged her as someone without much maternal instinct when we first met.

"If you didn't want kids, why would you keep getting pregnant?" I ask the question out loud. As if Rebecca can hear me. As if she can explain why she went through with four full-term pregnancies in seven years if she really didn't want to have children.

I remember how my sister was during her pregnancy with the twins. She said she loved being pregnant, but I always thought she did that to rub it in my face. Because as I recall, she was very tired, emotional, and had a lot of morning sickness. It must have taken a huge toll on Rebecca to be pregnant that many times in a row. Not just physically, but emotionally.

My knuckles are turning white—so I relax, loosening my grip on the steering wheel while I drive. I'm grateful to have my own vehicle. Taking an Uber from Rebecca's house to the city at this time of night, well, that's asking for trouble. Plus, I have a parking spot in the basement garage of my building, perfect for my new car —I paid extra for it, even though I didn't need it at the time. I figured someday I might. And someday has come sooner than I thought, because I'm not really heading to the airport to take a private plane to San Francisco. That was just an excuse to leave Rebecca's house for a few days. Because I had to get out of there.

I was so disgusted by her attitude surrounding Bailey and the pee-pants, I wanted to punish her.

Make her pay.

But I'm not generally the vindictive type. And the only thing I could come up with to punish Becks was to leave, forcing her to take care of her own children. She's been relying on me way too much to take the girls to school, to pick them up, do homework, bedtime routine, basically everything. I haven't minded because, as I've come to realize, I really love Sarah and Bailey. *Which is going to be a problem.*

Because Rebecca is their mum.

Not me.

So she needs to start acting like it—even if that means I have to take a step back and force her into it.

Navigating through the city while driving myself is a whole new experience. One I'm glad to be doing in the middle of the night, when there is presumably the least amount of traffic. Without too much difficulty, I park in my garage and ride the elevator up to my flat where I take some time to walk around, decompress, and unwind. I decide I should text Ekaterina, let her know I'll be gone for a few days. But when I look at the clock, it's only three thirty in the morning. I should probably wait and do it in a few hours, when she's awake.

To kill time, I putter around, take a shower, organize a few things in the kitchen and check some emails. Finally, at five a.m., I text Ekaterina. I don't really expect a response this early.

> Rebecca is going to ask you to watch the girls this weekend. Please, for the love of god, tell her NO. I'll give you five hundred dollars.

Much to my surprise, she responds almost instantly.

> OK

I wait for a few minutes, expecting her to ask me what happened or something else to figure out why I'd ask her such a thing. But when she doesn't say anything else, I decide that I should say something instead.

> You aren't going to ask me why?

> I don't care. I glad to say no. I'm not babysitter.

> Well, okay. Great. I'll pay you the money on Monday—I'm out of town for a few days.

> Fine. Monday. Don't expect me to ask what you up to. I don't care.

> Oh, stop acting like we aren't friends. I know you like me. And I know you care.

> Maybe. A little.

I chuckle and roll my eyes. Yes, of course she likes me. A woman like her would tell me to go fuck myself if she didn't. But friendly or not, I don't expect her to text me with a play-by-play of her conversation with Rebecca about babysitting.

No.

I won't find out about any of it until I see her on Monday morning. She'll grin at me and hold her hand out, waiting to get paid. Then she'll hold up her phone and show me a text exchange between her and Rebecca in which she denied babysitting services. Or she'll tell me about the phone conversation they had, which would mean Rebecca was desperate... I know how she is. She hates talking to Ekaterina on the phone.

The next morning while I'm making tea, I realize something—it's far too quiet in my flat. Yes, the sound of New York City is permeating my building: the rumble of trucks, the honking of cars, the buzz of air-conditioning units, all the sounds of a big city in action. But that's not what I mean. I mean the sound of little feet padding down the stairs and happy voices asking for breakfast. The noise from their favorite cartoon show, *Hilda*, playing on multiple televisions. The sounds of a salty Eastern European housekeeper arriving and making a big to-do about the political state of America before turning on the dishwasher, washing machine, and other loud appliances.

I guess what I'm getting at is that I miss Becks's house.

Maybe trying to punish her is not the right way to go about all of this. Because there is always the chance that while I'm gone she'll realize that she doesn't really want or need me around. Yes, she's verbally agreed to let me stay while my flat is being renovated. But that doesn't mean she can't change her mind and kick me out of her house if she thinks I've become a nuisance. And based on our last few interactions, I'd say I'm on the verge of being an inconvenience.

"Ugh..." I moan when I look around for something to eat after I've finished fixing my cup of tea. But there's nothing edible in my flat, besides a few stale biscuits and a couple of tins of sliced peaches that I like to dish over porridge, which I'm entirely out of. I haven't been here in over a month and didn't want to leave anything that might spoil or attract vermin.

I could just laze about and order delivery. "But that would be silly," I tell myself. Why order a single meal when I need food for the entire weekend? Plus, it might be nice to walk around the city for a little bit. Get out of my head.

"Sophia, right?" a man says behind me at the market while I'm trying to wedge a long baguette into my small basket without it falling out. I don't immediately register that he's speaking to me. I don't know anyone in the city who would be talking to me, plus Sophia is a common enough name.

"Aren't you Rebecca Hendricks's friend?" he asks.

This time I turn around and look. The young man is vaguely familiar. But I can't entirely remember where I've seen him before.

"I'm Justin, from the free clinic. We met once when you were there to pick up Sophia," he answers my thoughts. "Sorry, recognizing people and remembering their names is sort of my superpower." He smirks.

I do my best not to sigh. Americans and their obsession with superpowers. Instead I say, "Oh, yes, from the clinic—nice to see you again." I smile. "How have you been?"

"Well, aren't you sweet to ask? Honestly, I'd never thought I'd say this, but I kind of miss Becks. I mean, Rebecca," he says.

I smile, look around, then lean in and whisper, "I call her Becks too." As if it's some kind of secret we might share with one another. His face brightens.

"You know, she was kind of annoying to work with, always singing and dancing; everyone thought she was so full of herself. But she was always on time, never complained, and saw more patients than anyone else. You should see the new guy they brought in to replace her. He's the worst. Zero personality and I've never met someone who moved so slow." Justin seems thrilled to have someone to talk about this with. But my stomach is growling and I really just want to go home and eat something.

"Justin, I'd love to stay and chat, but I'm running late." I just realized that if Justin was to call Becks and tell her that he saw me, well, it wouldn't bode well. I'm supposed to be on a plane to San Francisco, not buying bread downtown in the city.

"Of course, I'm sorry for holding you up. Tell Becks I said hello," he says politely. It's refreshing to speak with a New Yorker who isn't a rude asshole. That's been my biggest pet peeve since moving here. The bad attitude of everyone I interact with. That was part of what I loved about Becks when I met her. She wasn't rude at all. She was so happy to have someone to talk to. As if...

"Justin, when was the last time you talked to Becks?" I ask.

"Oh, we haven't spoken since she quit. We weren't really friends outside of the clinic," he admits and I see a slight flush on his cheeks. Aha. So I don't have to worry that he's going to report back to Rebecca that he's seen me. Which means—

"Would you like to have drinks with me tomorrow night? I made a reservation eons ago at Spyglass Rooftop, and my friends from out of town had to cancel at the last minute. I was just going to cancel and stay home, but if you're free?" I ask.

"Oh my god, yes! My boyfriend, Luis, and I have been dying to go to Spyglass—would you care if I brought him?"

"Sounds lovely. I can't wait. Reservation is at nine thirty. See you there." Then I walk away from Justin and head for the front of the market to pay for my bread and cheese. I'll have to call Spyglass and see about getting a reservation tomorrow night.

I really don't know what possessed me to ask Justin to go out with me.

But maybe it will be fun. And I bet with some wine in his system he'll dish some gossip on Becks.

TWENTY-TWO
REBECCA

"What do you mean, *no*? I said I'd pay triple," I beg Mrs. Melnyk over the phone. I wanted to ask her in person, but she hightailed it out of my house as if her life depended on it the moment I walked in when I got home from rehearsal.

"No. No babysitting. I have to drive to Buffalo. Won't be back until Sunday," she says and hangs up the phone.

I call back, but it rings and rings with no answer.

I try once more and this time it goes straight to voicemail.

"Fuck!" I shout and throw my phone down on my bed. The nerve of that woman to tell me no, when I have been good to her. For years, I've been so good. I never make her work on the weekends. I don't nitpick over her methods of cleaning or doing laundry. I hardly ever ask her to stay late or help with the kids. If she was working for anyone else in town, she'd be miserable, because they wouldn't tolerate this kind of insubordination.

"Are you okay, Mommy?" Sarah asks. She peeks her head in my room and takes a step forward.

"I'm fine... Go play with your sister." I walk over, scoot her back into the hallway, then shut my door and lock it. I don't particularly care to have the girls in my room. Nor do I need them hearing me cursing or having a meltdown.

I should have been interviewing babysitters from that kidcare dot com website the moment Mitch said he was leaving for Amsterdam or Germany or wherever the fuck he's going off to now to teach. This is my fault. I was too reliant on Sophia, as if she'd always just be here, ready and able to watch my kids. Which is ridiculous. She isn't here to be my live-in, even if that's what Mitch keeps calling her. She is here as my friend.

Although even that I'm unsure of right now.

I wouldn't call what happened the other night a fight, but we definitely didn't leave on the best of terms. Ugh. I throw my hands up in disgust before flopping onto my bed.

There has got to be someone I can find to babysit—I desperately want to go out with the crew and actors tomorrow night. They are going to a rooftop bar in downtown NYC and it sounds like so much fun. I feel like I had a real turning point with everyone this week, and now they want me to be part of the group.

Chase, Violet, and Indra even added me to a private group chat. Not the one the director started with us for work stuff. Their private one, to talk non-work gossip.

I know I shouldn't be so nervous, I mean, I'm the freaking star of the show. They should all be bending over backwards, vying for my attention, not the other way around. But it's just taken me so long to get to Broadway. I have a serious case of imposter syndrome. So it's hard for me to believe any of this is real. Like any second the rug will be pulled out from under me.

I roll over and look up at my ceiling, trying to figure out who I can call to babysit, when my phone buzzes. I take a look and see that Indra has texted in the group chat.

INDRA

Becks, just making sure you got a sitter for tomorrow. You wanna come pre-party at my place before we go out? Say 6-ish?

I'd love to! Yes, I got a sitter.

CHASE

Is that an invite for all of us to attend your special
pre-party?

VIOLET

My place is bigger and I have more treats, if you
know what I mean. You wanna do it here instead?

INDRA

Great. Your place tomorrow at 6. And don't be a
smart ass, Chase.

VIOLET

Everyone bring a bottle. I'll put out some snackies.

CHASE

Dope.

I'm not sure if I need to say anything else in the group chat. But when I set my phone down, I start to panic. Maybe I should respond. Should I say *cool* or *rad* or echo Chase and say *dope*? Or I could say I don't have Violet's address. No, that's such a lame thing to say. I can just tell her to drop a pin tomorrow. I guess I could ask for one of them to clarify about the booze. Because when she says bring a bottle, I have no idea if that means a bottle of wine or a bottle of vodka or—oh my god, what if it means to bring a bottle of pills? Should I offer to share some of my meds with them? No, no, that's ridiculous.

An hour later, I'm still thinking about what kind of booze I should bring to the pre-party while I towel dry my hair. I've showered and thrown on a pair of pajamas. Since Mitch is gone, I'll probably sleep naked. But before I go to bed, I want to be comfortable.

Knock, knock, knock.

When I open my door, Bailey is on the other side, staring at me with those big, sad eyes. She reminds me of the cat from *Puss in Boots*. "I'm starving." She practically mews the words at me and rubs her belly in a circle with her hand.

"Didn't Mrs. Melnyk feed you dinner? What have I told you about not eating your dinner?"

"No, Mommy. She didn't make dinner. I know I have to eat everything on my plate like you taught me." She hangs her head.

I look at my watch. It's already eight p.m. Which is bedtime, not dinner. But crap, if I don't feed the girls something, I suspect they will both wake up early, crying and carrying on about being hungry. Which is the last thing I want to deal with first thing on a Saturday morning.

"Would you like some popcorn for dinner?" I ask. I'm not even sure what food is in the kitchen. Sophia has been doing most of the shopping and Mrs. Melnyk does most of the cooking. I just sort of come and go and eat what's served.

Bailey shakes her head. "No, Mommy," she whispers.

Is she always this small? Why does she seem so little and help-less right now?

"Well, let's go down and see what I can make. Maybe there's something left over we can heat up quickly. Or some pancake mix or toast," I say, listing off a few easy meal items I know she'll eat. Then I take her by the hand and we walk together down the hallway toward the stairs. Her hand clings to mine, as if she might blow away if I don't keep her close.

"Bailey, go back to your room," Sarah sticks her head out of her bedroom door and hisses. She looks startled when she sees me. "Oh, Mommy, I didn't know you were with her. Is everything okay?"

"Mommy's going to make me something to eat," Bailey says.

"Really?" Sarah asks with a hint of disbelief in her voice.

I'm not sure if I should take offense.

"Yes, really. I didn't know Mrs. Melnyk didn't feed you girls dinner. Do you want to come down and eat?" I ask.

Sarah nods and follows after me and Bailey.

Thankfully they want something easy for dinner. Pancakes. And Sarah even does most of the work, while I pour a glass of wine, find my laptop, and start searching for babysitters in my area.

It takes them about thirty minutes to eat and do their dishes. Too bad I'm not any closer to finding someone to watch them, everyone I texted said they already had a job lined up for tomorrow night. I guess I'm not the only mom in the suburbs who wants to go out on a Saturday.

"Like this?" I tuck Sarah's blankets in on the sides.

"Yes, just like that." She smiles at me. It feels like a long time since I've tucked Sarah in.

"Good night." I kiss her on the forehead and tuck her blankets in around her once more for good luck. "You did a great job helping me with making pancakes and doing the dishes."

She nods her head. "Thank you, Mommy."

"It's funny because I was thinking earlier how small Bailey seems to me. But you, on the other hand, if I didn't know you were eight, I'd think you were almost a teenager. You've really grown up a lot, Sarah. I'm proud of you." I want my daughter to know I recognize that she's using her brain and trying hard to be the best daughter she can be.

She smiles, then rolls over on her side.

I mean what I said. I am proud of her. I pat her once before leaving the room. And as I leave and walk down the hall toward my room, I get a wild idea. *Hmmm, I wonder if I could leave the girls home tomorrow night? Sarah could be the babysitter... No—that would be crazy,* I say to myself. I can't believe I just considered letting my eight-year-old babysit. But the more I think about it, the less crazy it seems.

I mean, she is very mature for her age.

She literally just made pancakes on the stove and did the dishes afterwards.

Plus, if I left at five, that's only three hours until bedtime. As long as the TV is on and they have enough snacks to eat, how much trouble could they really get into? We have a landline, so I could call and check on them before bedtime. We have a Ring camera and I can make sure I have the alert set on my phone.

Yes, yes, I think it will be perfectly fine. I'll just leave the girls here tomorrow while I go to the city with my castmates and the crew for the rooftop bar party.

I start humming to myself, then pour another glass of wine, before doing a high kick. I'm jazzed. I haven't gone to a party in longer than I can remember. Sure, I did the annual team building with the clinic staff once a year, but that's not the same. Not to mention it was absolutely lame as hell up until this last year, when I met Sophia. I mean, I love Sophia, but god, she can be so boring and stuffy and kind of lame. I cannot wait to go out with Indra, Violet, and Chase and have some actual adult fun. Eeeeek! I desperately need to cut loose.

I chuckle into my wine glass as I take a sip. Who would have guessed six months ago I would be here, with so many friends that I can rate which ones are lame and which ones I want to hang out with? And pick and choose between them. I mean, is this real? Is this where my life is headed? It's always what I dreamed about, growing up, that I'd be a star—that people would vie for my attention and friendship and do whatever it took to be part of my life. Somewhere after leaving home I lost that drive, that push, and I started letting the voices in my head tell me I wasn't good enough.

But not anymore.

I'm done listening to those voices.

I'm going to call Dr. Nakamura tomorrow and tell him that he was wrong. I'm not about to have a manic episode. I am one hundred percent about to have a beautiful, magical, exceptional moment in my life, because I'm finally getting everything I ever wanted. I'm going to be a star. I'm rising up and I can almost reach the stars. I stand on my bed and reach up in a stretch, trying to touch the ceiling to prove to Dr. Nakamura—I'm exactly where I want to be right now.

I'm even more sure of my idea to let Sarah babysit when I wake up the next morning. Because I was thinking about it last night when I tried to go to sleep—I'm not entirely sure I did actually go to sleep, but that doesn't really matter. What matters is that I am very sure I was babysitting my younger brother when I was Sarah's age. My mom loved playing bingo on Friday and Saturday nights at the church down the block. We used to go and sit at her feet or under the table. I'd sing softly and tell stories to keep my brother, Ryan, entertained. But by the time I was in third or fourth grade, I know she left us home. The more I thought about it, the more I remembered.

"If I win, I'll give you twenty dollars and you can put that toward your future," she'd say when she left. Dad was already gone, working evenings as a shift manager at Tera, the chemical plant outside of town. "If your father gets home early, just tell him I ran to the store to get milk and I'll be home in five minutes."

But he never came home early.

And she never brought home milk.

My brother and I were perfectly fine. We'd watch TV, eat microwave popcorn, then go to bed. No different than if my mom had been there with us, sitting in her favorite chair, reading a book or talking on the phone to her friends.

I racked my brain, trying to recall if anything bad ever happened, and nope. Dozens of weekends where I babysat and it was perfectly fine.

So it's settled. I'll leave the girls here while I go to the city.

Everything will be perfectly fine.

I park my car in my old spot in the garage, reserved for employees at the free clinic. It's after hours on a weekend, which means the spots are empty anyways, and I still have my pass—so no one should question it. I walk out of the garage, figuring I'll take a cab or the subway from here once I know where I'm going. I didn't want to take the train all the way into the city—what if there's an emergency and I need my car?

Stop it, stop getting in your head, I say to myself. I just need to find out where the fuck Violet lives and get to her place.

What's your address?

That's right, you've never been here. I'll drop you a pin.

See you soon.

Violet's apartment is in Morningside Heights. I take a cab, instead of the subway, and get out on the street in front of her building. It's a nicer neighborhood than I was expecting. I wonder how Violet affords to live here—I know she's been in at least three shows, but she's usually a background player. This is her first time as a supporting actress. Maybe it will come up naturally in the conversation, how she affords to live in this part of the city, otherwise I'll have to assume she's a trust fund baby. How nice for her.

When I first arrived in New York after high school, I rented a room from an elderly woman, Mrs. Hofstead, who never got up from her living room chair unless it was to demand her rent. She smelled like cabbage and laughed like Pennywise. I hated her. But it didn't matter, because I was hardly home and only used the place to sleep. That was when I was auditioning all the time. Sometimes I wonder if she's still sitting in her chair, where I left her, watching *Judge Judy*. I wonder how many other hopeful girls lived in the tiny extra bedroom of apartments in the city with their own Mrs. Hofstead?

Knock. Knock.

"Becks!" Indra shouts when she answers the door. I can see over her shoulder, Chase is inside and trying to waft smoke away from a giant glass bong.

I look at my watch. Six fifteen. And I thought I might be the first one here. Indra must see the confusion on my face and says, "Oh, Chase and I got here hours ago..." Then she leans in to whisper, "We all like to smoke weed and thought you probably weren't down for that."

"I don't care if you smoke," I reply and walk into Violet's apartment. Besides the weed, it smells like holiday candles and peanut butter.

"Becks, darling, you made it." Violet runs in from another room. She is clearly very high. She swirls and whirls before she gives me a hug and a kiss on the mouth. Her lips taste sweet and peanut buttery. "Come, follow me to the kitchen, have a drink. I was just feeding everyone my mother's famous peanut butter cookies. You're not allergic, are you? Ugh, it's such a terrible allergy." She grabs my hands and pulls me along with her.

Good thing I'm *not* allergic. I'd be going into anaphylaxis right now from that kiss.

"Your mother?" I ask when we reach the kitchen. I look around. There's a tray filled with cookies, but I don't see any other bottles of booze as I pull the bottle of wine I brought out of my bag and set it down.

"Her mother brings cookies and sweets all the time. She fancies herself the Martha Stewart of Manhattan," Chase teases. The three of them laugh, and for the first time I realize how snobby they all sound. Like they grew up with money. My husband laughs like that when he's around the other doctors—it's an entitled, fake laugh. But maybe it's just the way they all laugh because they are high.

"My mother loves taking baking classes, she always has. I should be a thousand pounds, the way she feeds me. Here, try one." Violet picks up a cookie and hands it to me.

Chase picks up the bottle I brought and opens it with a corkscrew. Then he pours a large glass and slides it to me.

I realize everyone is looking at me—so I take a bite of the cookie. It really is delicious.

"Mmmm..." I nod, then take a sip of the wine.

My three castmates laugh in unison. Then they launch into a story about the time Violet and Indra tried to bake cookies and used salt instead of sugar. I have a feeling this is going to be a long night... But this is what I wanted. To be the star of a Broadway show and to hang out with the other actors in the show.

So why do I still feel like I don't belong?

"Do you want a Xany? You look a little tense." Chase leans over and opens his hand. Without hesitating at all, I take one of the pills and wash it down with the entire glass of wine.

I don't even remember taking a cab to the bar.

But somehow, here we are. Sitting outside on the balcony, under a canopy of string lights zig-zagging overhead. I look up, staring into one of the bulbs, the stars in the sky, so dull and distant. Blocked out by the glow of the city that never sleeps.

"Rebecca, how you doin', you need another drink?" Chase throws his arm around me and leans in close to ask.

I nod my head, but I can't feel which direction it's nodding. So does that mean yes, I want another drink or no, I don't want another one? I should probably switch to water and take an Uber home. Yeah, it will cost a small fortune, but—

"Rebecca. Come, dance with me." Indra grabs my hands and tugs, pulling me off the chair and leading me to the small outdoor dance floor, where there's a DJ playing something with a beat. I know I thought I should go home, but I'd much rather dance right now. It's a completely out-of-body experience, the way my arms can move and float around and I don't even have to think about it. And my legs. My beautiful, thin, athletic legs. They are amazing! They can kick and twirl and I can pirouette and sway from side to side, and oh my god, we are so high up right now.

"Indra, look at the city," I say and grab her hand and pull her toward the edge of the rooftop balcony dance floor. We lean against the railing and look over and laugh at how high up we are and how far down the ground is below us.

We laugh and scream and hold our hands up in the air.

"I love you, Indra!"

"I love you, Becks!"

"Tonight is perfect." I look at her and smile and tears stream down my cheeks.

"So fucking perfect," she says, then she grabs my face in her hands and squeezes, then pulls me into a hug and tells me I'm a such a diva and she loves it and loves me. Over and over she tells me how much she loves me.

I never want this moment to end.

TWENTY-THREE

SOPHIA

Justin and his boyfriend, Luis, are waiting for me at the entrance of Spyglass, both looking extremely sharp, with fresh cuts and designer clothes. Dressed to impress. I appreciate it and I'm looking forward to spending some time getting to know them—and hoping maybe it could turn into more than a one-time event. Although, that sort of depends on whether or not they decide to tell Rebecca I lied and wasn't really in San Francisco this weekend.

"Justin. Hello." I wave as I walk over to him and his boyfriend. "Wonderful to see you again. Glad you could make it," I say and lean in to give Justin a quick, friendly hug. "And you must be Luis." I hold a hand out to shake.

"Oh, I'm a hugger too," he gushes and throws his arms around me.

It's actually nice to be hugged by an adult... It's been a long time (all my hugs lately are from children), and Luis is gentle and smells delicious. Once I get to know him a little better, I'll ask him what scent he's wearing.

"Thanks again for the invitation, Sophia. I cannot wait to see the view from the balcony. It's supposed to be one of the best in the city."

I'm just thankful I was able to bribe the VIP hostess with a five-hundred-dollar Venmo transfer for a spot on the balcony for a few hours. I think my accent helped. She kept asking if my real name was Emily Blunt and giggling that I was her favorite.

"Shall we?" I take a step toward the door. And just as the bouncer ushers us in, Luis lets out a shriek behind me. I spin around and look at him, then over at Justin.

Justin shrugs and asks, "Babe, is everything alright?"

"No. Look at this text from my mom—shit, she's calling." Luis answers the phone in Spanish and proceeds to have a quick and loud conversation. He hangs up, looking white as a ghost. I only picked up a few words, but I think someone was hurt.

"What's going on?" Justin asks.

"My sister, she's been in a car accident. We have to go—" He looks around in a panic.

"Oh my god, is there anything I can do?" I put my hand on Luis's arm.

"No, thank you," he says, trying to be polite. "Justin, we need a cab to Mount Sinai in Queens."

"Queens?" Justin sounds appalled.

That's when I know what I can do. "You guys can take my driver. He's downstairs waiting. It's all paid and he'll take you anywhere in the city you need to go, and wait for you all night long. I'll take an Uber."

"Are you sure?" Justin asks.

Luis is back on his phone and distracted, which I don't blame him for.

"Yes, it's fine. I'll call my driver when you're on the way down. His name is Petrov." I give Justin a goodbye hug. "You better go. Petrov will be waiting."

He smiles and nods, then runs after Luis, who's trying to get on the elevator. I quickly call Petrov and explain what's transpired. I know he'll get Justin and Luis to the hospital quickly. He knows all the best routes in the city.

Before I leave, maybe I'll go in and check out the view for a few minutes. Sure, I've been to other rooftop bars in the city since I moved here, and if you've seen one, you've seen them all. But I did pay for the table. I might as well go in and have a drink and take a look around before I leave.

The bouncer opens the door for me and I make my way to the VIP hostess near the balcony. I say hello and show her the reservation on my phone, and she seems a little sad that I'm not in fact Emily Blunt.

"Sorry." I shrug.

She gives me a wink and says, "You're probably her sister, right? Or agent?"

I nod and wink, just to give her a little thrill. She claps then asks if she can take a selfie with me. But before she can snap the photo, a group of what I assume are drunk socialites out on the balcony makes too much noise. A bouncer shouts at them to quiet down and waves at the hostess to join him.

"Sorry, I have to go deal with them. It's a group from one of the new Broadway shows," she says as she's running off.

Broadway?

No, it couldn't be Rebecca's show, could it?

I take out my phone and look. Ekaterina hasn't sent me a text saying she's babysitting. Which means, even if it is Rebecca's production, those are just her castmates and the production crew, clearly having too much fun.

The VIP hostess is ushering some of the members from the group out and I watch with fascination. That's when I hear someone saying, "Come on, Becks, let's get out of here. You can sleep over at my place." It's coming from a young, attractive blonde with sharp features. Total Broadway type.

"Aww, thanks Violet, you're the best. I love you."

I know that voice. I'd know it anywhere.

Rebecca.

I jump behind a potted palm, hoping she doesn't see me. But she and the blonde are teetering as they walk. Clearly both of them are pretty wasted and not paying any attention to anything around them. I'm sure she's not going to see me.

So, if Rebecca is here, in the city partying with the cast of her show, then who is watching Sarah and Bailey? Thankfully I saved Rebecca's house phone number in my contacts. I push to call and it rings, once, twice, three times. I'm nervous that no one will answer. Then I feel nervous that a stranger will answer. Which is foolish. Why should I be nervous to call the house where I live? I'm allowed to know who is there when I am away.

"Hello?" Sarah answers.

"Sarah, sweetie, it's Sophia. Can I speak with your babysitter?" Why is Sarah answering the phone? It's waaaay past her bedtime. Did the sitter fall asleep? Or maybe it's like the movies and the sitter's having a party or invited her boyfriend over, locking Sarah and Bailey in their bedrooms. No, that can't be it, I reassure myself —Sarah has answered the phone.

"Um... no, I'm sorry," Sarah says.

So I *was* right.

"Did the babysitter lock you in your room?" I ask.

"No... There's no babysitter for you to talk to." Sarah starts to cry.

"Oh, Sarah, honey, please don't cry. It's not your fault if the babysitter left." Well, thank god I called. I doubt Sarah knows how to use the phone to call Rebecca. Even if she had, would Rebecca have answered in that drunken state? Probably not. "I'm going to come home, okay? I'll be there as soon as I possibly can."

Sarah sniffles a few times and makes a sound like she's swallowing a hiccup. "Mm-hmm... but, um, Sophia... the babysitter didn't leave. Mommy left me in charge."

If I'd had a mouth full of liquid, I would have spat it out in one of those comical sprays, followed by a string of expletives. But this isn't a comedy show, this is real life, and I cannot believe that my friend Becks left her five- and eight-year-old daughters home alone while she came to the city to get bombed. I manage to tell Sarah goodbye and convince her to go to bed. I tell her when she wakes up, *I'll be home.*

Then I leave the Spyglass Rooftop Bar, wishing I'd run into

Becks on my way down the elevator, or out on the street while I wait for an Uber or try and hail a cab. This part of town is especially busy on a Saturday night, considering Columbia University is just around the corner. I don't see her or the drunken group she was with anywhere. It's probably a good thing overall. I'm not one for physical violence, but if I saw her right now, I'm pretty sure I'd smack her across the face. My hand pulsates with the imaginary feeling of my palm slapping her flesh.

"You stupid, stupid woman, I cannot believe you left your kids home alone," I grumble under my breath as I quickly order a car to come pick me up. I need to get back to my apartment and change and get my "mommy car" as Ekaterina likes to call it.

Maybe when I get back to the suburbs, I'll just load up Sarah and Bailey and bring them back to my apartment in the city. That would scare Rebecca straight tomorrow, when she finally drags herself home, to find the girls missing. Oh, and wouldn't Mitch have a complete shit fit to find out his wife lost his two living children? Now, I don't blame Rebecca for what happened to her first two children, not entirely. SIDS cannot be predicted, therefore it can't be prevented. And her second baby, dying like that, freezing to death in the car—I blame Mitch for getting her pregnant while she was still mourning the first baby. He should have had a nanny or someone there to help her.

Why did he leave her alone then?

Come to think of it, why did he leave her alone this time? Sure, Sarah and Bailey aren't babies, but they are still breakable.

My phone pings.

Thank god. My ride is here. Because the longer I stand here thinking about it, the angrier I'm getting.

"Sarah, sweetheart, I'm home."

"Mommy?" she asks in a sleepy voice, rolling over and rubbing her eyes. I can smell the mint on her breath, which means she brushed her teeth before tucking herself into bed. Something about that makes me feel weepy and I have to suck in a deep breath to calm myself down.

"I'm here... It's Sophia." I'm sitting on the edge of her twin bed, trying not to shake from the adrenaline. I drove here in under forty-five minutes, which has to be some kind of record, but there wasn't any traffic and apparently no cops on the road.

She smiles, scootches toward me, and puts her head in my lap.

"You and Bailey are safe and sound, you can go back to sleep now," I say and pet her hair for a few long minutes. When her breathing slows and I think she's fallen back asleep, I gently slide her from my lap and onto her pillow. Then I lean over and give her a kiss on the forehead and get up slowly so that I don't disturb her.

But before I'm all the way up, she exclaims, "Wait. Fifi," and reaches her arms out for me. "Hugs."

My bottom lip quivers.

Why am I being so emotional about this? It's not like I haven't tucked the girls into bed on at least two dozen other nights since

I've been here. But something about tonight feels different. A turning point maybe? I wrap my arms around Sarah, and she wraps hers around me.

She starts sniffling.

And as much as I try to control myself, hot, wet, stinging tears come pouring out of my eyes. Then, with much less diplomacy than me, Sarah's little body starts shaking and she cries hard and loud.

"Oh, honey, it's okay, I'm here. I won't leave you, I promise." I squeeze her.

Just then, the door creaks open behind me.

"Fifi? Is that you?" Bailey asks.

I crane my head to look behind me, while still holding on to Sarah. Then I temporarily release the grip I've got around Sarah to take one of my arms and hold it open for Bailey. She doesn't need me to explain it to her. She runs at full speed and leaps up, landing on me, and I pull my arm closed, holding her close to my chest. I'm a mama bear. Their mama bear. That's when I realize something—

"I love you girls so much," I sob.

"I love you, Sophia," Sarah says.

"My Fifi," Bailey cries.

Guilt consumes me when I think about leaving them up here in their rooms, without an adult across the hallway. But I am not going to sleep in Becks's room. And my back and bones cannot handle sleeping on the floor of one of their rooms. "I have an idea— do you girls want to come sleep in my bed? And in the morning, we can get up and I'll make some porridge with honey and berries."

"Yes!" they both shout and scramble from the bed.

As we walk downstairs, Bailey tugs on me. "Sophia, what's porridge?"

I laugh and pat the top of her head. "It's just the way I say oatmeal. But I like to cook mine with milk and honey."

"Mmmm, that sounds yummy," Sarah says.

"Yeah, yummy," Bailey says with a yawn.

When we get into my room, as I'm helping the little girls crawl into my bed, I remember something Rebecca said about Bailey. That she gets up a hundred times a night and cries and carries on and wants water, potty breaks, snacks, stories, and everything else under the sun in order to avoid sleep. I'm not upstairs during the night, so I don't know if that really happens, or if it's just Rebecca exaggerating for sympathy.

Then I think about Hannah—and how she never complained about Ruby and Rowen. She always said loving words about them and told cute anecdotes. Suddenly I appreciate her all that much more.

"You know one time, my dear friend Hannah was very sick, and I had to take care of her twins, Rowen and Ruby. And they crawled in and slept in the bed with me, just like this." The girls are on either side of me.

"Really, Fifi? What are they like?" Sarah asks.

"Yeah." Bailey yawns. "What do they like?"

"Well, they love *Bluey*," I reply, to which both girls squeal and wiggle up closer to me in bed and exclaim that they love *Bluey* too. "And they are funny and love to dance and play outside... Maybe tomorrow we can play outside."

"And watch *Bluey*?" Sarah asks.

"Yes, and that too."

It's so cozy having the girls snuggling with me, and maybe because it's been a hell of a day or because I'm just that tired, but I yawn once, close my eyes, tell the girls good night and everything goes black... Ahhhh, sleep, *my dear friend*.

"Sophia," someone whispers in my ear.

I stir. It's sometime after dawn, because even though my eyes are still closed, sunlight glows, warming my lids. My body doesn't feel overly exhausted, thank goodness, so I decide to open my eyes and look at the child next to me. "Bailey, is it time to wake up?" I ask.

She grins and tilts her head from side to side. Then she puts her hands on my cheeks and says, "Yes. Me and Sarah been awake for-ev-er."

"Oh, is that a fact?"

"Uh-huh. And we made you breakfast."

I fly up. "You what?"

"Come on, breakfast is getting cold," Bailey says, grabbing my hand and pulling me out of the room and toward the kitchen. I sniff the air. I don't smell anything and the house isn't on fire. But I'm still nervous. What on earth did they make me? However, as soon as we reach the table in the dining room, I see toy food and my shoulders relax. A smile spreads over my face. I guess I figured Sarah was too old to play with toy food, but I was wrong, because she's organizing my place setting with little plastic utensils.

"Ahhhh, breakfast, mmmm." I grin.

"Oh, this is just pretend. You still have to make us porridge with honey. You promised. But I did fill up your electric kettle to boil water for tea." Sarah looks up from her work and smiles.

"Brilliant." I love that she plugged in the kettle. When I walk into the kitchen, there is steam spewing from the teal-colored pot, and a mug and tea bag waiting for me to pour the water. I make quick work of putting some steel-cut oats together with the remaining boiling water and a heavy splash of cream and honey. I don't make too much, as I'm not sure the girls will enjoy what I call porridge.

Although, they did eat that horrifying red sauce their mother made the first time I had dinner here. What a weird night that was.

Maybe I should have known right then, on that night, that this thing with Becks was never going to work out. She was never going to be the person I needed, the anchor, the tether to the real world, so that I wouldn't get lost at sea while I was working with my international clients. Because it can be easy to lose your way. I've seen it plenty of times.

"You girls want to come dress up your porridge?" I shout.

Sarah and Bailey come racing into the kitchen.

"Dress up porridge?" Sarah asks, laughing.

"Yes, you can put honey, or butter, or fruit, or brown sugar, or—"

"Can we put chocolate chips?" Bailey asks.

"Marshmallows?" Sarah asks.

I stroke my chin and squat down, squinting an eye at the girls. "Hmmm, chocolate and marshmallows for breakfast?" I take a long pause. The girls wiggle and put their hands together in a begging prayer.

"Pleeeeease, please, pretty please," they both chant.

"Okay, why the heck not?" I throw my hands up in the air.

"Yaaay!" they clap and shout.

Rebecca finally shows up around two p.m. and comes slinking into the dining room where I'm sitting with the girls, like a college girl doing the walk of shame.

The girls and I just came in from playing outside for a few hours. Well—they played, I watched and cheered for them as they ran, skipped, hopped, and played hide and seek. Now they're coloring pictures of puppies while I'm doing some work on my computer—I'm trying to track down a piece of Incan art for a buyer in Shanghai. I'm right in the middle of paying a mercenary a thousand dollars to rough up my contact Eduardo, who I know is withholding the whereabouts of the art from me, when Rebecca lets out a long sigh. Today is not the day for Eduardo to mess around with me. Seconds later, Rebecca makes a clucking noise...

"Nice of you to come home," I grumble, refusing to look up from my screen. I need confirmation from the mercenary that he got the funds.

"I don't know what the girls told you, but I've just run to the store and come back, it's not a big deal at all. What time did your plane land?" she asks. "How was San Fran? I've always wanted to go there. Did you go to the piers? How was the food?"

Finally, the mercenary sends me a thumbs-up, so I slowly close my computer screen and look up at Rebecca. Her demeanor is completely off-brand. She's twitchy, and her eyes dart around the room. Is she high? Because I've seen hungover Rebecca and this is not it. I wondered when I saw the rest of her castmates last night if they were the kind who liked to party. I'd never taken Becks for someone who would participate in off-stage antics, though.

Guess I was wrong.

I decide to lie. "Just got here a few minutes ago, San Francisco was fine." Sarah looks at me, her eyes puzzled. Bailey is too busy coloring and singing her ABCs using a series of silly voices to care what we're talking about. I look at Sarah and shake my head, just enough for her to not say anything.

"Great. I'm pretty tired. Do you mind watching the girls? I'm going to go up and take a nap," she says and doesn't wait for me to say yes, or no, or anything at all. She just turns and heads for the stairs.

After we hear her bedroom door slam shut upstairs, Sarah narrows her gaze and says, "You lied to my mom."

"Yes, I did. But she lied to me first. She said she'd only been at the store for a few minutes. But that's not true. Is it? She left you here alone last night."

"I'm not mad that you lied to her," Sarah says.

"Then why'd you give me the stink eye?" I narrow my own gaze at her and purse my lips a little.

"Is that what that means?" she gasps and laughs.

"No. Stink eye is when you fart and your eyes go crossed, like this." Bailey stops singing and crosses her eyes. Then she makes a fart sound with her mouth.

Sarah and I burst out laughing.

"No. Stink eye has nothing to do with pooting." I reach over and tickle her. She giggles and wiggles in her seat.

"Are you sure, Fifi?" she asks. Then she waves her hand in a fanning motion in front of her face. "Excuse me..."

I sniff the air, getting a whiff of something toxic.

"Eww. Silent but deadly. Bailey, that reeks!" Sarah shrieks.

"Sorry, um, I think I have to poop." Bailey jumps up from her chair and runs out of the dining room.

I put my hand over my mouth and laugh. Not just a casual laugh, but like an uncontrollable laughter. I'm trying not to be too loud, because I don't want Becks coming down here screaming that we're being too loud and I don't want to embarrass Bailey, if she can hear me from the bathroom.

"Oh, you kids are so goofy," I finally say to Sarah once I catch my breath.

"You're so much fun," Sarah says and throws her arms around me in a hug.

I squeeze her tight and then pet her head.

After she sits back down and starts coloring again, I notice she's extra fidgety, peeling the paper from her crayons, then twisting her hair, and making little noises. Finally, when I'm about to ask if she has to go potty too, she opens her mouth and says, "Don't ever leave. I know she lied. But promise you won't ever leave us, Fifi."

"Who, Bailey? No, I'm pretty sure she had to go potty, she ran to the bathroom."

"No, my mom. She lies all the time." She looks down and lets out a very long sigh, for such a small girl.

I reach a hand over and put my fingers under her chin, lifting her head. "You don't have to worry. I have this ability where I can tell when people are lying, and then I can decide if I want to tell them I know they are lying, or let them go on and keep lying."

"Really?"

"Yep." I wag my eyebrows and smile.

"But why would you want someone to keep lying to you?" she asks.

"Well, you know how sometimes it's okay to tell a little lie to protect someone's feelings? Like, let's say I cooked you supper, but when you tasted it, it was bad. Would you tell me right to my face it was disgusting? Or would you be nice to me and eat it and try to smile?"

Her eyes light up. "Like Mommy's red sauce. It's yucky, but me and Bailey eat it anyway."

"Yes, just like that. And I wondered if it was my tastebuds or if there was something a little off about her sauce." I realize as soon as the words leave my mouth that I probably shouldn't bad-mouth Rebecca in front of her children. That's a kick-me-out-of-her-house kind of offense. Quickly, before Sarah can say anything else about the sauce, I jump up from my seat and announce, "How about we get Happy Meals and go play at the park?"

"Yes!" Sarah exclaims.

"Did someone say, Happy Meal?" Bailey comes running full speed at me and grabs my legs.

I wobble but catch myself before falling over. "Bailey. You goose."

"I'm not a goose."

"Yes you are, a very silly one. Now hurry up. Put on your shoes and let's go load up in my car." I jingle my keys and the girls rush out to find their shoes.

I contemplate texting Becks to let her know I'm taking her children. Instead, I grab a blue crayon and draw a big heart on a piece of paper. Inside of it I write:

French fries are life
Took the kids to McD's

I don't think she'll even come downstairs to check, but on the off chance she does, she'll know that's what we did. I hear whispers behind me, and I turn to see the girls standing in the entryway. Shoes on and hair brushed.

"Qui veut manger des frites?" I ask. "That was French for: who's ready for fries!"

They clap and jump up and down. "Teach me," Sarah says first.

"No, me." Bailey runs to grab my hand and I give it a little squeeze.

We exit the house and the girls talk a million miles a minute while I load them into my car. Something about it just feels so completely natural, almost like they are my girls. We laugh, talk, and then they serenade me with a song as we drive.

It's the most relaxed and perfect I've felt in all the time I've been staying with Rebecca. Like I have a real family who loves me and would miss me if I was gone. The funny thing is, it's not Rebecca who's caused it, it's the kids. But if they were actually my family, I'd never want to leave them...

"Okay, girls, ten more minutes!" I shout from the bench where I've finally parked myself. I'm exhausted from chasing them and pushing them on the swings. I splurged and ate some french fries with the kids, so I figured I better burn off the calories, which I think I've done and then some.

Buzz.

It's Barry.

"It took you long enough. I thought I paid extra for fast results... Tell me you have something," I say instead of hello.

"Yeah, I do actually. This guy's not just cheating, he has another life. He owns a home in Berlin, a vacation chalet in the Alps, and is engaged to a woman half his age named—"

"That's all I need right now, just text me the rest of the information." I hang up on Barry. My heart is racing as I watch the girls running and waving at me.

I wave back and smile. Hoping the girls won't be able to read my emotions. Oh, Doctor Mitch, you sneaky, sly son of a bitch. You're not just cheating on Rebecca, you have a second life! It won't be long and you'll be leaving her to move to another country. You're leaving Sarah and Bailey. You're ruining everything!

"Fifi. Watch!" Bailey screams and goes head-first down the tube slide.

I stand up and take a deep breath. "Girls, time to go home."

My phone buzzes—it's Barry. He's sent me a text with all the information about Mitch's mistress. Her name, address, where she works, pictures of her, pictures of their house in Berlin... It's all right there, in black and white.

I just have to decide how and when I want to use this information. No matter what happens, it's going to come out sooner or later, and things at the Hendricks residence are about to change forever.

PART 2

TWENTY-FIVE

REBECCA

The last six weeks have been nonstop and I'm ready for a break. Between conversations with my divorce attorney, finding the right realtor, going to rehearsals, and attempting to stay sane, it's been more than I want to deal with.

Oh yeah, all this shit started when Mitch came home from his second round of teaching in Europe and told me he wanted a divorce. Which really pissed me off, because why should that asshole get to go "live the life he was meant to live" and stick me with all the household responsibilities and the children?

Really, Mitch? The life you were meant to live? Blow me.

I actually debated killing him in his sleep.

Well, more than debated, I spent an entire week fantasizing exactly how I might do it. Pillow over his face? Gun to his temple? Bleach in his coffee? But Indra, Violet, and Chase talked me off the ledge. They reminded me that with Mitch in Germany permanently, I'd be free to sell the house, move to the city, and hire a live-in nanny—which would allow me to focus entirely on my career on Broadway. All without going to jail for murder. And that is one place I am not ever fucking going.

Sophia, on the other hand—she's been a regular snob over the whole divorce thing. Or as Indra likes to say, *a royal bitch*. Seriously, she's been taking it worse than the children. Over the last few weeks the number of times I've heard: *You can't sell the house. What about holidays for the girls? Where will I come visit when I'm in town? You're really going to give up the memories?* More times than I can count.

It would be nice if she would just relax a little. I can only deal with so much. I mean, who does she think she is, anyway? It's not like she's part of my family. Selling the house is honestly none of her business. If she loves it so much, she could fucking buy it.

But I think it's more than that. I get the impression that she thinks if I sell the house, I'm going to buy a one-bedroom condo in the city and leave my daughters on the curb with the trash. Maybe I have been a little short with Sarah and Bailey lately, but I can't deal with the constant crying and complaining every time I ask them to do something. Moving is a lot of work. They are getting old enough that they can help. It's not like I told them to pack up the dishes or clean out the garage. All I asked was for them to box up all the junk from the basement for the donation bin, and they acted like I was killing their beloved pet or something else dramatic.

Even if Sophia is far too opinionated about me selling the house for her own good, I am glad she's still here. She's taken over a lot of the duties with the girls, and the packing, allowing me to come and go as I need—which is making this so much easier on me. I haven't even been home in two weeks, besides popping in to grab clean clothes, check the mail, and leave money for Mrs. Melnyk. Now there's a woman I'm glad I won't have to see anymore. I'd fire her now, but that would really be asking a lot of Sophia. To do the cleaning and laundry on top of helping me with the packing, kids, and cooking.

I know she's been the one cooking because there are always neatly labeled and organized containers in the fridge. Mrs. Melnyk never did that.

I'm currently staring at a container with a green lid, labeled "Authentic tomato, basil, and garlic spaghetti." Even though I'm hungry, the thought of eating red sauce makes my stomach turn.

Instead I grab a blueberry muffin, nibbling on the soft, sweet edges as I walk upstairs to take a shower. I'm not surprised to find our bedroom empty. I'm sure Mitch is working late at the hospital. I don't want to see him anyway. I set my muffin down and grab some pajamas, but when I go to put them on, I notice how grimy my skin feels. Probably from all the costume changes tonight during dress rehearsal.

I smell my pits. "Yep, shower, now," I say to myself. I'll sleep better if I'm clean anyway.

After a long, leisurely shower, I leave my steamy bathroom and sit on the bed to rub velvety aloe vera lotion into my legs and arms. It feels strange to sit on my own bed. I'm not even that tired, even though it's one in the morning. That triple venti iced vanilla latte during our evening rehearsal probably wasn't my best idea. But I was supposed to go back to Chase's apartment to watch the full production playback, and take notes. I wasn't supposed to come home tonight.

Of all nights.

Mitch's and my anniversary...

Not the day we got married, but the one when he found me in the closet about to swallow all those pills.

"Please don't do that," he said.

"Why the fuck do you care?" I asked as I looked at him.

"My wife, she overdosed, and I'd hate to see another bright star be lost in the same way." He looked and sounded genuinely concerned for my well-being.

"Really? You think I look like a star?"

"Yes, absolutely. The Broadway kind... I bet you were captain of the cheer squad in high school. Maybe on the debate team. Or..." He narrowed his gaze, then put a finger to his mouth and said, "Hmmm... Girls' swim team—no, the theater. I bet you were the leading lady."

I remember blushing. Being enchanted by the fact that he

guessed so right about me. Like he saw me, he figured me out. I was putty in his hands—he saved me and I would do anything for him. Absolutely anything…

If I'd been with Chase tonight, he would've made me laugh and not think about my real life—the life I not-so-secretly hate, because of what happened. What I've done. What I'm capable of doing…

But Chase's new boyfriend called as soon as dress rehearsal was over and said he'd scored tickets to some off-off-Broadway show. So I ran over to Violet, who was so sorry, she was on her way to have dinner with her mom. Then I looked around, but Indra was gone too.

So that's how I ended up back here, tonight of all freaking nights! I wish my brain would just quiet down so I could go to sleep, but between the caffeine and this guilt of past sins weighing on my chest, even if I lie down, I'll just toss and turn. So I open my nightstand to look for a book, but nothing looks remotely interesting. Until I spot the soft pink leather from the journal Sophia gifted me right after she moved in. I haven't written in it in ages.

I'm not sure where to start this entry. I wasn't even supposed to be here tonight, I was supposed to be with Chase. He's probably the only person who could keep my head from spiraling right now. I haven't even told you about Chase. Wow, now that I think about it, so much has happened since the last time I wrote in you. First, I got the lead in Happily Never After. The role feels perfect for me, because she goes through such a metamorphosis. Becoming the woman she was meant to be. We open in two weeks. I've become best friends with my castmates, Chase, Violet, and Indra. They take me out in the city almost every single night, which is what I need right now, since my piece of shit husband Mitch asked for a divorce. Of course, he said he'll give me everything I want, because he just wants it to be over so he can move to Germany to be with his whore. I don't care. Really, I don't! But I have this nagging feeling that it's all hanging on by a thread— all it will take is one person pulling the end of it for me to completely unravel. Like, what if Mitch decides to use what I did against me instead of giving me the house? What if Sophia leaves and I have no one to take care of the kids? What if my new friends decide I'm lame and they never want to hang out again? What if our production is a flop and I never get another job on Broadway? Well, I'll kill myself. That's what. I will literally jump off the Empire State Building. I am never going back to working as a nurse in the clinic, or being someone's wife, or mother again.

I pause. I shouldn't have written that last part. I'll always be a mother.

I don't mean it like that. It's not like Sarah and Bailey are dead. I am a mother... Oh, never mind, this is stupid anyway. I don't know what I'm worried about. I'm getting everything I want. I have everything I ever dreamed of.

I frown at the words. It doesn't feel like I have everything I ever dreamed of. "Yeah, this is stupid," I say out loud, then shove the journal back into the drawer of my nightstand. An unexpected chill goes up my spine. Probably too much sugar from that muffin. I shake my head and reach over to turn off my side lamp... The moment it goes dark, the door creaks open.

"No, back to bed," I snap at whichever child it is.

"It's just me. I didn't know you'd be home." Mitch stumbles in, smelling like cigarettes and whiskey... I wonder if he was sitting in a bar, alone, mourning his losses. Regretting the day he ever met me. Is that why he's drunk? Or was he celebrating that he's leaving me and starting over, again.

"You must have taken the night off?" I ask.

"I fly out tomorrow, so yeah, I took the night off," he says and walks over to sit down on his side of the bed. He leans forward to untie his shoes.

Something about the way he says it rubs me the wrong way. I don't know why, but I thought maybe he'd say he took the night off because he was depressed. "Well, fucking excuse me, Mitch. How the hell am I supposed to know your schedule?"

"Huh?" He sits up and turns around. "Why are you so mad all of a sudden?"

Ooooh, now my blood is boiling. I can't stand when people accuse me of being mad when I'm not. Or at least I wasn't until he said it. I can't believe Mitch thinks he can just come and go whenever he wants.

"Who's watching the girls while you're gone?" I already know what he's going to say.

"Well, you, of course." He finishes removing his shoes, then his shirt, and stands to take his pants off. When he's done, he crawls into the bed, right next to me—in his underwear, no less. I'm sure his German bitch would love to know he's crawling in bed next to me practically naked. Not that it matters. Mitch hasn't made a pass at me in over a year.

"No. I'm not watching them. I told you, I'm going on a marketing tour for the show. I texted you and emailed you about this weeks ago. If you'd been paying more attention to me, instead of her..." Of course I'm lying. I didn't email or text him anything, because there is no such marketing tour. I'm just trying to prove a point.

"Well, I, uh, I'm not sure I recall—I didn't get your messages."

"How convenient. Well, you'll just have to cancel your trip and stay home with your children. I am not being your fucking babysitter so that you can go gallivanting around Europe with your little whore." I fling the covers off. I'm not going to lie here next to Mitch all night.

"Calm down. I never called you my babysitter. I understand you have a life, Rebecca. But I can't cancel my trip, I have several speaking engagements."

"Well, you need to figure it out before you go."

"How about we make Sophia watch them?" he says and pats the bed. As if I'm going to snuggle back in next to him.

"Are you serious? Make Sophia watch them? She's not our fucking nanny. She's my house guest." Well, more like a paid tenant. She gave me another "rent check" last week. This time for fifty thousand dollars... I was shocked, but she was so nonchalant about it. Said her apartment is almost done, but she'd like to stay here for a few more months. Something about her decorator being out of the country. I stopped listening after I saw the check with my name on it. I used it to open a new account so I didn't have to tell Mitch about the money.

"Well, Rebecca, this is still my house and I'm going to tell Sophia that she has to leave—or if she really wants to continue to stay, she can contribute like any other member of this family and watch the children. I'd wager my little finger that she'll agree." He wags his pinky finger at me. "Now, lie down and go to sleep. You always get so worked up when there's generally an easy solution right in front of your face." Then he yawns.

"I, uh, well..." I stammer. I don't think Sophia will appreciate Mitch's you-better-chip-in-or-get-out talk. Mitch doesn't understand how much Sophia is already doing. He's so fucking oblivious. Like, who does he think picks the kids up and takes them to school? Or makes all the dinners? Or does the grocery shopping?

"I'll ask her in the morning. I'm sure you have a lot to do if you're going on a marketing tour." Then he rolls over and stuffs and restuffs his pillow under his head.

I sigh, then slide back into the bed and set my hand on his shoulder.

"You don't have to speak with her about it. She's my friend, I'll do it. I'm sorry I was mad." I rub his bare flesh in a little encouraging circle. "I want you to have a nice trip."

He's snoring within minutes.

Even though I was lying about a marketing tour, maybe I will ask Sophia to watch the kids and I'll go stay in a hotel in the city, one with a rooftop bar. Yes. That's exactly what I'm going to do. I'm going to leave tomorrow, before Mitch even wakes up, or the girls...

TWENTY-SIX

I spent so much time lying in bed imagining my early-morning escape to the city before Mitch woke up, that I fell asleep at like four a.m. At least, that's the last time I looked over and saw the clock.

"Becks... Can you hear me?" Sophia whispers.

She is far too close for comfort—I know because I can feel her perfectly minty breath all hot and steamy on my face. I crack open an eye.

"Oh good. You're awake."

I wait for her to back out of my personal space before I open my other eye... Sophia has something in her hand and quickly hides it behind her back when she sees me eyeballing it.

I sit up and point. "What's that?"

She laughs, but it sounds fake. "Nothing. Just a hand mirror." She pulls it out from behind her back and shows me the small black-handled mirror. "I was getting concerned that you weren't awake yet, so I held it under your nose to make sure you were still breathing... Mitch asked me to keep an eye on you right before he left. He seemed worried about you."

Yeah right. Mitch worried. About me. I roll my eyes.

"Oh, he also mentioned something about you needing to leave for a marketing tour."

"No, it's dumb. You really don't need to worry about that, I'm not going." I wave my hands back and forth and shake my head. Damnit, Mitch, you piece of shit, I didn't want to tell Sophia about my fake marketing trip. I crawl out of bed, stand up, and attempt to walk to the bathroom, but Sophia is in the way.

"Not going? Why? You have to, you're literally the star." Sophia throws her arms around me for a hug I am not at all prepared for. "I will gladly watch the girls and take care of packing and everything else here while you're gone. Don't worry your pretty little head." She squeezes me once, then what I would consider prances her way out of my room. Rarely does Sophia get so physically animated. She's either really happy for me or up to something.

"I'm still not sure I'm going!" I shout after her, but she's already out of my room and off to play housewife and mommy.

Buzz.

I grab my phone off the nightstand, thankful to have someone besides Sophia to talk to.

It's Chase.

> Oh. My. God! You should have come to the show with us last night. Those off-off-Broadway Guys and Dolls are fabulous. We're going again tonight, all of us, there's a scene you have to see.

> Must be some scene.

> Oh, it is, sweetheart. When are you coming back to the city? Meet us for drinks and lunch at 2. I'll drop you a pin.

It's already twelve fifteen. I'll be cutting it close. I quickly text back a thumbs-up, then run into the bathroom to take a quick shower. I'll just have to let my hair air dry with some products, because I do not have time for a full blow-dry. Not if I want any chance of making it for at least a drink with the gang wherever they're having lunch.

But when I'm done showering and toweling my hair off, I realize I don't have any of my new hair products here. I left everything in the city at Chase's place. "Fuck!" I exclaim as I rifle through all the bathroom drawers and cupboards, desperately searching for some sort of taming product I can throw in my hair. But I can't find anything but some old gel, from when I was doing this slicked-back bun thing. Which is not the look I'm going for.

I run downstairs hoping—no, praying—that Sophia has something that will work in my hair. "Sophia, I need some hair products," I say, rushing past her and the girls toward the guest bathroom where Sophia keeps her beauty stuff. From the corner of my eye, I see the girls in aprons mixing up something blue and gooey in a bowl. Gross.

"Help yourself to whatever I have," Sophia yells after me.

"Oh, I will."

But as soon as I'm in her bathroom and standing in front of her things, I'm scared to touch any of them. I know from seeing ads, that bottle of spray is $300, and that serum is $500. But then I remember, I'm in a time crunch and I don't have time to worry about how much anything costs. She said to help myself. So I start squeezing, spraying, and dousing my hair, face and body in all of her expensive products. Not only do I have to look good, she has to believe I'm about to go on a marketing trip for a week.

"More. That stuff works, but you need to use a lot. Feel free to take anything with you on your trip," she says from behind me. It's like she magically appeared in the open doorframe.

My heart leaps. "Jesus, don't sneak up on people."

She smiles and shrugs. "Oh, sorry." Then she looks down at her nails and picks at the corner of one.

I'm watching her in the mirror while opening and closing the bathroom drawers.

"Becks, do you happen to know where the girls' passports are?" she asks.

I snatch several bottles of that gold leaf facial tonic that keeps showing on my TikTok "for you" page and shove them in the pocket of my bathrobe. She did just say I can take whatever I want. Wait, did she just ask about passports? "Why do you need their passports?"

"Oh, good, so they do have passports."

"Are you taking them out of the country? Because I'm not sure I'm comfortable with that." Although, I'm sure Sophia would watch them like a hawk. I probably wouldn't need to worry.

"No, no, nothing like that... For identification. If there was an emergency and I had to take one of them to the hospital or something, I just figured an official passport would be better than their paper birth certificates."

I turn around and look Sophia in the eye. She looks bored. That excitement she had for me upstairs to go on this pretend marketing trip is waning. Probably because she's suddenly thinking about all the things she needs to think of, like freaking passports! I need to defuse her indifference as fast as I can so I can get out of here and head to the city...

The more that I think about it, the more I realize this fake marketing trip is going to be incredible if I can pull it off. My husband is already gone. Sophia won't expect anything from me for a week, maybe even two. And I bet she could get the entire house finished by then, which means I could list it for sale and be living in the city by the end of the month!

"Yes, great idea. Their passports are in Mitch's office in that little fireproof safe he keeps behind his desk. The combination is written on a piece of paper taped to the back of the safe."

Sophia perks right up, but I'm in too much of a hurry to decipher her mood shifts.

"Thanks," she says and walks away. I'm done hunting for beauty products and I'm out the door right behind her. But I turn and go down the hall the other way, and around and up the front set of stairs. I don't want to see the girls and have one of them stop me to ask silly questions about where I'm going or what I'm doing.

I can literally feel the clock ticking down.

And it's giving me anxiety.

TWENTY-SEVEN
SOPHIA

It's easy enough to find out if she's lying, which she most definitely is. All I have to do is text my old pal Grant, the director. I don't even know if that's necessary, because all that matters is Rebecca is going to be gone for a week. Maybe longer. Which gives me plenty of time to take the girls to get physicals, any vaccines they need, haircuts, new play clothes, and have them fitted for private school uniforms.

I've decided to transfer them to a private school.

After that horrible nonsense surrounding Bailey's bathroom accident, I can't risk leaving them in public school. Even though it was entirely Rebecca's fault, those mishaps are the sorts of things that can scar a little girl for life. I do feel quite certain something like that would never happen at the private Northbridge House school in Primrose Hill—the quaint and upscale neighborhood where my *London* house is located.

Yes. My plan is to move the girls to London. With me.

Becks is one hundred percent ill-equipped to handle single motherhood after Mitch officially leaves her. Which is going to be soon. There's no way he's going to wait until their divorce is final. I bet he's gone for good by the end of the month. He's already started to quietly move out his personal belongings. I've seen him leaving with boxes in his arms when he thought everyone was still sleeping.

Not that Becks would notice.

Especially while she's been pursuing her dreams of stardom.

If her production of *Happily Never After* does as well as she keeps bragging it's going to, then I have no doubt Becks will get offered the leading role in another show. That's when she'll realize that she's not prepared to care for her daughters *and* be a star at the same time. I'm going to speed up the process by taking a trip for a few weeks, leaving Becks alone with her daughters.

When I return, I'll be her lady-knight in shining armor, there to offer her a marvelous solution. I'll take the girls with me—to London—for school. It's perfect! They'll get a first-rate education, while she has all the time she needs to rehearse for her new show. I'll make sure she knows she can FaceTime them as often as she likes and I'll bring the girls back to see her during school holidays. It's doubtful she'll want them back, but I'll offer nonetheless...

But there's one little problem with my plan.

Okay, two problems.

First, it repeatedly leaves Sarah and Bailey with a woman who has already accidentally killed two of her other children. Yes, maybe "killed" is a strong word. SIDS was not her fault... Was it foolish for her to let a newborn sleep in her bed? Yes—if you believe that co-sleeping is a contributing factor of SIDS. However, baby number two's accident, being left in the car seat in the garage and freezing to death, was totally preventable.

So the question is, do I really want to leave the girls with a woman who's capable of accidentally harming them? They aren't babies, so that should give them some additional layer of protection. But I've read articles about women who drowned their school-aged children in bathtubs or stuck them in a vehicle with the carbon monoxide pumping in through a hose and claimed it was all a big accident. They didn't mean to hurt their children, when in fact they'd murdered them. You'd think Sarah and Bailey would fight back if she was trying to harm them, but I've seen those children eat an entire plate of her rancid tomato sauce, just to please her. So if she told them to sit still while she held their heads underwater, they might just do it. It's something I'll be having their new therapist discuss with them. I'm going to get them the best professional help money can buy once we arrive in London.

But I have a second problem with my plan.

Mitch. There is still a chance that he might object to me taking the girls. I've worked it out in my head that I can get Rebecca to sign over custody to me as long as I reassure her it's strictly for enrolling them in school. Plus, the check for $100,000 I'll wave in front of her face will probably help seal the deal if she's having any doubts. I'll call it her "travel money" to come see them whenever she likes. But we'll both know what it really is.

Mitch on the other hand, he won't be so easily bought.

I'll have to get Barry to dig up more dirt on him.

If he hadn't asked for the divorce already, that would be easy, his affair. But since that's out in the wide open, I'll have to figure out something else. Hmmm... He is a surgeon. Maybe he's killed someone and covered it up? Or taken bribes from a medical device company? If Mitch has done something wrong, which I'm almost a hundred percent certain he has, *I will find out.*

"Whoa, that's a lot of shaving cream." With quick reflexes I snatch the can out of Bailey's hand mid-spray.

"But, FiFi, I want it super squishy," she whines.

I stick my hand in the bowl of blue slime and shaving cream and squeeze and wiggle my fingers around. "It's already squishier than a bowl of Jell-O on a sunny day."

Both girls giggle, sigh, and say, "FiFi," at the same time.

"What? I'm just saying, you can only make it so squishy before it becomes pudding." I shake my head, then tickle Bailey behind the ear and ruffle Sarah's hair. With my clean hand of course. Then I pretend my blue-goo-covered hand is toxic and that it's going to attack them. They're squealing and laughing.

We're in the kitchen—making slime and other silly, messy concoctions that small children love putting their hands in. Something I never could have imagined myself doing a year ago. But it's actually kind of fun.

Five minutes ago, Rebecca just not-so-casually swiped a thousand dollars' worth of beauty products from my collection in her attempts to get out of this house as fast as she can. Thankfully, in exchange, she gave me the information on where to find the girls' passports. The things I need if I'm going to take them to London. They are locked in the fireproof safe in Mitch's office.

But I have to check she's telling the truth.

"Sarah, sweetie, can you keep an eye on Bailey, and stay here and play with your slimes? I've got to go grab something in the other room real fast. I'll be right back."

"Can you leave music for us?"

"Of course." I grab my phone and turn on Spotify. The only music I have is Broadway, which has lost its appeal. "Have you girls heard of Lady Gaga?" I ask. A smile spreads over my face as I think about Hannah—and her insistence that I learn about some popular music.

The girls nod their heads and continue squeezing and stirring their bowls of slime. They are laughing and elbowing each other and are really too busy to care what music I turn on.

I leave my phone on the end of the table and walk briskly down the hall toward Mitch's office. I have to hurry—because once Becks leaves this house there's a very real chance that I might never see her again. That's not me being paranoid or some veiled threat, that's the absolute truth. New York City is dangerous and Becks's behavior has been reckless recently. There's a million things that could go wrong over the next week, while she thinks she has carte blanche to misbehave. Things I can't control, even with all of my money and connections...

Which means, all I can worry about right now is taking care of these two perfect, precious little girls. "So far, so good," I say to myself as I reach around the safe and find the small piece of paper taped to the back of it, just like Becks promised.

Written in Mitch's handwriting are the numbers 48-31-17.

The code. I quickly punch it on the digital keypad and hear the locking mechanism clicking in the safe. The door pops open and inside I find the girls' passports, birth certificates, and other important documents, like the deed to the house and Rebecca and Mitch's marriage certificate. I wonder why Mitch keeps that other file hidden in his desk drawer and not in the fireproof safe?

Unless it's because he knows seeing those things will upset Rebecca.

Or seeing them upsets him...

Later that night, after I've tucked the girls in to bed and Rebecca is long gone, the house is calm and quiet. There are no sounds of TVs or computer keys clacking or showers or music or singing or any other sounds of life from within the walls of the house. The hair on my neck stands up. I look over my shoulder once, but there's no one in the hallway. I was about to head downstairs to pour myself a drink and curl up with a book for an hour before bed, after tucking in the girls, when I notice the door is cracked open to Rebecca's room.

"Hello?" I whisper.

I could have sworn the door was closed.

There's no way Rebecca came home and I didn't realize it, right? No, that's silly. One of the girls probably opened it during our bedtime routine and I just didn't notice. But I better go in and check. I shiver when I enter. There's just something about Rebecca's bedroom that gives me the creeps. Maybe it's because a baby died in this bed. Sure, it's probably not the same mattress or sheets and comforter, because it's been over ten years. But Rebecca isn't the best decorator... She's not changing things out very often, if at all.

I squint and look at the bed. Then I feel the comforter. It's old and thin, like it's been washed too many times. Why have I never noticed that before? I should have insisted she buy herself new bedding.

It doesn't matter now, but still, maybe tomorrow I'll order her some new bedding. For my own personal sanity so that when I walk by this room, I don't think about a dead baby. Too bad I can hear Ekaterina's harsh voice echoing in my head, *You stupid woman, waste money on new bedding for a woman who never sleep here.*

I chuckle. Yes, maybe I am a stupid woman. But I have more money than I know what to do with. And for my own mental health, I'd love to not think about what might have happened on this bed. "So why don't you shut up, Ekaterina," I scold the woman, and she's not even here.

That's when I notice a pen sitting on the nightstand. Hmmm... Maybe Rebecca wrote something interesting in her journal. Although, I'm sure it's a long shot—she hasn't written anything in it in months. She was probably just practicing signing her autograph for her fake marketing tour.

My hand jerks open the drawer on the nightstand and there, right on top, is the pink journal I purchased for her as a gift when I moved in all those months ago.

"Okay, Becks. Let's see if you have anything interesting to say." I sit down on the floor, because sitting on that bed really freaks me out. I turn the pages of the journal—past all the entries I've already read. There is only one new entry. From last night when she got home after the girls and I were asleep. She was complaining again, about what she'll do if things don't work out the way she wants them to.

"What does that mean?" I ask, reading the line, *What if Mitch decides to use what I did against me instead of giving me the house?*

Now that I know I'm alone in the house, I don't have to freak out, and I can snoop around as much as I want. I'll dig around in Mitch's office and see if I can find anything about what Rebecca might have done that he's holding against her. However, right now, I want to get out of this bedroom and go downstairs and have a few minutes with my book before my eyes are too heavy to comprehend the words. I used to have such terrible insomnia, but lately, it's as if I can barely keep my eyes open. I'm always exhausted.

But I guess chasing after children will do that to a person.

I have a lot more sympathy and compassion for my sweet friend Hannah these days. I really should reach out to her. Maybe once I'm in London with the girls. I know Hannah always wanted me to return to the UK. Then I shove the journal back in the drawer, turn off the lights, and close the door, making sure it latches, as I leave. God, I can't wait to get out of this house for good.

Buzz.

My phone rings.

I groan and roll over. My book flops off my chest. Damnit. I guess I fell asleep reading. I hardly remember making it back downstairs after snooping in Rebecca's room. I wonder what time it is? And who could be calling me at this hour?

I grab my phone and squint at the glowing screen—even at sixty percent it's too bright.

"JUSTIN" is flashing across the screen.

I haven't heard from him since the rooftop bar. I've been wondering what happened to his boyfriend, Luis, and the sister who was in a car accident. I've texted a few times to see how he's doing. But no response. You'd think he would have at least messaged me back with a quick update since that whole thing. To at least let me know if the sister survived.

I really hope he's not drunk calling me just to use my driver. I sit up in bed and rub my eyes. I don't answer in time—Justin hangs up. But I have a feeling he's either going to call me back or he's going to send a text.

> Sophia, I'm so sorry to bother you this late… But we have a little Rebecca problem.

Oh great. What now? There are so many ways this could go. But before I can respond to ask what kind of Rebecca problem, he sends another series of texts.

> Are you awake?

> Sorry I was MIA. Luis's dad unexpectedly passed away the week of his sister's car accident and we had to take his body to the Dominican Republic for the burial and funeral.

Well, now I feel a little shitty for being annoyed that I hadn't heard from him since the Spyglass Rooftop.

> Please pick up.

> Yes, I'm awake now.

Buzz.

He calls again. And this time I answer.

"What's wrong with Rebecca?" My voice is middle-of-the-night groggy. "And I'm sorry to hear about Luis's father." I throw that last part in so Justin doesn't think I'm heartless. Obviously it's sad. But I have no idea what kind of man his father was. Maybe he was a drunken pedophile and Luis is glad he's dead.

"Thanks, girl," he says. "And I'm so sorry to call this late. Luis and I just got home and decided to go out, you know." His voice is a little slurred. I can imagine after spending weeks with his boyfriend's family in the Dominican that he was ready to blow off some steam. "We went to the park to see Bethesda Fountain before going home. And that's when I saw her."

"You mean Rebecca?"

"Yes!"

"So Rebecca's at Bethesda Fountain?" Even I know that's the big fountain in the middle of Central Park. It's a huge tourist attraction.

"Yes. Or, well, at least she was. The park is closed now. When I saw her she was only half dressed and dancing around the edge and splashing in the water. She fell in, then ran over and was vomiting in the bushes. Her friends were all still dancing. No one seemed to care she was so fucked up. I'm scared that if the paparazzi find her, she'll get fired from her show." Justin sounds pretty worked up, his voice is shrill and he's breathing heavily. "I'm sending you picture evidence."

Buzz.

I tap on the text message and zoom in on the picture as soon as it pops up on my phone.

That's Rebecca all right.

If I was standing there next to her, I'd say, *Jesus, what's wrong with you, Becks? Just because it's Saturday night does not mean you have to party like some wild NYU co-ed.* But I'm not standing in Central Park. And it sounds like she'll have moved on anyway, if the park is closed. I doubt her friends and co-stars would risk getting arrested.

"I'm not sure what you want me to do, Justin. I'm at Rebecca's house watching her daughters. I can't just drive to the city and go hunting around Central Park for her."

"No, of course not. But do you think you could call her? Tell her she needs to head home? Maybe send your driver to pick her up?"

I open my mouth to say no. Because why should I bail out Rebecca? Plus, Justin's fear of the paparazzi identifying a drunken, vomiting Rebecca at two a.m. is pretty ridiculous. No one even knows who she is, for now. Maybe after opening night for her Broadway show, some diehard fans might recognize her. But right now? No way. So no, I'm not sending a driver to find her. By now she's probably stumble-walking with one of her friends back to their apartment where she'll sleep it off all day tomorrow.

But then, another thought crosses my mind. A devious, evil, horrible thought. And I know I'm a changed woman and my heart is full of love now, because of Sarah and Bailey. But maybe Rebecca doesn't deserve love. She clearly doesn't show it to her daughters. She didn't show any to her husband. And she didn't show it to me.

I leap from my bed.

"Thanks for the call, Justin." I need to get off the phone so I can think. "Yes, I'll call her and get my driver to pick her up." Lies.

"You're the best," he says. "We should get together again and really do a night out."

"Yes, I'll call you." Then I hang up and exit my room. I quietly go up the stairs, taking them two at a time, and I go into Rebecca's room—heading right for the nightstand to retrieve her journal. I want to see it again, exactly what she said.

What if our production is a flop and I never get a job on Broadway again? Well, I'll kill myself. I will literally jump off the Empire State Building.

And I believe her. I really, truly, believe her.

TWENTY-EIGHT

Is it evil that I want Rebecca to die? That I can picture her standing on the ledge of a giant steel-framed skyscraper, overlooking New York, with the wind in her hair, teetering on the brink of death? I'm not saying I'd push her. I just want her to walk off it by herself. Is that so terrible? Yes, for some people, I imagine it is.

Evil is such a complicated subject.

Just like my relationship with Rebecca.

A few months ago, I would have called her my best friend. But now, I want to take her children and flee the country. So—I suppose that means our friendship is over. Sad, really. We had so much potential, Rebecca and I. We could have been like sisters.

But her death would make this entire thing so much cleaner for me. If Rebecca is dead, I'm sure Mitch will sign over custody. I doubt his new fiancée wants to take responsibility for his children from his first marriage.

Especially if what I've discovered while stalking the new future Mrs. Mitch's social media is true. She's expecting a little boy in a few months. The perfect, bouncing baby boy that Rebecca could never give him. Even if she had, would he have survived? Rebecca doesn't have the greatest track record with infants.

It's been a few days since that two a.m. call from Justin, and

I've had time to think about how to metaphorically push Rebecca off the ledge. I have to give myself credit for coming up with it. Because, well, it really is quite clever.

I've got the girls situated in the living room with a snack and an episode of *Hilda* so that I can make a phone call. I'm standing in the kitchen when I dial the number.

"Hello?"

"Justin. I'm so glad you answered."

"Oh my god, Sophia, I was going to call you and apologize. I definitely drank one too many Red Bull and vodkas the other night and, well, I should learn to mind my own business," he gushes.

He actually sounds embarrassed. Great. He'll be willing to do whatever I ask. "No, Justin, please, don't apologize. You were looking out for Rebecca. That's what friends do. Which is why I wanted to call you and see if you might help me with something."

"Yes of course. Anything," he says.

"Are you sure? Because it kind of needs to be top secret... It might not be very ethical—but I promise, it's to protect Becks." I set the trap and now I'm biting my lip and holding my breath waiting to see what Justin will say. If I'm right, he'll offer to help.

"Oooh, well, this sounds juicy. What do you need my help with?" he immediately asks.

A smile spreads over my face. I knew he wouldn't be able to resist.

"Do you happen to know where any of the Broadway critics hang out? Like the bars or clubs or any of that?"

"Oh my god, Sophia. Are you going to bribe the critics? Or threaten them?" he gasps.

Well, yes actually, that's exactly what I want to do.

But I don't want him to know that. "No, my god, Justin, what sort of woman do you think I am?" I pretend to be taken aback.

"I, uh, um..." he stutters.

"Sorry. And no, I was just thinking that if I knew where the critics hung out, maybe I could go after the press preview of *Happily*

Never After to see what they are saying, so I can tell Rebecca before the papers come out in the morning. Give her a heads-up, so she can mentally prepare herself and a statement for her social media."

"That is actually such a brilliant idea. You're so right. Becks is the kind of person who would want to know. Warning her before the official reviews come out—good, bad, whatever they are—will make her feel so much more in control. Um, let me make a few calls. My old roommate Clive is a wannabe Page Six blogger—he might know."

"Wonderful." I knew he'd do it.

"And don't worry, I'll be super discreet. I'll let you know as soon as I find out anything," he says. "And sorry, for accusing you of bribery."

"Don't worry about it," I say, hiding the smile in my voice, because that's exactly what I'm going to do. Bribe the reviewers. Or at least one. One is all I need... like a snowflake that starts an avalanche.

I'm about to say goodbye and hang up when Justin says, "She really is fragile, isn't she? So much more than she ever allowed any of us to see at the clinic. It makes me wonder—do you think she really was all those things she said?"

"What do you mean?" I ask.

"You know, when she was growing up—she said she was like the queen of everything. A cheerleader, in theater, show choir, voted most likely to succeed, all that shit. I just think if that was real, she'd be more confident."

"Oh, she was all of those things, and more. There are shelves filled with her trophies and awards in the attic." I remember how creepy it was the first time she invited me over for dinner. She took me up the little staircase to the attic, opened the door to show me all the rows and rows of gleaming trophies. I couldn't believe how many she had. It was quite overwhelming, and it's going to take a lot of work to pack them all up with bubble wrap so they don't break. Which gives me an idea... "Sorry, Justin, I, uh, gotta go." I hang up and run as fast as I can up the stairs, and fling open the door to the attic.

There in front of me, the shrine Becks keeps to memorialize her glory days. It gives me the heebie-jeebies... All the blue first-place ribbons of varying sizes pinned all over the room. And the gold-plated trophies. Some of them are three feet tall and too big for a shelf. How can one woman have so many awards?

"Well, Rebecca, you said you wanted to get rid of stuff..." I say out loud, thinking about how she forced Sarah and Bailey to pack up and get rid of most of their toys. Calling it "junk."

I found it rather cruel. So I'm going to use the same technique to hurt Rebecca.

I'll box up every single ribbon, trophy, and award and put them all on the curb for trash pick-up. Then I'll text her a picture of it with a caption like:

"Taking out the junk."

Or "Getting rid of all that attic trash."

Or something else equally as shocking.

But after looking around for a few minutes and checking my watch, I realize this is the last job I really want to spend my day doing—maybe I can convince Ekaterina to do it on Monday morning. And if she doesn't want to do it, maybe there are some teenagers at her church who would be willing to come over for a few hours after school to help box it up and haul it downstairs.

The cleverest part will be when I text Rebecca the pictures of her beloved high school mementos. I wonder if I should do it right as the trash men come and load them up? So there's no way for her to rush home to save them. They'll be long gone.

I rub my hands together.

Okay, so maybe now I am embodying the whole "evil" push-Rebecca-over-the-edge villain character. But it is such a delightful plan. I can hear her now, screaming and freaking out.

Then, because I'm curious, and I've never inspected Rebecca's awards up close, I decide to pick up the trophy closest to me. It's heavier than I expect. The base looks like a small piece of marble and the glimmering golden girl on top is swinging a golf club. I didn't know that Rebecca played golf.

I look at the name plate to see when and why she won it. Did she win a tournament? Or is it just for participation?

PEEWEE LEAGUE '94
ANGELA PARKER

What is Angela Parker? Is that the name of the team or the league or the town? Because it can't be the name of the little girl who won it, otherwise it would say *Rebecca Forester*—Rebecca's maiden name. I place it back on the shelf and pick up another trophy, this time of a girl swinging a softball bat.

GIRLS' 8-10 '95
AWARDED TO:
ANGELA PARKER

Okay, now I'm confused. It says "Awarded to: Angela Parker" which definitely means that is the name of the girl who received the award, not the name of the town or league. Maybe this shelf is for awards from a friend or relative of Rebecca? Because every single one in this section is for Angela Parker.

I take a few steps deeper into the attic and pick up a bigger trophy. This one doesn't have a girl with a club or a bat on top, but a great big golden cup.

CHEERLEADING '99
DANIELLE JONES

I set it down and check the rest in this area. They all say Danielle Jones.

"Who the fuck is Danielle Jones?" I'm completely bewildered. I move to the last corner of the attic and finally come across a few trophies that say Rebecca Forester on them. I look around for a while longer to see if there are any other names, but it appears they are all either Angela, Danielle, or Rebecca. I snap a couple pictures of the name plates as evidence. Of what, I'm not really sure yet.

My lips purse and the muscles on my face tighten. I rub my thumb between my eyebrows to smooth out the creases, then massage my temples in a circular pattern, trying to make sense of what I'm seeing. *Why are there so many awards for girls other than Rebecca? And—when was the last time I had a Botox appointment?*

I feel like I've fallen into the middle of some bizarre episode of the BBC Sherlock Holmes mystery series, and any second Benedict Cumberbatch and Martin Freeman will step out from the shadows to point out all of the mistakes I've made and how obvious the solution is.

Well, I'm not a detective.

But I know someone who is. Sort of.

"Damn it all to hell," I curse myself as I walk out of the attic to call Barry Whitemore. I'm going to ask for his help, which is what I should have done all those weeks ago when I had him digging up dirt on Mitch's affair.

Then I remember something. I turn around and run back for the box marked "Yearbooks, Journals & MISC". Maybe there will be something interesting in the box. But I can't sit up here all day to go through its contents and leave the girls alone in the living room. So I pick it up to bring back downstairs with me.

I'm sure I'm making a much bigger deal out of this than I need to be. But there's always a chance for things to be more than they first appear. I mean, look at my poor friend Hannah. She had no idea she was married to a monster. If she had started digging around sooner, she might have figured out her husband was living a double life before it escalated.

Maybe she'd be an ex-wife instead of a widow.

Then I shake my head.

No. Blake was never going to let her leave—that prick deserved to die. Sometimes—late at night when I can't sleep—I recall the way it felt to kill him. To avenge my sister, Lauren, and her children and to protect Hannah and hers.

Before I call Barry, I set the box down on the kitchen table, then I stick my head into the living room. The girls are watching *Peppa Pig*—and I smile, thinking about the first day I met them and they thought I sounded like Mummy Pig.

"Do you girls need anything?" I ask. "Refills on your chocolate milk, more snacks, what about blankies?"

"No thank you, Fifi." Sarah looks over her shoulder and smiles at me. I blow her a little kiss, then walk out of the living room and to my bedroom. I shut the door and dial Barry's number.

He answers the phone on the first ring. "Hello?"

"Barry, I need your help. I found something really strange, some women's names in the attic. I'm not sure if they are friends or relatives of Dr. Mitch and Rebecca, but I need you to find out who they are."

"Let me guess—are the names you found Angela and Danielle?" he says.

"Barry, what have you been hiding from me?"

TWENTY-NINE

I'm not entirely surprised that Barry found other things out about Mitch and Rebecca and didn't tell me. That's the name of the game in private investigating. You don't give away information that you can later sell to your clients.

Barry hums and haws and shuffles papers and it sounds like he's getting ready to tell me what he knows, but then he goes nearly silent.

"Anytime, Barry." I try to coax it out of him.

"Well, see, Ms. Carter, when you originally called—you said you wanted to know if Mitch Hendricks was having an affair and with whom. So that's what I found for you. The answer was yes, he is having an affair with a German woman, Emilia Mueller. They are engaged, she is pregnant, and they recently purchased a home together in Berlin. Well, you know, all of the information I emailed to you as proof."

"Yes, yes, I know... But what about Angela and Danielle? How do they fit into all of this?"

"My fee, well, uh, I was thinking that technically..." Barry stammers, mentioning bills and how bad the economy is these days and—

I quickly PayPal him the same amount as before just to shut him up.

"I paid you. Now stop blubbering and tell me about Angela and Danielle," I hiss.

"Oh, oh, yes, well, thank you... So during my investigation, I found out the good doctor was married before he married Rebecca Forester."

"I knew it!" I blurt out. "Rebecca was extremely cagey when I asked her how long she'd been with Mitch. I'd guessed he was married or in a relationship when they met, making Becks the other woman."

"Actually, he was married twice before. First to Angela. Then to Danielle."

"Jesus, a serial husband. Gross."

What else is gross are all those trophies and awards in the attic. Why does Rebecca still have them? Why didn't Angela and Danielle take their awards with them when they divorced Mitch? And how on earth has Mitch managed to land four women in the first place? Every time I've spoken to him, I have to pinch myself to stay awake. Dr. Mitch is so fucking dull! Literally the most boring man I've ever met in my life. But he is a surgeon... I guess that part alone would attract some types of women.

"If that's all, I should probably get going," Barry says.

"Barry, you know, you could have just told me about Angela and Danielle with your original investigation. I'm not sure a couple of prior marriages warrant your entire fee... Maybe I'll have my man Petrov pay you a visit." I am absolutely not asking my driver Petrov to pay Barry a visit, but he doesn't have to know that. And I'm sure Barry's used to being threatened.

He coughs and clears his throat.

"No, that won't be necessary, Ms. Carter, um, oh, wait... I'm looking through my notes here and I just recalled, the first wife, Angela—they didn't get divorced. She died. Rather tragic actually. She killed herself, after their baby died of SIDS."

"What?" I whisper.

"Yes. It looks here like it was actually on the same day. I found a police record..." He pauses. I can hear him shuffling more goddamn papers. What a disorganized buffoon. "Ohhhh, yes, that's right. Angela Hendricks swallowed a bottle of pills while the police were in the home investigating the dead child. Rather ironic, don't you think? I wonder how often someone kills themselves in the presence of the police?"

My heart is racing.

I thought it was Rebecca.

I've spent the last couple of months feeling sorry for her. Giving her a free pass for some of her behavior because I believed she'd had a baby that died of SIDS. But that wasn't Rebecca! It was Angela. Mitch's first wife. The one whose golf award and softball trophy and other ribbons are in the attic. So wait. Does that mean that...

"And I found it rather odd that Dr. Mitch's next wife, Danielle, also had a baby that died. But at least she didn't kill herself, from what I could tell, anyway," Barry says.

"Barry, truly, I'm disappointed in you. Why didn't you tell me any of this before!" I exclaim. "And what do you mean, she didn't kill herself *from what you can tell?* Someone is either dead or not."

"Oh, she's dead alright. I just meant, she didn't do it to herself. Elmhurst listed her death as—oh, hold on, let me find the paper," he says. The phone bangs—he must have dropped it.

"Barry, just put me on speaker phone and set it down. Use both hands to look." I shout into it so he can hear me.

"Here, I found it. Yes, yes, that's right, she was committed after the accidental death of their daughter," he explains. "She seems to have been sleeping and the baby froze to death. Horrible, isn't it?"

I remember looking at the highly redacted papers I found in Mitch's desk drawer. I put Rebecca's name into all the blacked-out spots, never imagining it might have been about a different Mrs. Hendricks.

"She was released a few months later, then arrested for breaking and entering Mitch's home. Looks like he'd filed for divorce and put a restraining order against her. She was placed back into the custody of Elmhurst."

"He filed for a divorce while she was recovering from the death of their child? What a dick."

"Yes. Tragic ending to their love story. She died a few months later anyway, saved her from the heartache of a divorce."

"Jesus, Barry, this isn't Romeo and Juliet here. What do you mean she died?"

"It means her life expired. I was suspicious so I did a little digging. Private facilities like Elmhurst are notoriously hard to get records from. But I was able to find her death certificate—it says she died from an accident, not a suicide."

My mind is spinning.

"Accident? What kind of accident can you have in a mental hospital?" I ask.

"Oh, plenty. Falling down the stairs. Choking on your food. Disagreeing with an orderly and having your skull bashed in and they lie about it."

"BARRY! Is that what happened to Danielle?"

"No, no, not Danielle. But that did happen to a client of mine. Well, an ex-client. Or rather, they were a current client that died—anyway, you get the point. Accident might not mean accident."

"FIFI! Where are you? Sarah, noooo!" Bailey screams in the hallway outside my door. That's quickly followed by the sounds of two little girls running and shouting. And then something breaking.

"Shit. Okay, I have to go... Can you send me whatever documents you found on Angela and Danielle?" I ask in a hurry, getting up to leave my room to go find out what the girls are doing. It's my fault, I shouldn't have left them out there alone for so long.

"Of course. And my apologies for not disclosing this information sooner, I, uh, didn't realize you'd need it."

Yeah fucking right, you old duffer, you just wanted more money, I say in my head. "It's fine, Barry. Don't forget to send me all the documents you found." I hang up the phone. Barry really pisses me off. I wish I'd had this information weeks ago. But at least I have it now. The only thing is, I have to figure out exactly how I can use it to my benefit.

Dr. Mitch Hendricks has two dead wives and two dead children.

But he also has two very alive children.

Who are standing in the living room, staring at a broken vase.

I shove my phone in my back pocket, put my hands on my hips, and say— "I always hated that vase. One less thing for us to pack for your mum. Let's get the broom and dispose of the evidence. And please, no more running in the house."

"Yes, Fifi!" they exclaim at the same time.

"And when we're done cleaning up, how about we go outside and play freeze tag?"

A few hours later, the girls are in their rooms, playing quietly.

I'm staring at my phone. Justin has texted me the location of where the Broadway critics like to hang out for a drink after shows. I don't know if they'll be there tonight or if I even want to go through with this... I told Justin I wanted their information so I could use it to protect Rebecca after the preview performance— which happens to be tomorrow night.

But really, I wanted to poison the press against her.

My plan was to spread gossip and spill her secrets and let the reporters take it from there. Or maybe even pay one or two to guarantee they put an article in the *Post* or the *Times*. Something to push a fragile Becks over the edge.

But things have changed...

Now that I know the truth.

"What's wrong, Fifi? You look sad," Sarah says. I didn't even hear her come down the stairs, but she doesn't startle me. Instead, her presence warms my heart. I set down my phone, close my laptop, and reach around to give her a big hug.

"Nothing's wrong now that you're here," I say and give her a squeeze. My instinct to protect the girls is so strong it nearly consumes me—but the more that I think about it, my fears aren't as warranted as I originally thought.

I convinced myself the only way to fix Becks was to help her achieve her dreams of being on Broadway. I thought it would make up for her husband's behavior, make her more loving towards the kids. Then I found the file in Mitch's study and thought she was suffering some kind of long-standing depression from the loss of two babies. That she could snap at any moment and hurt Sarah and Bailey. And still I clung to the idea that once the show opened, being a Broadway star would make her happy. Happy enough to appreciate how great her life is, even though she'd experienced the tragic loss of two children.

But those weren't her dead babies.

They were her husband's.

"Fifi, you're making that face again," Sarah says.

"Oh, sorry, sweets. I guess I just have a lot on my mind. I'm trying to figure out what to do about a situation," I explain.

"What kind of situation?" she asks.

"Nothing you have to worry your pretty little head over." I smile. "Now, why don't you join me in the kitchen and I'll teach you how to make shepherd's pie for dinner." I get up and head for the kitchen.

"Pie for dinner?" She tilts her head like a puppy.

"Not a sweet pie, it's a meat pie, but with mashed potatoes for the crust," I try and explain. "You'll just have to see it."

"Meat pie?" Sarah questions. "That sounds yucky, buuuut I love helping you cook... So maybe it will be okay." She shrugs.

"Brilliant. Here, I'll start passing you the ingredients." I hand her a bag of flour to thicken the gravy. She's helped me make things before and knows to start stacking ingredients on the far counter. "And I promise, it tastes better than it sounds. If we're going to live in London, you'll need to know what shepherd's pie is—" I pause as I pull the carrots from the fridge. Oh my god, why did I just say that? I should smack myself in the face with this rather limp bunch of carrots.

Going to live in London.

I'm an idiot.

I don't want to scare the girls or give them the wrong impression. What if they tell Rebecca or Mitch? Or one of their teachers? I need to fix this fast, before Sarah starts asking a bunch of questions.

"What did you say, Fifi? Sorry, I uh..." Sarah says when I turn around. Her little cheeks are red and she points at the floor.

"Oh, Sarah," I gasp. The bag of flour has tipped over on the counter, spilling half the contents on the floor in a pile shaped like a volcano. Just as long as no one disturbs it, we might be able to sweep it up...

"What's this?" Bailey comes skipping in, pauses at the pile of flour, then pulls her leg back and—

"NO!" Sarah and I scream at the same time. But it's too late. Bailey punts the pile of flour. It explodes in a huge cloud of snowy white powder.

"Wheeeeee!" Bailey runs into the cloud, covering herself from head to toe.

Sarah and I look at one another, then at Bailey.

My mistaken comment about London is long forgotten (I hope), and instead this new delightful mess has taken full control of the kitchen. Sarah runs into the cloud and grabs Bailey by the hands. They spin around and jump up and down and giggle and squeal...

Be still—my heart.

This is the happiest I've ever seen them. And all at once and everywhere, in the dissipating cloud of flour, I understand my life's purpose.

It's not just about keeping them safe.

It's about making them happy.

THIRTY

When I wake up the next morning, with two sleeping children next to me, I am so glad I didn't end up driving into the city last night. I mean, I thought about it, I really did. I visualized the entire thing in my head. I pictured myself standing with the Broadway critics with flutes of expensive champagne in their hands. All eyes on me as I wove an irresistible story filled with all the high-stakes drama that takes place on the set of *Happily Never After*.

Drama that I would invent, since I've never actually been on the set of the production, but it would be well worth it.

Becks would wake up tomorrow morning and gasp at the articles, sobbing and crying out, *Oh, woe is me, who would say such horrible things? Maybe it's true, maybe I am a sad and pathetic woman without a drop of talent.*

She'd continue to cry and carry on, and ultimately implode before the big opening night, giving me exactly what I want. A pliable Becks who is all too happy to sign custody over to me because she is planning on jumping off a building.

But after such a long day and all of that crazy information about Mitch's dead wives, I was completely exhausted. And by the time we finished making shepherd's pie, cleaning up all the flour mess, it was time for the girls to take a bath and go to bed. There was no way I could drag Sarah and Bailey into the city and leave them with a hired sitter.

Who am I kidding?

I don't have a hired sitter! At least, no one I can trust.

On that subject, I agree with Rebecca. How can you ever trust a stranger with your children? Just because they have credentials on some website, or they're the teenager who lives next door, how does that qualify them to care for kids? I mean—what if something goes wrong? It takes a special kind of person to watch and care for young children.

I'm going to have to start interviewing quickly when we get to London. I don't particularly want a full-time nanny since I am not planning on working much, except for when the girls are in school. My clientele will be very limited, strictly ultra-high-end, royalty and billionaires. But those sorts of clients can be demanding, wanting a piece of art on a Sunday at three a.m. Okay, so maybe a full-time nanny is a must.

I'll put out an advert now, because I know it's going to take me months to find the right person. Which means I can't lie here in bed any longer. So I move little arms and legs and crawl out of bed, tiptoeing to the kitchen to make a cup of tea. Armed with my laptop, I curl up in the armchair in the living room. It's a mess, with boxes and packing materials everywhere, and really starting to grate on my nerves. I should just call someone to come and finish this.

But Rebecca doesn't even have a plan.

Where does she think she's going to go? An apartment? A house? Maybe I should just buy this damn place so I can stop having to look at the boxes.

You buy it over boxes? Why? You live here forever? Pathetic. I can hear Ekaterina's voice in my head, ridiculing me if I was to buy this house from Rebecca and Mitch, just because I'm frustrated by all the boxes. God, she can be so annoying. But she's also right. What the fuck would I do with this house? Stay here?

Laughable. My entire reason for being here has fallen apart. So now I need to take the girls and go. So I open my laptop and start typing up an advert for a nanny in London.

Single mother seeking live-in...

No, that's not right. What will I be to Sarah and Bailey? Not a mother, or an aunt... I'm their Fifi. Maybe I'll just skip the part about my title.

Seeking professionally trained nanny for a live-in position...

As I'm typing the character traits I require of a nanny, I realize I'm describing Ekaterina Melnyk. Now wouldn't that just be the perfect solution? She loves the girls and I can trust her—plus, I can tolerate her. More than tolerate, I actually think she's rather funny when she wants to be. Dry, yes, but witty nevertheless. And she never smiles, which is perfect for London.

I'll give her an offer she can't refuse. Enough that she can retire in a few years when the girls are teenagers and don't need a nanny anymore.

I wish there was someone here I could gloat in front of for such a clever idea. But it's Sunday, so Ekaterina is off, and obviously Becks and Mitch are gone. Well, now that I don't have to waste my morning writing up an advertisement for a nanny, maybe I'll search the web for any news about Rebecca's upcoming show.

As soon as I type her name into Google, my phone rings.

It's Becks.

Apparently her ears were burning.

"Hey, Becks, tonight's the big night. Preview!" I say with a smile.

"Sophia, um..." Her voice is deep and husky.

"Are you alright?" I quickly ask, even though I can tell something is clearly wrong.

"No. No, I'm not alright. Um, I need you to come get me. Please," she begs. Her voice is shaking. I can tell she's scared.

"Of course, I'll be there as fast as I can... Are you in immediate danger?" I ask.

"Um. I don't know. Please, I need your help. I'll text you my location." Then she hangs up.

I wonder what Becks has gotten herself into, I think as I jump up from my chair. I highly doubt that whatever is going on is something she wants her children to see. So I make a quick call to Ekaterina. She haggles with me on the price but eventually agrees to come and watch the girls so I can deal with Rebecca.

"Rise and shine, sleepy heads. I have a little emergency in the city I need to deal with. So Mrs. Melnyk is going to come over and play with you today until I get home, okay?"

The girls both groan.

"What is that about? Why all the moaning and groaning? You like Mrs. Melnyk." I say as I hand them each some play clothes to put on.

"Yeah, we like her, but she's not very good at playing. Not like you, Fifi," Sarah explains.

I try to hide the smile on my face. Does that mean they think I'm good at playing? Me? Well, isn't that cute. I suppose I had some practice with Rowen and Ruby... but besides that, I don't recall playing much when I was a child myself.

I grab the hairbrush and start brushing Bailey's bedhead.

"Okay, maybe I misspoke, you don't actually have to play with Mrs. Melnyk. I'm sure she'd appreciate it if you left her alone to read her Bible or knit or whatever it is she'd like to do, since it's technically her day off. She won't be cleaning or doing laundry or any of that. You girls can play in your rooms or color at the dining room table or watch TV. But she'll be here if you need anything."

"Yes, Fifi," they say simultaneously. Then Bailey runs out of my room with only half her hair brushed.

"Don't forget to brush your teeth!" I shout after her.

"Is something wrong with my mom?" Sarah asks.

"Now why would you think that?" I ask.

"Because... she's..." But before Sarah can finish talking, we hear the front door, and Ekaterina yells:

"I'm here!"

"Sarah, sweetie, we can talk more about this tonight. But I've got to run." I grab my purse and sweater and give her a kiss on the top of the head, before darting out of the room. Ekaterina and I lock eyes on my way out. She nods once. Yes... I think we have an understanding, Ekaterina and I. And when the time comes, I think she will go to London with me. But now I have to drive to the city and clean up whatever fucking mess Rebecca's made. And I have a sneaking suspicion it's something bad.

Very bad.

THIRTY-ONE
REBECCA

I thought being entirely "free" from my responsibilities for a week was going to be fun and exciting. I thought not having to worry about checking in with Sophia, or dropping money off to pay Mrs. Melnyk, or thinking about Mitch and the divorce—well, I thought it would make me feel better. But instead I feel worse.

Though, that might also be the binge drinking.

And the uppers Chase gave me to wake myself up enough for our last week of rehearsals.

Or the muscle relaxers Violet gave me yesterday after I took that big fall off the stage and nearly impaled myself on some of the equipment the musicians were setting up.

Or the pills Dr. Nakamura prescribed for my anxiety...

Which I've been eating handfuls of to keep myself calm.

After that big fall, but before all the muscle relaxers, I went into Baker's office to give him a piece of my mind—only to find him snorting a line of cocaine off a mirror on his desk.

"What the fuck are you doing? I almost died. I fell off the stage into the music pit!" I screamed.

"If you don't know where the apron ends by now, Rebecca, well then, maybe you should fall off and die," he replied while wiping up the white powder from the mirror and rubbing it across his gums.

"Are you for real? What's happened to you?" I asked with an incredulous laugh.

"To me? HA! It's you, Rebecca. You and that fucking woman happened." He threw his hands up in the air. "Everyone thinks getting money will make your life easier. But it doesn't. Do you hear me? It doesn't. It just makes it that much fucking harder. Harvey left me... and he took everything. The money. The furniture. Even the goddamn cat! And now, he's running all over the city telling everyone our show is gonna be a disaster—because of you."

I narrowed my eyes and pointed my finger at him and said, "Grow the fuck up, Baker." Then I stormed out of his office, only to turn around and march back in, my back throbbing in pain from my fall. My head swimming from the handful of Xanax. "And what do you mean, me and that woman? What woman? What money?"

And that's how I learned that Sophia, my dear, rich, lying best friend, had paid for my leading role. A million fucking dollars. I mean, what was she thinking? And what was Baker thinking by accepting it? Of course this would come back to bite him in his flat (probably hairy), ugly ass.

And NO. I don't believe him when he says he would have hired me anyway.

I was rejected how many times when I used to audition?

Dozens... no, hundreds of times. By men just like him. For years and years.

Even if I did believe him, my head is so full of doubt, there's nothing anyone can say or do to make it go away now. At this point, it will take winning a Tony Award to prove I deserve to be on this stage.

That's why I tossed and turned all last night on Chase's couch. Someone is going to find out Sophia bought my part by bribing Baker with a million dollars. They are going to print it in the news and post it all over social media. Which means, I'll never get the chance at that Tony Award anyway. No matter how good I am. The Tony Awards have all kinds of strict rules about those sorts of things. That's why all day, during rehearsals, I've felt three steps behind everyone. I mean, how else am I supposed to feel?

"The show must go on, people," Baker screams and claps his hands to get our attention. Everyone looks around confused. "You —stage left! You—stage right! Come on. Aghhh!" Every vein in his face is popping out. His two assistants are going nuts. One is fanning him and the other is holding up a can of Fresca with a straw. "Places, people. Am I speaking Greek? What's haaaaappening?"

"Jesus, what's his problem?" Chase leans over to ask. Chase, Indra, and Violet, and I have all been standing on our mark for the last fifteen minutes. Just patiently waiting for Baker to yell, "Action."

"Oh, this is nothing, you should have seen my director on *Baby in the Rain*. He was a crying mess for days before we opened. Fetal position and everything. We literally thought he was going to throw himself off the roof," Indra snickers.

Sweat beads at my hairline.

I'm the only one who knows the real reason why Baker is acting like a freak show. Because of me. Because if this show is a flop, and word gets out that my best friend—or whatever the fuck Sophia is to me—paid for my part... it will ruin him.

But not just Baker. It could get every single actor and crew member on this set blacklisted. And they will all hold me person-ally responsible.

My stomach gurgles and before I know what's happening, I run off stage and vomit behind the curtains. It's mostly stomach bile and it stings and smells like booze. When was the last time I ate any real food?

"Don't worry, the nerves get to me too." Violet comes up behind me and rubs my back. "We just have to make it through the preview night tomorrow and everything will settle down. Every show gets easier, I promise."

Wait? Preview is tomorrow? But wasn't it a week away? What day is it? I look at my watch, but my vision is blurry. "I need to get out of here... Can you take me home?" I ask. The word *home* triggers a longing for my real home. The one on Long Island. The one where that traitor is living. I can't believe she paid for my part. I don't know why she'd do that. Didn't she believe in me? She acted like I was the best singer and dancer in the world, but all along she kept this secret from me. She just wanted me out of the house. Because she couldn't stand me.

Just like Mitch.

Just like my daughters.

Just like my mother.

"Of course I'll take you home, come on. I doubt Baker will even notice, look, he's on his phone now... I'm sure everyone else will start to leave soon anyway," Violet says, wrapping her arms around my shoulders and guiding me away from the puddle of vomit. She looks over her shoulder and says something to whoever is behind us. The words sound muffled, like I'm underwater.

"It's just nerves," I try to convince Violet, who's flipped on a weird motherly switch. It doesn't work for her.

"Are you sure? I'm worried about you, Becks. Seriously, you don't look well. Maybe you're coming down with the flu. This one time when we were in Italy, I caught the flu and—no, wait—I was just hungover. But anyways, my mom made me this tea and it really helped." Violet sets a mug of steaming liquid on the coffee table in front of me. Then she wraps a blanket around me. "I know. Do you want to smoke a joint? That always calms my nerves." She doesn't wait for me to respond—she pulls a joint from her front pocket, then lights it up and sits down next to me on the couch.

Rebecca, I'd strongly advise against smoking marijuana. You're coming down from a manic episode. You need to eat and get some rest or you'll never be prepared for preview night tomorrow, Dr. Nakamura says.

Shut up, I hiss.

"I didn't say anything," Violet says. Then she hands me the joint. The sweet, skunky smell actually does make me feel calmer. Even if Dr. Nakamura is trying to kill my buzz. I take the joint, put it to my lips, and take a very long drag.

You worked so hard to get your bipolar under control. To overcome what you did. To have a normal life with Mitch and your daughters. Getting an advanced degree. Working as an APRN at the clinic. Why did you give it all up? he asks. Then he starts clicking his pen, over and over, click, click, click...

Stop clicking the goddamn pen, Doctor. I suck in a second puff from the joint. Then pass it back to Violet. *And it's none of your fucking business. I can give up whatever I want.*

"Are you okay?" Violet asks.

"I'd be perfectly fine if Dr. Nakamura over there would stop clicking his goddamn pen!" I stand up, a little wobbly on my legs.

"Doctor who?"

I look around—I could have sworn we were at Violet's apartment, but I guess she brought me to Dr. Nakamura's office instead. What a sly girl. "You are sneaky, aren't you, Violet? You thought you could bring me here, trick me into spilling my guts to the doctor. Well, like I told him the last time I was here, I'm not going to talk about what happened to Danielle."

"Who's Danielle?" Violet asks, taking another puff of the joint.

"Who's Danielle? Are you fucking serious right now? You know, Danielle, the girl from the trophies. She goes by the name 'Dani.' That skanky device rep, the one who was married to Mitch. The one who killed her baby when she found out I was fucking him."

"Whoa." Violet coughs. "She killed her baby? That's insane." She takes another puff then hands me back the joint.

I'm not sure you need any more of that, Dr. Nakamura says in that fucking condescending tone he loves to use when I'm not entirely focused on him.

I glare at his smug face, then snatch the joint from Violet. I take a huge hit, hold it for as long as I can, then hand it back to her. I start pacing in front of the big picture window overlooking Central Park.

"I mean, that's what I thought happened, that she killed their baby. That's what Mitch told me happened. He made me quit my job at the hospital and take a job at Elmhurst. He wanted to make sure she wasn't running her mouth. Part of me didn't believe it, that a woman could intentionally kill her own child—how could someone do such a thing?"

Violet sits up at full attention. "Becks, stop pacing. Come, sit, tell me about Dani. I want to know—did she do it? What did you find out at Elmhurst?"

A smile spreads over my face. I've always wanted to tell someone this story. I'd thought once I'd tell Sophia, but she never really seemed all that interested in the difficult topics. She was always trying to make my life better, easier, happier, healthier. But maybe that's not who I am or what I need. Maybe I'm a fucking mess, and I always have been.

I take a seat next to Violet, whose eyes are sparkling with anticipation for my story. I try not to look over at Dr. Nakamura—he's shaking his head and furiously writing notes on a yellow legal pad.

"Dani was crazy. That's what I found out. She was a crazy fucking bitch. So I pushed her down the stairs and she broke her neck."

Seems excessive, Dr. Nakamura says.

"She was going around telling everyone that Mitch killed the baby! Not that it was an accident and she didn't do it, but that it was Mitch! Don't you see, she was gonna get Mitch in trouble? I couldn't have that, she had to go."

Violet looks at me. Instead of the relaxed, chilled vibe she had a few minutes ago—her eyes have gone all big and wide. "Wait. Becks. You killed her? You killed Dani?"

Now you've done it, Dr. Nakamura says.

I blink a few times to clear my thoughts. Did I just admit to Violet that I killed my husband's wife? Shit. Fuck. Yes, I did.

"I'm sorry," I whisper as I grab the mug of tea off the coffee table. With one quick motion, I smash it against Violet's head as hard as I can. It happens so fast that she doesn't scream or flinch or anything. She just slumps over on the couch, blood oozing from the side of her head where the blow split open her scalp.

I stand up, brush myself off, and walk into the kitchen. I open and close the kitchen drawers until I find what I'm looking for. A paring knife. I hold it up to the overhead light. The edge of the blade gleams.

Sharp.

Then I walk back into the living room.

I wouldn't do that out here if I were you, Rebecca, Dr. Nakamura says and lets out a long sigh.

"Shut up," I tell him. What does he know anyway? If he knew anything at all, he wouldn't have given me all these drugs. He knows I'm hypersensitive to them. I always have been. I pick up Violet's limp arm and hold the paring knife up to her flesh. I'm about to drag the point of the blade over her wrist, when I realize: No one would slit their wrists on the couch.

They would do it in the bathroom.

Yes. In the shower. And that's how she got this bump on the side of her head—from falling.

So I put down the blade, and awkwardly pick up Violet's body, under the arms, and drag her into the bathroom.

"Jesus, fuck, you fat cow," I yell at her. She looks a lot lighter than she really is. And I'm still sore from falling off the stage. I'm going to need to see a chiropractor after this.

In the bathroom, I undress Violet, tossing her clothes on the floor, just like she does when she showers. I hoist her naked body into the shower, take the blade and slit her wrists. Making sure not to get any blood on me. Jesus, I must have really knocked her out good with that blow to the head, because she isn't twitching at all.

I take her head and slam it once against the shower tile where I already hit her with the mug, just so there's some evidence of a fall in the shower. Then I turn on the water, hoping the hot steam will help leach the blood out of her system even faster.

This is a thing, right?

People slit their wrists in the shower? As a nurse I feel like I should know the answer to this. I close my eyes and try to recall some of my training about emergency care for suicidal patients.

And that's when I remember. It's not the shower. It's a fucking bath. Shit! They slit their wrists in the bathtub. I slump on the floor and rest my head on the wall. I look over at Violet. She's also sitting on the floor. Inside the ornately tiled shower. The glass partition is starting to steam up, blocking the view of her naked body. At this point it's too late to try and move her to the bathtub, I'd just get blood and water everywhere. Well, even if a shower suicide looks suspicious when the authorities arrive, she had to die...

I told her about Dani.

And no one can know about Dani.

THIRTY-TWO

2016

I started sleeping with Mitch almost as soon as I started working at the hospital two years ago. I didn't know he was married. Which is my fault, he *was* wearing a wedding ring, which he pointed out to me afterwards. But I was distracted. I hadn't been an RN for very long—and I worked in the emergency room, which was a regular bloodbath and honestly really hard to handle emotionally.

New York City on a Friday night?

Gunshot wounds, homeless wandering in, pedestrian hit-and-runs, domestic violence, child abuse, it all came through our doors, every single hour, all night long.

Not like Mitch's precious pediatric floor three levels up. The ER was insane from the moment you clocked in to the moment you clocked out. And I hated it. Plus, I was still auditioning for parts on Broadway pretty regularly in my free time. Which was giving me more anxiety than I was capable of dealing with.

Needless to say, when I met Mitch, I was mentally distracted. I'd just gotten to the hospital for my night shift after a hellish audition that ended with a director screaming in my face. I was in the supply closet, crying, ready to end it all by swallowing a fistful of pills I'd swiped from the med cart, when a very handsome Mitch Hendricks swooped in and rescued me. At least, he looked handsome in the moment—or like an angel, the bright light behind him, that white physician lab coat, the smile with one dimple on the side.

Clearly I wasn't paying attention to his ring finger. Just like he wasn't paying attention to the signs that I suffer from bipolar disorder and was having a manic episode. Why else would I be in the closet trying to eat stolen meds, and then follow a doctor I just met into the on-call sleeping quarters and let him fuck me without a condom as a thank-you for saving my life.

That's not normal behavior.

It also cost me eighty-five dollars, because I had to go to the pharmacy the next morning and buy the morning after pill.

"Yeah well, I'd just come off a twenty-four-hour shift, Rebecca, how was I supposed to know you were having an episode?" Mitch says to me while we're in the bathroom getting ready. We are arguing, again, about my bipolar disorder. Mitch keeps implying that I tricked him and that he never would have gotten me pregnant if he knew I had bipolar disorder. While I keep trying to tell him that all the signs were there. Why didn't he notice, especially as a distinguished surgeon?

The problem is, I'm seven months pregnant and I can't take my meds.

Which means I'm not doing the best, mentally. Physically, I'm great. I'm still dancing, working out. Trying to stay fit. But I quit working a few months ago and I'm not all that good at just sitting around this house. It's still got so many reminders of Mitch's former wives. Which sends me spiraling. I've had a few episodes and I think it scares Mitch. But whose fault is that? I really don't think it's mine.

"If you want to go pointing the finger—how about you point it at yourself. You were fucking married when we met! And you'd already been married once before that."

"Completely different, Rebecca," he says.

"Hmmm... I don't think so. I didn't disclose that I was bipolar before we got married. You didn't disclose that you had one dead wife and one wife in the loony bin when we started officially dating. I'd call that even."

"Two dead wives," he corrects me. "We've gone over this. I don't want anyone to know we started dating before Dani had her accident and died. As far as anyone is concerned, we met after that."

I shoot him a nasty look. Like anyone fucking cares. But Mitch, he has this dream of being some world-renowned surgeon, and he's so worried about his image. He even hired an expensive PR firm to help scrub the fact that he was married twice before and had two children—all four of whom are now dead—from having any connection to his name. He used the money he got from Dani's life insurance policy.

Like anyone wants to search for my husband online. Who does he think he is? A fucking Kennedy?

The baby kicks and my stomach morphs like there's an alien inside of me. I put my hand over it and send it a secret message. *Baby, I'm sorry for all the fighting with your daddy. He's a big, fat, self-important idiot.*

"Oh, just so I'm clear, because I don't want to embarrass you when we're out at a function. What you're saying, Mitch, is that you don't want me to tell anyone you made me quit my job at the hospital and take a job at Elmhurst. Or that I pushed Dani down the stairs so you could collect her life insurance policy and so you didn't have to spend months trying to divorce a crazy person. Is that what you're saying, Mitch?" I say it so flippantly while spritzing myself with some body spray, that it doesn't even feel or sound real. Like I can't remember the way her flesh felt on my hands, through the thin gown she was wearing. Like I don't see her face in my dreams, haunting me at night.

"Jesus Christ, Rebecca! What are you talking about? Dani fell down the stairs. It was a tragedy. You can't go around making up that sort of thing." He looks around nervously.

"I'm not 'going around making up that sort of thing' like some goddamn crazy person. That's what happened, Mitch, whether you like it or not." I use air quotes and that voice he hates, to mock him. "You've got to stop treating me like some uneducated medical assistant that cleans bedpans for a living. You know I graduated from NYU magna cum laude and they are always begging me to go back and get my master's in nursing. I could work independently as a provider."

He smiles, then his smile turns into a chuckle, then his chuckle turns into a great big belly laugh. "Sure, sure, Rebecca. Between a new baby, a household to run, those foolish auditions you go to, and being bipolar, you're telling me you're going to get your master's degree and be an independent practitioner." Tears are coming out of his eyes, he's still chuckling and laughing.

"You know what? Fuck you. That's right, fuck you, Mitch Hendricks, big-time pediatric surgeon. I can do anything I want to do. I can go to school and raise children and run a house. I don't need you telling me I can't fucking do something. God! You are so arrogant." I throw my hands up in the air, then I storm out of our bathroom and head downstairs to find my phone.

I'm going to call that recruiter at NYU who keeps harassing me to sign up for the master's program. And then I'm going to call Dr. Nakamura. He was recommended to me by a girl I met during my last Broadway audition. She said he's helped her immensely, with managing her anxiety.

I will prove to my husband that I can do it all.

Or die trying.

No. Scratch that... I'm not going to die. His first two wives might have, but I am here to stay. If anything, I'm walking out of this as the widow.

THIRTY-THREE

SOPHIA

Present Day

As soon as I pull up to the old money Upper East Side building where Rebecca said to pick her up, I know something is terribly wrong. There are four police cars parked in the fire lane and I have to circle the block three times before I get a spot as someone else pulls away. I have no idea what to expect when I get inside.

But I've come prepared.

I have an attorney on speed dial, a purse full of cash, and a loaded handgun—I stopped by my apartment quickly to change and stock up on supplies just in case. I figured by the sound of Rebecca's voice that I might have to talk, buy, or shoot her way out of whatever mess she's gotten into.

I walk slowly up to the front of the building. I'm in a tight black dress, bright red heels, drenched in diamonds and a fur wrap with sunglasses and a silk scarf tied around my head. I take a moment to peer through the glass doors—the lobby is full of police officers. There's no way I'm making it to the elevator without having to identify why I'm here. But maybe I can use a service elevator or something. So when a couple walking a dog comes up and the bellman lets them in, I slip in behind them. They head for the elevator, and I stay close to the bellman.

I slide my sunglasses down and say to him. "Jesus, what's going on?"

"Sorry, ma'am, no guests today," he says.

"No problem, I'm not staying, I'm just here to pick up a friend. I'll call her and tell her to come down and meet me." I smile, then I slide him a hundred-dollar bill. "Do you know what happened?" I whisper. "Should I be worried?"

He looks at the bill, smiles back at me, looks side to side, probably making sure the cops aren't watching us. Then he leans in and says very softly, "A resident committed suicide. A Broadway star. The daughter of a New York socialite."

I pretend that I don't know anyone by that description, making a polite shrug. But the truth is I do know someone that matches that description. Violet Ogelman. One of Rebecca's castmates and friends in the city that she's been hanging out with all this time.

I'd looked her up as soon as I found out who was cast alongside Rebecca. I assumed Violet's mother made a deal, similar to the one I had, with the director Grant Baker. Considering her reviews in previous shows were neither good, nor bad. They were just fine. Average. Violet was average at best. But those aren't the kind of girls who keep landing leading roles like Violet. Unless their mother is a mega-rich socialite.

So Violet is dead. Very interesting.

I need to find Becks and get her the hell out of here. Let's just hope that she didn't have anything to do with Violet's suicide. Because if she did and she gets caught, well, a messy murder trial is not on my list of to-dos this year. Not to mention something like that could haunt Sarah and Bailey for the rest of their lives.

Their birth mother, a murderer?

I shake my head as I call her, but it goes to VM. So I quickly shoot her a text.

> I'm in the lobby of the building. It's swarming with cops. They won't let me in.

...

I think she's going to respond, but after a few minutes, nothing. Maybe she's talking to the police...

"Any luck reaching your friend?" the bellman asks.

"Yes, well, she said the elevator is blocked. Is there any way I can go up the stairs to meet her?" I lie, slipping him two hundred this time.

He looks at it, then his watch.

"If you and your friend aren't down in ten minutes, I'll have to tell them you snuck up," he whispers and his eyes dart towards the police.

I grab his hands and squeeze them. "Thank you. Yes, ten minutes, we'll be back down." The only problem is I have no idea what floor Becks is on. I do not want to wander up and down each floor, calling out for her. Especially not in these shoes. I look down at my red Louboutins.

> I'm coming up the stairwell to help you escape. What floor are you on? Are you being held?

> I'm in the hallway on the 4th floor. And yes, sort of.

> Be right there.

Four flights of stairs doesn't seem like a lot. But with the high ceilings in this place it really is. I suck in through my nose and out through my mouth, so that I'm not out of breath by the time I reach her floor.

I want to be completely calm and composed, because if the police are "sort of" holding Rebecca captive, they must think she's somehow involved in this. And based on the tone of her voice this morning? The urgency. The panic. Well, she probably is.

As soon as I step out of the stairwell into the hallway, Becks gets up off the floor and runs for me. She hugs me and whispers, "I'm sorry. I wasn't sure you'd come..." Then she pushes me away from her. "Jesus, you took long enough!" she yells.

I don't know what to say, I'm confused. Is she glad I'm here, or upset?

"Ma'am, you can't be up here, this is an active crime scene," an officer rushes over and says to me. "And you, I told you to sit down," he snaps at Rebecca.

Rebecca wobbles on her feet then plops down on the floor. Something doesn't feel right. But I can't put my finger on it.

"Becks, what's going on?" I bend over to get closer to her. She looks at me and seems surprised to see my face.

"Sophia." She tries to push herself up from the floor, but her arms give out and she sits back down.

"Honey, please, just sit there while I talk to someone," I say to her.

But instead she puts her arms out, catching me off guard. "Help me get up." She waves her hands. I take them and pull—she struggles but makes it to her feet. Her eyes are black and she's grinding her teeth. She does not look well—almost like she's about to overdose.

"I said *sit down!*" the officer shouts at her and reaches a hand out, like he's going to push her back to the ground. But I wedge my body in between them, shaking my head. I don't care what bullshit Becks and I are going through right now, I will not let her be manhandled by the police. I shake my head and chuckle.

"You did not just tell this victim to sit her *ass* on the floor, like a fucking animal. Did you?" Then I take my phone and quickly turn it to video. "I'm filming you until my attorney can get here. Because you cannot hold this woman here without an attorney or medical attention. You cannot force her to sit on the floor. Where's your superior? I want to speak to a superior officer right now."

"Sophia, I don't feel good," Rebecca slurs.

"Becks, you're coming with me. They didn't arrest you, did they?"

She shakes her head no.

"Ma'am, please, put that phone down, before I, uh—well, you can't be here," the officer stammers.

"I can. And I'm taking this woman. You have no right to detain her if she's not under arrest."

"Well, we need her to come down to the station and—"

"Becks, come on, let's go." I drag her with me toward the stairwell. I can tell, just by dragging her, that she's lost weight this past week. She looks breakable. She looks distracted. She looks—if I'm being completely honest, she looks like an addict.

She doesn't look like the woman I met six months ago, the woman who I was so ready to make my second home. The mother of two beautiful girls, the wife of a surgeon, the nurse who claimed she loved her job. When did this happen? When did she turn into this?

Why haven't I noticed sooner?

Tears well up in my eyes.

"Jesus fucking Christ, Rebecca, I'm really fucking disappointed in you," I hiss at her when we get in the stairwell and start weaving our way down and around the stairs toward the exit of the building. "DON'T say a word until we get out of here and into my car."

She lets out her breath and slows her pace, but I just squeeze her hand harder and pull even more.

"Ouch, Sophiaaaa, you're hurting me. Look, it was an accident, okay? Don't be like this, I didn't mean to—"

"I said, don't say a fucking word." *Oh my god.* I shake my head. She did it. She killed her. Rebecca killed Violet... That's what she was about to say, that killing Violet and making it look like a suicide was all some big fucking accident. And here I am, dragging her away from the crime scene, instead of letting the police have her. I should have just left her there.

I clench my jaw as we emerge from the stairwell.

"Ten minutes on the nose." The bellman shakes his finger at me.

I roll my eyes and pull Rebecca out of the building as fast as I can and across traffic to where I parked across the street. I get her in and buckle her up. She leans her head on the door, and sniffles and whimpers as I drive down the road. I don't know where I should take her. I can't take her home to Long Island, not like this, she would scare the girls. I can't take her to the theater, because how can there be a show if Violet is dead anyway?

"Fuck me." The only place I can take her right now, where we won't be seen, is my apartment. The apartment that's not supposed to be finished. The reason I'm living with her in the first place. But whatever, she's a liar too. She lied to me about Mitch. About his other wives. About his dead daughters.

She's been lying to herself too.

Because whatever happened last night, between her and Violet, didn't just happen out of the blue. I didn't peg Becks as a lesbian, but I also didn't peg her as a drug addict. Maybe she and Violet had a lovers' quarrel? Or maybe Violet was her dealer and she cut Becks off? Or maybe I should just ask her instead of surmising all of it. "Rebecca, I need you to tell me what happened so I can figure out how to protect you. I have a great attorney. And based on the fact they hadn't arrested you yet, it makes me think—" I look over...

She's foaming.

"Oh shit! BECKS! BECKS! Wake up. Wake the fuck up, you goddamn junkie!" I scream, slamming on the brakes. My tires squeal and the back end of the Range Rover slides as I whip over to the side of the road.

"Becks!" I slap her face. "What did you take? Becks? Wake up. Please. Becks." Shit! I wasn't wrong when I thought she seemed like she was overdosing. I need to get her to a hospital where they can pump her stomach and give her meds to reverse whatever she's done to herself. But I don't want them to know who she is. So I take her phone, and I find her wallet in her pocket. Then I quickly look up where the closest ER drop off is and program it into my directions.

Thankfully I don't get pulled over on the way to the hospital. Because I really should, I mean, if there's a cop anywhere—I'm stomping on my gas and weaving around taxis and Ubers and honking and basically driving like a fucking maniac. But I guess today is not my day to lose my American license. I make it to the ER in mere minutes and pull up to the loading/unloading zone, behind an ambulance, throwing my car in park and leaping from the driver's door with it wide open.

"You can't park there!" People are screaming at me and waving their arms.

And I'm screaming back, "Fuck you, she's overdosing or dying or I don't know!" and I yell something about her being a strange woman in the middle of the road and I'm just trying to be a good Samaritan.

I literally hoist Rebecca's limp body from my vehicle and set her on the sidewalk right in front of the ER. Then I get back into the vehicle. Her ID and phone are sitting in the cup holder. Do I give them to her? If I do, they will know. There's no hiding that she's Dr. Mitch Hendricks's wife and she'll be at risk of losing her nursing license. But if I keep them, and they can't identify her, and something goes really wrong—then what?

What am I supposed to do?

"Fuck!" I yell and bang my hands on the steering wheel.

Sit here with her? When she's literally overdosing and potentially just killed someone.

Nope.

I have to go home and get Sarah and Bailey ready to go to London. Because I have a feeling we are going to be leaving much sooner than I thought. I throw my car in drive and speed away. When Rebecca wakes up, if she wakes up, she can tell the hospital staff whatever nonsense she wants about who she is and what she's doing. If she wants to lie about her identity, that can be up to her.

While I'm crossing the bridge, driving home toward the house and the girls, I roll down my window and chuck her phone and wallet out, hoping they'll reach the water.

Then, instead of crying, which is what I want to do—I call someone I've spent the last few months completely ignoring and avoiding.

"Hello? Is everything okay?"

"No. It's not. Rebecca is indisposed. You need to get on the first plane to New York. I'll explain when you get here."

When I hang up, I run through all the things in my mind I'll need to do in the next twelve to twenty-four hours to stay ahead of whatever's happening with Rebecca—then I make another phone call.

"Mrs. Carter, what can I assist you with?" my attorney answers on the first ring. I've trained him well.

"Those papers I asked you to draw up about a month ago? I'm going to need them."

"I'll have a courier bring them by first thing tomorrow," he says.

"No. I need them today—let's say, two hours."

"Yes, I see. The situation you were afraid of must have—" He pauses, realizing that he should stop talking. I pay him for his legal skills. Nothing more. "Of course, Mrs. Carter, I'll have them delivered to you in two hours. Signature lines will be flagged, as I'm sure you recall from our prior dealings." He hangs up, letting me fantasize about the thing I've wanted, yet been so afraid of. At least this way, everything will be legal. And they will be mine.

THIRTY-FOUR

I'm surprised with the speed at which Mitch is able to get home to New York. He must have chartered the first plane from Germany, because he's walking into the house and it's just a little after nine p.m. I put the girls to bed around eight, earlier than usual, but we spent hours playing in the yard this afternoon—because I couldn't just sit around and wait for my phone to ring, or watch the news, or social media.

Tonight was supposed to be the preview of *Happily Never After*. But with Rebecca in the hospital and Violet dead, there's no way the production isn't postponed. I avoided looking it up, because, well, I just didn't want to deal with the drama. Instead, I was trying to focus on the girls, our exit strategy, and what I was going to say to Dr. Mitch when he showed up.

"Sophia, what the hell is going on? Where's Rebecca? I've tried calling a thousand times and she won't answer," Mitch says as soon as he walks into the dining room. He sets down a small bag and throws his coat over the chair. It's almost comforting in a way, his familiarity.

"Would you like to have a seat?" I ask. I'm at the table with a cup of tea.

He's more handsome than I recall—maybe it's the new life in Europe. Maybe he's getting better sleep. I'm sure he's eating better... Rebecca's such a horrible cook. Before he sits down, he looks around nervously. I wonder if he thinks Rebecca's going to jump out and yell "Surprise!" while wielding a knife.

I mean, I wouldn't blame him if that's what he thought.

Rebecca is an unpredictable psycho.

"She's not here, if that's what you're worried about. Just sit down and I'll explain everything."

"Sophia, you're scaring me. Where's Rebecca? The girls?"

"I'm not the one you should be scared of, Mitch. But I think you already know that. And the girls are fine, they're upstairs sleeping. Rebecca's in the city—I dropped her off at the ER this morning after I picked her up from Violet Ogelman's apartment."

"Why did you drop her off at the ER?" he asks.

"I'm pretty sure she was having a drug overdose."

"Jesus Christ. What..." He looks panic stricken.

"Well, according to what Rebecca told the police—Violet had committed suicide in front of her, which if that were true, I suppose would be cause for her to accidentally overdose as a coping mechanism..." I narrow my gaze and put my finger up to my lips, as if I'm really thinking hard about what happened. "Or maybe, in a drug-induced stupor, Rebecca killed Violet and just said it was a suicide. Does that sound like something she'd do, Mitch? Would Rebecca kill someone?"

Mitch scoffs, then he shakes his head, rubs his hands over his face and shakes his head again. "I, uh, Sophia, I don't know what to say—I mean, this is the last thing I expected you to tell me."

"Really? Which part seems unexpected, Mitch? Your wife overdosing? Or that she might have murdered someone?" I shrug. "Because the more I learn about Rebecca, the more I realize this type of behavior reflects her true personality. But I think you already knew that."

I spent all afternoon going over it in my head. All of Rebecca's behavior. The ups and the downs. Her fixation on things, like, well —me, Broadway, the trophies upstairs... That's when I remembered the box of old journals and yearbooks.

So during one of our breaks from playing in the yard, while the girls watched episodes of *Hilda* and *The Owl House*, I spread the old diaries and journals out on the table. It was then that I slowly pieced together the story of Rebecca. A troubled woman with a history of blackouts and self-indulgent behavior.

> *Dear Diary,*
>
> *Mom took me to see Dr. Nakamura again. He said if I don't start taking my meds, he's going to stop seeing me. I told him to fuck off. He knows the pills make me feel gross and I lose all motivation to go to cheer practice and dance and if I'm ever going to make it to Broadway, I can't turn into some fat-ass slacker. I flushed the pills down the toilet.*

> *Dear Diary,*
>
> *Dr. Nakamura makes me so mad! He asked me about what happened at Stone Bridge. I told him it's none of his business. He said just because I'm having a manic episode and feel invincible, doesn't mean I'm actually invincible. But I survived the jump, so I guess the jokes on him. He's so annoying. I'm sorry if Alexis died jumping off the bridge. I didn't force her to do it. Okay, maybe I told her I'd go to the mall with her if she jumped. I can't help it if I'm popular and desperate little idiots like Alexis will do anything to spend time with me. It's not my fault!*

Dear Diary,

I can't wait to move to New York so I never have to see Dr. Nakamura or my mom again. They just want to control me. They said I hurt people when I don't take my meds. But that's not true! I'm so much more focused when I don't take them. How can I be on Broadway and memorize lines if I take this shit? I guess I'd rather be crazy and famous than a zombie on lithium. The only person I hurt is myself. Okay, sometimes I intentionally hurt my little brother. But Ryan is a brat.

"I brought a box down from the attic today. It was filled with these—" I lean over and pick up the stack of journals and notebooks and set them on the table. I try to gauge Mitch's reaction when he sees them.

"Sophia, what's your point? You found old journals from Rebecca. I really don't want to get into all of this right now. Just tell me what hospital she's at so I can go take care of her," Mitch says.

"Really? You want to take care of her? Because, last time I checked, you wanted nothing to do with her." I slide a big yellow manila envelope that came in the mail the other day across the table. Their no-contest divorce. All signed and ready to go to the state to be recorded and finalized. I know this because I opened it and resealed it.

Bailey's glue sticks to the rescue, again.

"I know she's not my responsibility, but I, umm..." He pauses and gulps.

"Look, I don't know what Rebecca has over you, but it's clearly something. That's why you got on that plane today. And it's why you're dying to get up and leave right now, to find her and see what she said and to who."

Mitch literally gave Rebecca full custody of the girls, the house, half his pension, all the furniture, the cars, their cabin in Maine, absolutely everything. At first I thought—wow, he really just wants to get to Germany to be with his new woman.

But then I remembered.

Mitch is Alaska. Meaning, he has a big ego. He is a celebrated surgeon, after all. So why would a guy like that give a fucking nut job like Rebecca absolutely everything? And that's when it hit me.

He's scared of her.

He's scared of what she might do, yes—but more importantly, he's scared of what she might say. Which is why he's trembling right now. Sweat is forming at his brow, his eyes are darting around, and he's fidgeting. Yes. Dr. Mitch is guilty of something, and Rebecca knows what it is. Maybe it has something to do with his first two wives or his two dead daughters. Or maybe it has something to do with his job as a surgeon. Or maybe it's something entirely different.

The thing is...

I don't fucking care.

But he does. And that puts me in control.

"I, uh, Sophia, I have no idea what you're talking about." He stands up—his face is red, he looks like he wants to get angry, but he's a pathetic man. What can he get angry at me about? This was his life and it's his mess.

Then I slide a different envelope across the table. "Please, sit back down."

"What's this?" he asks.

"Custody papers. I want custody of Sarah and Bailey."

Mitch opens his mouth to say something, but I put my hand up. "Mitch, don't let your ego get in the way of this. You just agreed in those divorce papers to give Rebecca full custody of the girls. But she's not in any position to care for children. Not if she might have just killed a woman and then tried to OD afterwards."

"Do you really think she did it? Killed her co-star?"

"Her actions make her seem guilty." I'm keeping my tone even, reasonable.

He puts his head in his hands and exhales loudly. "Not again, Rebecca, not again."

"What do you mean, not again?" I ask. "Is this about what her journal entry said, about the girl that jumped off the bridge?"

"No. It's about someone else. We don't have to get into it right now. You're right, she's in no position to take care of the girls." He opens up the manila envelope with the custody papers and looks at them. I'm trying to be patient, but it feels like my entire forever rests on whether this man will sign these papers.

"Signing doesn't have to mean goodbye forever. It just means that you're protecting them." Although, I hope it means forever. I'd love nothing more than to never hear from Mitch again. But, if the girls want to see their father someday, I wouldn't take that away from them.

He sighs. "Am I a failure?" He takes a pen from his pocket, signs the papers, and hands them back to me.

Mitch's phone rings.

"I need to take this." He answers his phone and says something in German, then walks away speaking in hushed tones, before I have a chance to answer his question. Is he a failure? Well, yes, I'd say so. But I won't say it to his face. The man did just sign over custody of his children to me. I do hate to think about what a disappointment he'll end up being to his unborn child and fiancée. Mitch is literally the worst.

But whatever. Not my problem.

I quickly snap photos of the pages and email them to my attorney. Once they get filed, my attorney will fast-track it with one of the judges who accepts envelopes full of cash as a thank-you. Which is good for me and even better for the girls. And once the judge signs it, there will be very little Rebecca or Mitch can do to reverse the custody agreement, especially if she's put on a psychiatric hold or if charges are filed against her. Not that Mitch would try. Honestly, I'm surprised he hasn't already grabbed his bag to head back to the airport after hearing about the mess his soon-to-be ex-wife has made.

Oh wait, that's right. He knows Rebecca cannot be trusted. And she has some kind of dirt on him. I really don't care if Mitch and Becks want to get into it and fight about their secrets. As long as it's far away from me and the girls.

Because Rebecca Hendricks is dangerous...

THIRTY-FIVE
REBECCA

Equipment beeps and whirs. The air smells recycled. Muffled voices float through the thin walls. Without opening my eyes, I know I'm in a hospital of some kind. The only thing is, which one, and am I here of my own free will or am I a prisoner of the state of New York? Because the last thing I remember, I was in Violet's apartment and I'd just smashed a coffee mug over her head. Although, I'm not entirely sure why I did that?

Did we have an argument? Had she attacked me?

Hmmm... I lift my arms up. Okay, they work. I wiggle my fingers. Yes, they work too. I feel my face, my nose, my head. Everything seems to be where it's supposed to be and I'm not in a great deal of pain or anything. So I must not have been in a physical altercation with Violet, or anyone else for that matter.

So why am I in this hospital bed?

I guess there's only one way to find out.

I open my eyes, look around the room, until—bingo. The whiteboard with the notes on it that the nurses leave as reminders and information for the nurse on the next shift who takes over my care.

Under diagnosis, the nurse wrote, "OD".

"I had a drug overdose?" I sit up and practically shout the

words. And that's when the headache hits me. "Ooohhhh, ouch." I lie back down.

I look at the whiteboard again, to make sure I'm reading it correctly—that it's really about me. The patient name says, "JANE DOE".

I look at the side table, checking for my wallet and phone or anything of mine. But it's empty. I look down and I'm in a hospital gown. I honestly can't even recall what I was last wearing. There's a hospital bracelet around my wrist that reads, "JANE DOE".

Holy shit.

So they really don't know who I am. Maybe that's a good thing, because I can't remember what happened or how I got here.

Are you sure you can't recall anything? That's very unusual, Rebecca, unless... Did you forget to take your medicine? Dr. Nakamura walks into my room. He walks up to the monitors and looks at them, then jots things down on his clipboard.

"Jesus, of course you'd be here." I sigh and cross my arms.

"Who, me? I'm flattered, but I'm not sure we've ever met before. I'm Mackenzie Douglas. But you can call me Mac. I'll be your nurse today, Mrs...."

"Mrs. Hendricks. And don't play stupid with me, Mac. I'm sure you've already called my husband and this whole Jane Doe thing was his idea. God forbid anyone find out his wife overdosed on too many of her anxiety pills."

Mac lights up. "Well now, Mrs. Hendricks, what did you say your first name is? Now that you're awake, I'm going to help you get out of here just as fast as we can," Mac says. And for some reason, I believe her.

With good reason too.

Apparently last night was a full moon. Which meant admissions in the ER were at their monthly high, and every bed was needed, for real patients—with stab wounds and broken bones and actual emergencies. Not the wife of a surgeon who accidentally took too many Xanax with a bottle of wine and was dumped at the ER by her lousy friends.

At least, that's the story I'm going with, and it seems to do the trick.

Mac is quick to help get me cleared to leave. She even lets me use her cell phone to call Mitch. Because I'd rather be the one to tell him, before someone here decides to.

"Hello, this is Dr. Mitch Hendricks," he answers.

"Mitch, it's me."

"Rebecca? I'm almost there. Sophia called me and I flew home as soon as I could."

"Huh?" Now, how does Sophia know I was in the hospital? Interesting. I glance over at Mac, who's casually tapping her toe, faster each second. "I lost my phone. I'll be out front waiting." I hang up and hand the phone back to Mac.

"Good luck, Mrs. Hendricks," she says with a smile and heads off to deal with her next patient. As I walk down the hallway toward the lobby and to the front doors, two police officers walk past me. My heart flutters, but I'm not sure why. I look over my shoulder, and one of the officers looks back and stares at me.

And that's when it hits me, like a truck, and I'm the stupid jaywalker.

Violet's apartment. Filled with police officers. Police that arrived, because I called them—

Oh shit, oh god, that's right. When I woke up, I thought Violet had killed herself—so I called the police. It wasn't until they were screaming at me about what happened that I remembered—I'd killed her and covered it up. But I guess I was so convincing as a drunk, stoned idiot who'd fallen asleep and woke up to find her friend dead that they let me go.

But how I got to the hospital, I have no idea.

And how Sophia knew about any of it and called Mitch? Well, maybe I called her? I mean, before I lost my phone.

Mitch was right when he said he was close. As soon as I exit the hospital, he pulls up and I get in. "Before we go home, can you take me to the theater? I have to figure out what happened to our show—last night was supposed to be our preview performance."

"I'd really rather not. I think we need to go somewhere and discuss what happened. Jesus, Rebecca, you look like you haven't eaten in weeks. And is that marijuana I smell on your clothes? And cigarettes? What has happened to you?"

"Ugh, really, Mitch? You fly all the way home from Germany so that you can fucking berate me for losing weight and smoking? Isn't that exactly what every European bimbo does? Smokes, drinks, and starves themselves?"

He looks at me and rolls his eyes. The muscle in his jaw twitches. "I'm being serious, Rebecca. You know what, maybe you're right. We should go to the theater, so that you can quit the production in person and collect any personal effects you might have."

"I'm not quitting. What are you talking about?"

He makes a quick left turn, heading toward Broadway.

"No, no, no, you can just turn this car around. I'll deal with the show myself later. I don't need you turning into some weird over-protective husband figure right now. I digitally signed all those fucking divorce papers a few weeks ago anyway." I don't know why he's acting like this. I'm never quitting my show—just because Violet is dead doesn't mean that the show can't go on. We each have an understudy, which means someone else can step into Violet's shoes.

But Mitch isn't slowing or turning around, he's heading right for my theater.

"What do you want from me? And if you say, 'quit my production to be a stay-at-home mom,' I will scream at the top of my lungs."

"God no, I don't want you anywhere near the girls."

I'm about to ask him what the fuck that means when he pulls up to the red loading/unloading zone behind the theater.

"You can't park here." I point to the sign.

"Watch me. Now you can stay here if you want, but I'm going to go have a little conversation with your director. What's his name again? George? Gerry... no, Grant. That's right, Grant Baker."

I'm mildly impressed that my soon-to-be ex-husband knew which theater our show is debuting at and that he knows the name of the director. Does that mean that during our family dinners maybe he was actually listening and paying attention to me?

But I'm still not sure why he wants to speak to Baker when he knows I'm not going to resign from the show.

I've been sitting in his car, contemplating why, and then I realize— "Shit. Mitch, wait for me!" I shout as I get out and start chasing after him. Sneaky son of a bitch. He's already so far ahead of me, and I'm not sure how.

The floor feels soft, like I'm walking on Jell-O, and I put my arms out to balance myself. Maybe I should have eaten something at the hospital. I'm feeling a little light-headed. I go into the back of the theater, trying to keep up with Mitch.

"Mitch, please, wait for me!" I shout.

The hallway is painted black—normally there are people and costumes and sounds of rehearsing coming from every direction in the theater. It's always alive with activity. But not today. Today is dark, quiet, lonely. This must be for Violet. A day of rest, a day of remembrance. Baker probably hated to give everyone the day off from work, especially with having to sub in an understudy.

"Absolutely not. She's a sick woman!" I hear my husband shout.

"You are not her keeper, sir, and you can get the fuck off my stage!" Baker yells back. Aww, are they up there fighting over me? Well, that is sort of sweet, isn't it? Wait, no, what am I thinking? It's not sweet, they sound like a couple of idiots. I can hear them huffing and puffing and feet scuffing on the floor. Wait, are they actually fighting? Like, with fists? I run around from behind the stage, up the stairs, and find them standing very close and whispering to one another. I can't make out what they are saying, but Baker is shaking his head, then he folds his arms over his chest and heaves a big sigh. Mitch stops talking and rubs his hands over his face, while Baker is saying something.

Finally, I've had enough of whatever this is and I walk toward them. "Hello. I don't know what the two of you think you're doing. But I'm not quitting the show, and Baker, I don't need you getting all buddy-buddy with my ex-husband."

They turn and look at me. I don't know what they think they see, but their faces change, twisting and contorting, like I'm some sort of hideous leper with rotting flesh falling off of me and dripping on the stage as I walk toward them. Is it me, or do they keep moving away from me? I'm confused and suddenly so unsure of myself. Am I supposed to smile? Or frown? Or start crying?

This is supposed to be my show—I'm the star and no one should look at me like that! Especially Baker and Mitch. I've got to get a handle on this before it really sours.

"Baker, I'm surprised to see you. We just stopped by because I've lost my phone, I thought maybe it would be here." Then I hold open my empty hands. "Nope, not here." I chuckle uncomfortably for a minute. Baker looks over at Mitch then back at me. "Since we're here and all, maybe you could tell me when our next rehearsal is. I'm assuming we're going to rehearse with the understudy, since Violet is dead?"

"Well, um, you see Rebecca, I was just telling Mitch that I think it would be best if... well, you see, you know your understudy—Pauline? So um, I was speaking with her and I think—"

"Jesus Christ, Baker, spit the fucking words out. What are you trying to say?" I throw my hands up in disgust.

"Rebecca, please, let the man speak." Mitch takes a few steps away from Baker, toward the edge of the stage, presumably to give us space to talk. But then Baker takes a few steps away from me, toward Mitch. Oh my god, this man is such an idiot.

"Fine. Speak, Baker, what are you saying?"

He exhales loudly. "I'm saying that I've replaced you, Rebecca. You're too much of a liability. You're not bad, but the fact that your lady friend paid me for your audition... and now to find out you were with Violet when she killed herself. I'm just very unsure of having you on set. It's going to be a distraction and—" He's still talking. Words are coming out of his mouth, but I can't hear them. I can see his lips moving, and when I look over at Mitch, he's nodding and semi-smiling in that fucking condescending way.

"Oh, look, I think I see my phone," I say loudly and point. Baker and Mitch both turn and look.

I run at full speed toward my husband, who is closest to the edge of the stage. I know it won't kill him because I've fallen off the stage myself, but maybe it will shut both of these two idiots up. And scare some sense into Baker. I am *not* giving up my part. I don't care what kind of backlash it causes him.

"Tough titty said the kitty," I say through clenched teeth as I shove Mitch off the stage. He doesn't scream, but there is a disgusting crunching sound. "Oh, shit. I probably shouldn't have done that. He's going to be so pissed at me if I just broke one of his hands."

Baker squeaks and slaps his hand over his mouth.

"Oh, shut up, Baker. I'm sure you and your ex pushed each other around every now and again." I walk over to the edge of the stage and look down. "Mitch, don't be such a baby—" I gasp. Mitch is face down, impaled on a metal music stand post. The ones I warned Baker about. The ones he said he'd take care of before previews. I spin around and look at Baker.

"What did I fucking tell you about those things?" I shout at him.

He doesn't say anything, he just stands there, shaking.

"Are you serious right now? You're not going to say anything? You just killed my husband!" I run over and give him a shove too.

He falls backwards, landing on his butt. He sobs and cries out. "Please, Rebecca, I don't want to die."

"Why are you looking at me like that? You're the one who just killed my husband. Get up, Baker." I kick him and he cries out. "Don't be such a fucking baby. Come on, let's go to your office. I need to use your phone."

Baker crawls to his feet and walks slowly toward his office. His shoulders are slumped and he's shuffling his feet. "Oh my god, old man. What's with the dementia shuffle? You coming down from all those uppers? Need a little pick-me-up, Baker? Yeah, well, me too. So let's go see what we can find in your office."

An hour later Baker is slumped over on his desk, blood dripping from his nose. I just forced him to snort every last drop of coke he had in his desk, plus any other powder I could find in the building. Some face makeup from the costume department. Some salt from a shaker sitting on a file cabinet. A packet of Splenda by the coffee maker. I would have kept going if he hadn't fallen face forward, smacking his head on his desk.

What a wimp.

Seriously, I would have imagined a guy like Baker should be able to keep up. I'm sure he's going to vomit or maybe his heart will go out or he'll fall to the side, have a seizure, and hit his head on something. Whatever it is, there is no coming back from what I just made this man do.

Now, to take Mitch's car and get home before someone shows up here and calls the police. I'm not really in the mood to put on a performance. But I will if I have to.

THIRTY-SIX
SOPHIA

I guess I expected Mitch to call after he found Rebecca. To give me some kind of status update. Is she going to jail? Or being temporarily institutionalized? I really want to know what's happening. But it's been five hours and he hasn't called or sent a text. I suppose this sort of thing takes time for regular people. If it was me, I'd use cash and my attorney, speeding up the process tenfold. But this is Mitch we're talking about, using his I'm-a-doctor charm instead. Which takes more effort.

Thankfully, Ekaterina came over earlier and kept my mind off things. She helped me pack the children's suitcases—all the things they will need right away in London. The rest we put into boxes and had them picked up by FedEx to be shipped. They should arrive shortly after we do. I've booked a red-eye flight for the four of us tomorrow evening. Ekaterina has agreed to go with me and the girls. Unfortunately, she will have to fly back to deal with her apartment before moving permanently, but I'm grateful she can come for the first few weeks when we arrive. I'm hoping her presence will make the transition a little easier on the girls.

This move to London is happening fast.

I'm not sure how the girls will react when I tell them.

I guess in the back of my mind, I thought Rebecca would be

out of the picture, permanently. But she's not and now this sense of urgency is because Rebecca is so damn unstable. I have to get the girls out of here to keep them safe. But how can I tell them that?

Hey, kiddos, your mom is batshit crazy and may have killed several people, so we have to get out of here before we're next.

Not exactly the kind of conversation I want to have with an eight- and five-year-old. Even if I tell them the truth about what Rebecca's done, they still might not want to leave her. She is their mother and I do think they love her. They don't understand that they need to be protected from her.

I will tell them everything, eventually, when they are older. Because they deserve to know the truth. But right now, I just need to get through the next twenty-four hours. And if I knew where the hell Mitch and Rebecca were, it would make me feel a whole lot better. Actually, there's no reason we have to stay here, in this house tonight. I'll just finish up and load up the girls and we can go stay in the city at my apartment.

I sigh and smile, feeling a whole lot better.

Buzz.

Justin is texting me. Oh god, I'm sure he's heard something. I'm almost scared to read the text from him.

> Hey! Oh my god I'm being so nosey, but I just heard that someone from Rebecca's show died? Obvi I won't ask her about it. But I thought you might know something.

> You're such a gossip.

> Gasp! And duh.

> No, I don't know any of the details. Just that it happened and they cancelled the preview performance. Rebecca's phone keeps going to voicemail. Maybe the director made them turn off their phones? To avoid the press?

> Oooh, I bet you're right!

> If I hear anything juicy, I'll be sure to text you.

said getting records from Elmhurst would be difficult, but for the right amount of money, anything is possible.

"Fifi, someone's in the house," Sarah shakes me out of my daydreaming.

"Hmmm, oh, um, maybe it's your dad." I say and blink a few times. I jump up to go downstairs when I hear Rebecca.

"Oh, children! Mommy's home! Come give me a hug!" Rebecca is using her singsong voice. She sounds like a creepy villain in a Disney movie. "I have some terrible news about your piece of shit faaaaaatherrrrrr!" she sings even louder.

Sarah and Bailey start shaking like puppies in a thunderstorm.

"Shhhhhh... go hide in your closet. Take my phone and call 9-1-1, okay? Tell them there are people fighting inside your house and you're hiding in the closet. My passcode is 0-3-1-3."

"My birthday," Sarah whispers.

I give her a quick wink, then scoot her and Bailey into the closet, closing them in before I lock Bailey's bedroom door from the inside, pulling the door shut as I leave. That should slow Rebecca down for a few minutes—she'll either have to kick it down or pick the lock.

Glass shatters downstairs in the living room.

"Oh, lovely, she's in a breaking-things kind of mood." I'm glad I'm wearing Skims leggings—they are easy to move around in. I have a feeling I'm going to be dodging projectiles. Too bad I'm barefoot.

There's another loud crash in the kitchen.

I hope the police get here soon.

THIRTY-SEVEN

"The police will be here soon. You should probably stop breaking things and just sit down and wait for them to arrive," I say as I take the last step off the staircase into the living room.

Whoosh! A dining room chair whizzes by my face and splinters against the wall behind me. I swing my head in the direction the chair just came from.

Becks is smiling, and I swear to god all she needs is some white-and-red face paint and I'd be standing with the Joker. I don't waste my time with movies like that, but I know the gist. Crazy goes even crazier and likes to blow things up and kill people.

"Rebecca, darling, if you want to break things, that's fine, this is your house." I turn on the voice I use with my clients when I'm trying to convince them to spend a lot of money (which is always). "But could you please refrain from throwing the furniture at my head."

"Why should I, you fucking bitch? You've ruined my life. So maybe I'm going to ruin yours. Hmmm... How about that? A chair leg jammed in your skull?" Even across the room I can see her eyes are black again. "Or a picture frame?" She launches a small frame. I duck, but her aim was off anyway—it smashes against the wall to the right of me.

"Better men, and women, have tried." I feign boredom, even though my heart is racing and my throat is tight. Where is Mitch? He must have brought her home. I can't believe they'd let her out of the hospital on her own accord when she's acting like this.

"They must not have tried very hard. It took me, like, a combined ten minutes total to kill three people today."

"You can't be serious..."

"Oh, I'm serious. First Violet, then Mitch, and lastly Baker. I can tell you all about each death if you like." She looks like she's seconds away from rubbing her palms together and throwing her head back to cackle. She has turned herself into a true show-stopping villain—just like what happens to her character in *Happily Never After*.

I shake my head. "Rebecca, you have bipolar disorder and you make things up in your head. This is not real. You did not kill them. These are delusions." I just can't believe it. There is no way she killed Mitch and Baker. God, I wish I had my phone so I could try calling Mitch again.

"Nothing about this is fake, Sophia. Unlike your friendship... I am one hundred percent serious. They are all dead. And the incredible thing is—I'm going to blame it all on you. Because *you* were having a torrid affair with Mitch, and then with Baker. One man just wasn't enough for you."

"Excuse me?" I practically choke.

"Today it all came to a head when you discovered Mitch and Baker were going to leave you, for each other." She sounds so proud as she tells me her nonsense.

I don't mean to, but I laugh. The thought of me having an affair with Mitch. "Is that the best you could come up with? An affair with your husband and the extremely gay director of your Broadway show?"

Her face turns red. "You might think it sounds stupid. But there are witnesses! Sarah and Bailey will tell the police they've seen you and their daddy in bed together. You can't stop this."

"Fuck you!" I snap when she mentions the girls. She would make them lie? To frame me? Over my dead body.

"Ohhhh, does that touch a nerve?" She grabs a lamp and throws it. I put my arms up to catch it or stop it, and Rebecca screams and runs toward me.

"No!" I exclaim as she smashes into me. My back slams into the mirror on the wall behind me and it drops to the ground, shattering glass. Little shards scatter all over the floor. Larger shards hit the back of my legs, slicing through my leggings. "Jesus Christ, Becks! Stop!" She's a lot stronger than she looks.

She doesn't stop. Instead, she pulls back her arm, balls up her fist, and punches me in the face. Pain explodes from my nose. "Oh my god, you punched me!" And much to my surprise, she hits me again. I fall down, cutting my palms on the broken mirror when I try to catch myself.

Rebecca laughs. Then she picks up the broken chair leg. "Did you really think you fit in to this life? My life? I didn't even fit in. I kept wondering why the fuck a millionaire, or billionaire, or whatever you are, would want to stay here for so long. And that's when I realized—Sarah and Bailey. You want the girls."

I look up at her as she holds the chair leg. Blood drips from my nose.

"Yes, I want the girls. Someone has to protect them from you."

"Oh, please. Protect them from me? They are just like me! Dr. Nakamura performed a full evaluation on both of them and they are Just. Like. Me."

"Dr. Nakamura? Your childhood psychologist from Ohio?" I question her. I don't believe her for one instant.

She blinks a few times, giving me the seconds I need to scramble up off the floor. I run toward the kitchen, hoping to see police lights coming. What the fuck is taking them so long? Sure, we're pretty far out in the suburbs, but not that far.

"Where the fuck do you think you're going?"

Thump.

Pain explodes from my head and I fall to my knees. "Just leave the girls out of this," I warn as I scramble to my feet. Blood pours from the massive gash on the side of my head, where Rebecca just hit me with a chair leg. I drag the back of my forearm over my face, trying to clear the blood away.

I choke out a cry when I step on a piece of glass.

The police should be here soon—I just have to keep Rebecca from going upstairs and finding the girls. I limp from the dining room, calling her name, heading into the kitchen. I strain my ears, hoping to hear the sound of sirens racing through our neighborhood. The police should be here soon—I just have to keep her from going upstairs and finding the girls.

"SARAH! BAILEY!" she screams from the living room.

I pivot and run toward her, ignoring the sharp pain in my foot.

"Don't you fucking say their names," I growl and lunge forward with my arms out, slipping on some of the broken glass and falling to the floor. "Oooof." The air escapes my lips.

She laughs at my crumpled body. "You're pathetic," she spits the words at me. Her eyes are blazing like she's possessed by the devil.

I grab her ankle before she can take a step up the stairs. "Please, I'll do anything. Leave them alone!" I cry. Then I muster enough upper body strength to pull her leg out from under her, but she doesn't fall. She leans down and pounds my head with her fists. "Let go of my leg."

"Fuck you." As long as she doesn't go upstairs, I'll take every beating she can dish out. That's when I hear something, between the punches, like a child whimpering in the hallway. I think I see Sarah holding my phone up, but I can't be sure. Between the fist hitting my head and the blood in my eyes, everything is a blur.

Police sirens wail down the block.

She starts screaming even louder at me. My head feels like I'm underwater.

Thankfully, I see red-and-blue lights through the windows as the police pull into the driveway. They'll barge in any second and save me and the girls.

But Rebecca's a smooth talker—she already said her plan is to pin everything on me. Which means there won't be anyone to protect Sarah and Bailey. So with the Herculean strength of a mother lifting a car that's rolled on top of her child, I shove her away from me and get on my feet, grabbing the first thing I see.

Mitch's prized "Doctor of the Year" award.

Rebecca turns to run toward the police officers shouting in the foyer. But there's no way in hell I'm letting her reach them and spew more of her lies. So without any hesitation, I slam the award, point first, into the back of her neck.

She doesn't scream as the glass severs her spinal cord. Her body just tumbles face forward in a heap of flesh.

Then I collapse.

"Mommy and Fifi were fighting," Sarah sobs.

"Are they dead?" Bailey asks.

"Sophia, I'm so sorry this happened to you," a familiar voice says. Slender fingers wrap around my left hand, giving it a little hopeful squeeze. I flinch because everything is sore, even my fingers. "Are you awake? I felt you move."

My throat is dry. I'm not sure I'll be able to speak, but I'll try anyway. "Hannah," I whisper her name.

"Yes, hi, it's me. I'm here with you. Should I go get the doctor?" Her fingers loosen and I can feel her shift.

"No." I try to grasp on. I don't want her to leave me yet. I'm not entirely sure I'm alive—this might be a dream. The last thing I remember was lying on the floor at Rebecca's house while she beat my head with her fist, possibly a hammer.

My eyes hurt and I try to open them, but they are swollen so badly they can only open partially. The lights in the room are dimmed, but I'd recognize her anywhere. Hannah McMillian. She smiles and reaches a hand up to my face to gently stroke my forehead and move my hair. It's very intimate and kind—my bottom lip quivers and tears well up in my eyes. After everything that happened between me and Hannah, the fact that she's here right now, and seems to care about me...

"I got on the first flight here when the hospital called," she explains. "You still have me listed in your phone as your emergency contact."

I don't even remember putting Hannah as my emergency contact, but that was smart of me. I really don't have anyone else, I guess. But now, I have two little girls that depend on me. So if I'm here, where are Sarah and Bailey?

"The girls," I croak and try to sit up.

"Relax, it's okay. They are absolutely precious and very worried about you. Also, a little traumatized. Thankfully Ruby, Rowen, and Bailey have joined forces. Sarah, on the other hand, she's pretty quiet. But Ekaterina has been teaching her how to crochet, which is at least keeping her mind busy."

So Hannah *and* the kids flew to New York to take care of me. If I could smile, I would. But if she's got the girls, does that mean Becks was telling the truth? *Did she really kill Mitch?*

"Listen, you don't have to worry. I'm not going anywhere until you've been released and you're well enough to take care of the girls on your own. Your attorney came by earlier to let me know, well, to let you know—the custody papers were fast-tracked due to the circumstances. Everything has been approved."

I choke out a cry. "Really?"

"Yes, well, that Sarah of yours. She's a smart cookie. She had the wherewithal to film most of the fight between you and Rebecca."

I thought I saw Sarah filming before I blacked out. But I wasn't entirely sure—it could have been a figment of my mind, a way to cope with the pain I was suffering at the hands of Rebecca. My bottom lip quivers and I can't really say anything. I just nod.

Hannah opens her arms and leans in. I throw my arms around her neck, even though I'm so sore I might vomit, but I need a hug right now.

"Oh, Sophia. Everything will be fine. I promise. And when I

heard that Mitch gave you custody of his daughters before his death, I was so happy for you. I know you never saw yourself with a family before—but now, it's amazing. Those little girls are going to need you now, more than ever."

"Thank you," I reply. I'm going to have to send my attorney a Bentley or something for his expeditious filing of the custody papers. That's one thing I don't have to worry about now. That some relative of Mitch or Rebecca will come out of the woodwork and try to take the girls. In the last six months, there's never been any real mention of grandparents, aunts, uncles, cousins. Becks told me her mom died a few years ago. And her younger brother died when they were teenagers. But I know that at times like this, when there's an idea that there might be money, the roaches come out of the drain. I'll have to alert my attorney to take care of any mysterious relatives that appear.

"Well, I should probably get the doctor, let them know you're awake," Hannah says. "And then you should get some rest. You've got two little girls who are very anxious for their Fifi to get better. Oh, that reminds me. The kids colored you 'Get Well' cards." She digs around in her bag and pulls out construction paper cards with color crayon and marker drawings on them.

I don't want her to leave, I want her to stay with me, to keep me company. But I know she's right. I need to rest if I want to get out of here and back to the girls.

"Thank you, Hannah. Truly."

THIRTY-EIGHT

Hannah is a godsend. She's stayed with the kids for nearly two weeks while I've been recovering. I had a broken nose, multiple fractures to my face and ribs, plus some internal bleeding that needed to subside before they'd release me.

There's not much that Hannah hasn't finished by the time I get home from the hospital. Well, not home to my apartment in the city. Or home to the Hendrickses' house. No, that fucking nightmare with Becks is over—I'm never going back there again, unless it's to burn it down. Which I just might.

Hannah took charge. She cleared out the Hendrickses' home and hired a realtor to get it ready to sell. Not to mention she rented a cute little vacation house near the beach big enough for all of us. The children have set up a fort in the living room, complete with blankets, pillows, twinkle lights, and their stuffies. I'm so grateful, I'm not sure where to begin. Even Ekaterina is staying with us.

She flung open the front door when we pulled into the driveway yesterday and came to help me out of the car while Hannah carried in my belongings.

"Look what happens when I not around twenty-four-seven to keep eyes on you—you get beat up." Ekaterina looked me up and down. It felt like I hadn't seen her in ages. She refused to come to the hospital—something about demons and the devil.

"Clearly I need you, Ekaterina. I hope you've made arrangements so you can come to London with us permanently." I leaned against her shoulder as she helped me out of the Range Rover.

"Yes, yes, I come with you and stay. Keep close watch. No more beating up."

I threw my arms around her neck and cried a little. "Thank you."

"Ahhh, so you a hugger now? Like your friend, miss happy blonde."

I stood back, wiped my tears and chuckled. "Hannah does like to hug—and she is an unusually happy person, isn't she? But don't get the wrong idea about me... I'm still a cold British woman at my core." I said that last part as clipped and sterile as I could, just to prove it. Ekaterina just rolled her eyes. Then hugged me again.

I knew it meant she was grateful I'd survived—if for no other reason than to take care of Sarah and Bailey and raise them in a loving home.

She loves them too...

Today is less about hugging and more about ironing out our travel plans to get to London. Hannah and the twins are leaving tomorrow. They have to get back to the farm. Apparently they have a goat about to give birth. Or multiple goats. I'm not entirely sure... I just know farm animals are being born.

"Fifi, can we get a baby goat?" Bailey asks.

"No, dear heart. No goats in London."

"But, Fiiii-fiiiii, goats are so much fun," Hannah bleats out my name, while holding a goat stuffed animal up to her face. Then she uses the stuffie to tickle and chase Bailey around the dining room.

"Yes, goats might be fun, in a poop-balls-everywhere and getting-rammed-by-horns sort of way. But I don't think we're zoned for them." I shrug. "But, I suppose, I could bring Sarah and Bailey to visit the farm during a school break. What do you think, Rowen?" I ruffle his hair.

"Yay!" he shouts. "You hear that, guys? Fifi said she'll bring you to visit our house. I can show you the chickens and the tree house too!"

Ruby, Bailey, and even Sarah cheer and jump up and down and clap. Hannah smiles and winks at me.

"Good, then it's settled. Bailey, no goats in London. Now, who's ready to take down the fort? We're leaving tomorrow, so we have to start packing."

"Nooooo!" the children shout and go running and diving into their fort.

"Fine, thirty more minutes," I tell them, then sit down at the table.

Hannah takes a seat next to me.

"Well, I'm happy to hear you tell the girls you'll bring them to visit the farm. I imagine London will be pretty exciting and a bit overwhelming. It might be nice to spend some time in the country."

"Yes, I imagine so," I reply. I look over my shoulder into the living room. It sounds like the kids have turned an episode of *Bluey* on in the fort. I'd recognize those Aussie pup voices anywhere at this point. I smile. Who'd have guessed I'd even know the name of a children's cartoon show a few years ago when I was living in Beijing? And now look at me. I'm the guardian of two little girls.

"What are you smiling about?" Hannah asks.

"Oh, just what a strange journey the last few years have been. For both of us, really." I take a sip of my tea.

"Strange, yes—but also exhilarating and thrilling. We all have a chance at long and happy lives from here on out," she says. Her eyes sparkle. She's put on some weight since the last time I saw her, and her hair looks thick and healthy. She's got a bit of a tan—and she's not wearing nearly as much makeup as she used to. I'm not sure she's even picked her phone up to check her socials once.

Yes.

Being widowed has done Hannah a world of good.

The children start giggling. "Do you think they'll be okay? Bailey seems very resilient. But Sarah—I'm a little worried."

Hannah takes my hand and squeezes.

"You know, I was worried about the twins, after everything that happened. But I just made the commitment to be there for them. I think it was hardest on Rowen, and sometimes it's not easy parenting him. But every day I show up with a smile."

I remember that Hannah's mom abandoned her at her great aunt's farm when she was about Sarah's age. I know it was hard on her, but it was the best thing for her. Her aunt Tippy has been a rock and guided Hannah, even if she wasn't always the warmest person early on. I think she's turned into a pretty caring woman now.

It gives me hope.

Hope that I can be there for Sarah and help her overcome the loss of both parents. And the bizarre behavior of Rebecca in the end. And before I arrived in their lives, there might have been all kinds of strange behavior, because there is so much about Rebecca I don't know. I called Barry when I woke up in the hospital and had him send me everything he could dig up. And wow, Rebecca had a history. The fact that she killed one of Mitch's wives during a manic episode leads me to believe she was always capable of murder. For all we know, there were others.

She was good at hiding in plain sight, until she wasn't.

THIRTY-NINE
REBECCA

2021

"You're sure she's capable of babysitting the girls?" I ask Mitch. It's been so long since we've gone out. But ever since he signed on to be the face of the Velature system, he's been around less and less. They've got him traveling the world showing other surgeons how amazing their device is. Not to mention all the teaching and speaking engagements. I'm not even sure he operates on patients anymore, the amount of time he spends traveling.

"Yes, I'm sure. I've known Brittney for a while, she used to work at the Bur—I mean in the records department, at the hospital," he says.

I look at him and can see the lie on his face.

Something inside me bubbles.

But before I can say anything to him, the doorbell rings downstairs. I'm not done getting ready, I only have half my makeup on and I'm still in my bathrobe.

"I'll get it. You just take your time getting ready... I'll show Brittney the house and how to use the TV remote and what to fix the girls for dinner." Mitch smiles, then gives me a kiss on the top of my head. As soon as he leaves and walks downstairs to answer the door, I tiptoe across the hallway to Bailey's room. She's in her crib, sleeping. I go into her closet, then I move the box of baby clothes that have gotten too small, revealing a panel on the wall. I slide the panel slowly so it doesn't make a sound and I crouch down and crawl in. It's kind of a tight fit, but I've done it enough times, I know how to squeeze in.

I don't really know why this space exists. I found it when I was cleaning out the closet, which Mitch had jam-packed full of his first wife's clothes and shoes. She had a real shopping addiction.

The door in the room below me closes—and I can hear perfectly and even see a little through the edges of where the light fixture was installed. If I get down on my hands and knees and peer with my eye, I can see Mitch's desk.

This space is right above Mitch's office.

"Are you sure we should do this with your wife upstairs?" our babysitter Brittney asks.

"She'll be up there for at least twenty minutes getting ready. Plus, she never comes in here, she says it gives her the creeps," he says.

"Why would your office give her the creeps?" Brittney giggles.

"Who knows. I keep telling you, Rebecca is crazy," Mitch says and laughs.

Oh, you sorry sack of shit, I say to myself. Then I move my head lower, to try and get a better view. I can see the edge of Mitch's shoulder, but not much else, so I shift my body to the left so I can see more, trying to stay as quiet as possible.

I watch as he kisses Brittney and gropes her breast, then kisses down her neck. She's got her eyes closed and her head tilted up.

"Oh, Mitch, you're so naughty." She smiles and giggles.

The skin on my arms crawls. I don't know why I thought it would be different, after we had Bailey. That he'd stop cheating on me. First it was Jessica, then Madison, and now Brittney. I'm really getting sick and tired of this.

Then ask him for a divorce, Dr. Nakamura says.

Oh right, because a guy like Mitch Hendricks is really going to grant me a divorce. He's a world-famous doctor, I lament.

I'm a world-famous doctor, what does one thing have to do with the other? Dr. Nakamura asks.

You're not world-famous. I roll my eyes.

"Oh, fuck me harder," Brittney begs.

I adjust my position again. I can see Mitch fucking the babysitter over the edge of his desk. And now I'm supposed to walk downstairs and pretend like nothing happened and leave my children in her care.

I sigh.

I know what I have to do tonight when we get home from the gala. Which means, I better go finish getting ready. Mitch will want to leave soon—and god, he's going to be such a cocky asshole all night, he always is after he fucks them.

"Babe, do you mind paying Brittney? I'm exhausted, I just want to go up and shower and go to bed," Mitch says when we pull into the driveway.

It's after midnight, the house is dark. Brittney never once texted to bother me about the girls. I assume that means they behaved for her.

"Of course, no problem." I pretend-smile. Mitch leans over to kiss me and I turn my head so he gets my neck. I don't want his mouth on me. Before he fucked her, he must have gone down on her. His breath smelled fishy all night.

I could see the nostrils flare on his fellow doctors when they leaned in close to whisper whatever bullshit they do at these big hospital gala functions. Things like, "My dick is bigger than your dick" or "I fucked your wife last night" or "Smell my pussy breath."

Whatever it is they do, it makes me sick.

So I stood in the corner of the room, sipping on a drink, deciding just how I'd kill Brittney. I settled on a car accident.

. . .

The moment we walk into our house, Mitch runs up the stairs to shower.

"Here you go," I say and hand Brittney two hundred dollars.

"Wow, thanks, Mrs. Hendricks. I'm finishing up my last year of nursing school, this will come in handy," she says.

"Lovely," I reply. Jesus, Mitch really has a type. I bet she was a high school cheerleader too.

"I have to go get diapers," I say, when she looks confused as I follow her out of the house. I get into Mitch's BMW and start it at the same time Brittney starts her Audi. Pretty nice car for a college student. I wonder if my husband bought it for her.

She backs out of our driveway and turns left. So I back out and turn right. Then I flip off my headlights and pull over to the side of the road. If she looks in her rearview, she'll just think I've driven off toward the gas station for diapers, instead of going into town. I can see the glow of her cell phone screen—which means she's distracted. Probably texting and driving or calling her real boyfriend.

"Oh, Brittney, you stupid little idiot," I say with a smile on my face. I whip my car around and start following her with my headlights off. It's dark, but I know this road well. Then, after a few minutes, I turn my full beams on and speed up, getting really close to her back bumper. Naturally, as my headlights get closer to her, she speeds up. She's still texting, I can see it.

I'm sure she doesn't know it's me.

I speed up even more, until I'm mere inches from her. And it's just her natural reaction, in the dark, to speed up again. I know we're getting close to the turn near Mills Bridge and she's going to have to slow down to go right into town or left over the bridge, but does she know that? I speed up even more. She puts her phone down, and I'm pretty sure she turns around to look over her shoulder at me. So I flip off my headlights, speed up, and tap her bumper with the front of Mitch's car. Then I rev the engine and it's enough...

Brittney jerks her steering wheel and the front end of her Audi gets away from her. She slams on her brakes and the momentum sends her car spinning. The front end clips the cement barrier at Mills Bridge and her car careens sideways into a barrel roll. So as I turn right into town, her car is rolling down the ravine toward the creek.

I don't slow down at all. Instead I speed up, make a right at the next stop sign, and take the back roads home—hoping to get there before Mitch realizes I've even left the house.

Thankfully, when I walk up the stairs and slip into our bedroom, Mitch is in bed and snoring. I take off my dress, put on a pair of pajamas, and crawl into bed.

"What took you so long?" he asks.

"Just putting Bailey back to bed—she needed her diaper changed and a fresh sippy cup," I reply.

"You're such a good mom," he mumbles in his sleep as he snuggles up next to me. I roll over on my side, to get away from him. I fall asleep dreaming about putting a knife in Mitch's gut.

The next morning I get up early before Mitch or the girls—I'm not really sure I ever reached REM sleep. I felt like I was consciously dreaming most of the night. I don't use my phone to check about the accident... Instead, I go downstairs and turn on the Sunday morning news with the volume down low.

Little Sarah comes into the living room shortly after I do, and snuggles up in the chair with me. "Hey, sweets, did you sleep well?" I ask.

She nods her head. "Yes, Mommy."

Before I can ask her if she wants breakfast, a picture of Brittney flashes on the TV screen. I turn the volume up just enough to make out what the reporter is saying.

"*In local news, twenty-two-year-old college senior Brittney Monsolovich died last night in a single rollover accident,*" the news reporter says.

Ding-dong.

A smile spreads over my face.

I quickly change the channel to *Peppa Pig* for Sarah.

"Coming!" I yell.

Whenever I've had to speak to the authorities, I always take it as an opportunity to give them a show. I know I've never landed a role on Broadway, but I've been preparing for it my entire life. Even at my day job, as a nurse at the free clinic, I prepare.

Justin, one of the silly gay medical assistants, is constantly badgering me about going to auditions again. He loves Broadway and loves to say, "Becks, you're too good for this place." It really is the most foul-smelling, tragic medical office in the world. But it's another chance for me to perform. Every day I put on a happy face, fighting against the urge to kill someone, and sing for my patients. Sometimes I even dance a little. It really seems to brighten their pathetic days.

I smile, thinking about it. That I, Rebecca Hendricks, could brighten someone's day—considering how often my husband tells me what a worthless piece of shit I am.

I take a deep breath, smile, then open the front door.

Showtime.

EPILOGUE

SOPHIA

Six Months Later

LONDON

"Justin! Luis!" I roll down the window and shout when I see them exiting Heathrow Airport. My driver gives me the eye in the mirror. "Oh, stuff and nonsense. They're American, they're used to shouting."

"Sophia! Babes!" Justin screams when he sees me waving out the side of the limo.

I jump out of the vehicle as soon as my driver stops and I rush over to hug Justin. It's funny how close he and I have become since I moved to London. We talk almost every day. I'm so excited to see him again in person.

"Oh my god, you look fabulous," he says.

"I love the hair," Luis chimes in.

"Thanks, it's sort of an accidental haircut. Bailey fell asleep with gum in her mouth in bed with me, and no matter what Ekaterina tried, we couldn't get it out. So I said, what the hell. A bob it is."

"Aww," they both say at the same time. I see the shared glance, that twinkle in their eye. It's what people without children do when their friends with children launch into anecdotal stories. I've become that woman.

And god, do I love it.

"Now, I've booked you a suite at the Savoy. And all your meals, drinks, and room service are paid for. So please, anything your hearts desire, enjoy."

"Aww," they both say again—this time that sparkle is for an entirely different reason.

"You really didn't have to do all that for us," Luis says.

"I know. But I wanted to, I'm just sorry I couldn't be there for your wedding. But it was still too soon for the girls. I couldn't leave them and I didn't want to bring them back to New York."

They both nod as they get into the limo.

Ever since Rebecca and Mitch died and the lies began to unravel, the media has gone nuts. Fortunately, there are very strict rules about paparazzi in England. Courtesy of the Royal Family. So here in London, I can shield the girls. But if I took them back to the States, it would be a TMZ media free-for-all.

It only took a few true crime podcasters a month before they unraveled Rebecca's lengthy web of lies. It helped that Violet's mom, Mrs. NY Socialite, was offering a fifty-thousand-dollar reward for information on her daughter's suspicious suicide. Very quickly Rebecca was linked to that, and then to a string of other murders in her wake... I can't believe I was living with a woman like that.

Technically, she's considered a serial killer.

Her first "known" kill was the girl in high school—the bridge jumper. Whether she'd have been convicted of that in a court of law is of much debate in the true crime circles. Either way, they consider that the first one. Then it was the landlady she lived with when she first moved to New York, Mrs. Hofstead who was found dead in her apartment—shriveled up and mummified, tied to a chair watching TV. Next was Dani. Mitch's second wife, the one who left her baby in the car and it froze to death. But—it's still a hot-button issue, whether it was Dani or Mitch. Personally, I think Mitch told his wife to take a nap and he'd get the baby and forgot. But whatever, Becks admitted to pushing Dani down the stairs. After that was Brittney, a babysitter who'd been fucking Mitch. Then Violet, Mitch, and finally Grant Baker III. She would have killed me too, if I hadn't shoved that glass award in her neck, finally putting an end to her years of killing.

My attorney has been busy shutting down all the outreach from the true crime junkies, streaming networks, and news stations. Everyone wants to know more about Rebecca. Everyone wants to know what made her tick. But it's not my job to tell them. Or my problem.

My one job right now is to protect the girls.

I do not want *my* daughters connected to Rebecca Hendricks the serial killer.

Yes, since arriving in London, I've officially adopted Sarah and Bailey and changed their surname. We've all taken my family moniker—Egerton.

"Now, this trip is your honeymoon, I seriously do not expect to see you again. I just wanted to give you both a hug and tell you I'm so happy for you," I say when we pull up to the hotel. I give Justin and Luis each a big hug before they get out of the limo.

"Uhhh, but what if we want to see you?" Justin asks.

I smile.

"You say that now, but once you get up to that luxury suite and kick off your shoes, you'll be thankful not to have to worry about seeing me again. Seriously. I love you both. Congratulations again." Then I blow air kisses in their direction. They wave and blow kisses back at me as my driver pulls away. I feel good knowing I could give them a nice honeymoon gift.

When my driver pulls up to my house on Primrose Hill, I see

two little faces in the front window. I get out and run up the stone steps, and fling open the front door. "What are you gooses doing in the window?" I laugh when I rush into the front room. I lunge forward with my tickle hands out, and Sarah and Bailey shriek with joy and run around dodging me as I wiggle my hands. Finally, we all collapse on the couch, wheezing and laughing.

"Ekaterina said when you got home we could all go to the park!" Sarah exclaims.

"Can we get ice cream, Fifi?" Bailey asks.

"Oh yes, can we get ice cream, Fifi?" Ekaterina walks into the room and teases.

I stand up, narrow my eyes, put my finger up to my lips, and pretend—like I'm thinking really hard about it. "Hmmm. What about gelato? I heard there's a lovely new place a few blocks from here."

"Yay!" Sarah and Bailey clap and jump up and down.

Then they run for the front door and I wink at Ekaterina. She opens the door and the girls charge down the front steps.

"You think they have pistachio?" Ekaterina asks as we walk much more slowly out of the house and down the stairs to the street.

I frown and give her a little nudge with my elbow. "Do you think I'd suggest a place that doesn't have your favorite flavor?"

"Yes," she teases.

"Oh, please," I laugh. The girls are already running halfway down the block. "Shit... Sarah! Bailey! Wait for Fifi!" Then I take off in a sprint toward them. I don't want things to ever change. I love them so much at this age. Young, inquisitive, happy to try new things and glad they live with me.

I worry about when we hit those teenage years.

Ekaterina tells me not to invite trouble by worrying about tomorrow.

I'm really trying.

So far neither Sarah or Bailey have shown any signs of bipolar disorder... Their therapist is pretty confident that with regular visits, we'll be able to diagnose and treat before it becomes an issue. I often wonder what Rebecca's childhood looked like. My only real glimpse was her diaries and journals... Hannah got rid of those when I was in the hospital recovering. Along with all the trophies in the attic.

None of it matters anyway.

I don't believe in all of Ekaterina's religious witchcraft, but she's not wrong about focusing on the present. It's like what Hannah said about Rowen: It's not easy, being a parent is hard, but she shows up every day and does her best. Which is where Mitch and Rebecca failed. They were narcissists. Only concerned with showing up for themselves and their own personal ambitions and desires—never putting the children first.

I'm trying. I'm really trying.

Like agreeing to try a taste of Sarah's bubble-gum-flavored gelato, even though the thought of it turns my stomach. But, for her, I would literally do anything.

"Okay, I'll try it." I close my eyes and open my mouth. She shoves a spoonful into my mouth. It's not at all what I expect. It's creamy and mildly sweet. It makes me nostalgic for a holiday on the Isle of Wight. Maybe when we get home I'll plan a trip there. I bet the girls would love the airboat ferry ride and bike riding in the countryside.

"Do you like it?" Sarah asks.

I look at her and smile. "Delightful. Thank you for sharing." I give her a little boop on the nose. "Now, who's heard of the Isle of Wight? Because I was just thinking we should take a little holiday..." I talk the entire walk home, while the girls skip and eat gelato. Ekaterina nods and makes hmmm and ahhhh noises between bites, and my life feels more complete than I knew it possibly could.

A LETTER FROM THE AUTHOR

Huge thanks for reading *The First Widows*. I hope you were as intrigued by Sophia and Rebecca's twisted friendship as I was writing it. If you'd like to keep in touch with all my new releases with Storm Publishing, you can sign up below.

www.stormpublishing.co/se-reed

And if you want to join other readers in hearing all about my new releases and bonus content, you can sign up for my newsletter.

www.writingwithreed.com/subscribe

If you enjoyed this book and could spare a few moments to leave a review, that would be hugely appreciated. Even a short review can make all the difference in encouraging a reader to discover my books for the first time. Seriously, thank you so much.

If you read *The First Wives* (book one in this series), you know that I clearly have strong feelings about adult friendships. They can be full of love and joy or messy and complicated—especially if you work full-time, have children, a spouse, and family obligations. I wanted to continue to examine those feelings with this book. How cultivating a new friendship can easily turn into trying to fix details in another person's life, potentially fueling resentment and anger (as what happened between Sophia and Rebecca). Although this book is a work of fiction, whenever I write I like to draw inspiration from my own life.

Thanks again for being part of this amazing journey with me, and I hope you'll stay in touch. I have so many more stories to entertain you with!

xo
S.E. Reed

tiktok.com/@writingwithreed

x.com/writingwithreed

instagram.com/writingwithreed

ACKNOWLEDGMENTS

First, I want to thank my husband Brian for all the love and all the years. Thank you. To my children, Shannon, Jackson, and Kassidy, for being silly, fun-loving, and the best kids a mom could ask for. I love you very much. Cheers to the adventures we've had and those yet to come. I'm so lucky to have a family like you!

Daddy, I love you more than all the stars in the sky, because they go on forever and ever. Give your little buddy Albert a pet from me.

To my Nebraska/Iowa family for your love and encouragement. I love you, Brenda, Dawn, Brooke, Madison, and Amber.

To Emily Gowers, my kind-hearted, nurturing, and witty acquiring editor and mentor at Storm Publishing. You are wonderful to work with and I feel blessed every day to be on this writing journey with you. I love our six a.m. brainstorming sessions.

To Dana Hawkins, my twin flame and best gal pal in the universe. What would I do without you? Nothing. That's what. My life would be boring as hell without you. I love you xoxo.

To my delightful literary agent, Jenna Satterthwaite, for believing in my writing abilities, career vision, and wanting to take a chance with me. Working with you is a joy.

To all of my agent siblings, thank you for welcoming me into the fold! I appreciate you guys so much. I'm truly inspired by your talent.

To my Sunday writing group, Ginny Myers Sain, Casie Bazay, Jenni Howell, Alyssa Villaire, Tracy Truels, and Vanessa Montalban. Our calls and emails over the last few years are something I cherish and look forward to.

To Theresa Green, E.L. Johnson, Diane Billas, Mariah Stillbrook, Benjamin Ryan, Abby Wild, Bruce Buchanan, Amy Nielsen, and Demi Michelle Schwartz—thank you for your friendships and wisdom.

Hugs and love to my friends at BRPSC. I consider you all family.

To all of the lovely readers who have supported me on this journey, thank you!

And finally, to all my other friends and family around the globe. I love you! I'm always grateful for the conversations, encouragement, and laughter whenever we connect or see each other in person.

www.ingramcontent.com/pod-product-compliance
Lightning Source LLC
Chambersburg PA
CBHW011555190726

48287CB00010B/2901